A Girl At The Tiller

Titles from Geoffrey Lewis:

Flashback

ISBN 978-0-9545624-0-3

Strangers

ISBN 978-0-9545624-1-0

Winter's Tale

ISBN 978-0-9545624-2-7

Cycle

ISBN 978-0-9545624-3-4

Starlight

ISBN 978-0-9545624-5-8

A Boy Off The Bank

ISBN 978-0-9545624-6-5

A Girl At The Tiller

ISBN 978-0-9545624-7-2

A Girl At The Tiller

Geoffrey Lewis

ISBN 978-0-9545624-7-2

Printed and bound in Great Britain by
Creative Print and Design (Wales)

First published in Great Britain in 2008 by

SGM Publishing
35 Stacey Avenue, Wolverton, Milton Keynes, Bucks MK12 5DN
info@sgmpublishing.co.uk
www.sgmpublishing.co.uk

For Brian:
The man whose love of the waterways
did so much to inspire my own.

Acknowledgements

Like *A Boy Off The Bank,* this story is set against a factual background, and it is, in my mind, a crime for an author to write a historical novel without doing his best to make sure that his background is accurate! I have, of course, drawn upon my own knowledge of the canals, but many others, with wider experience than mine, have given of their memories and skills in support of my efforts: David Blagrove of Stoke Bruerne, and Ron Withey, an ex-boatman who remembers the hopes and horrors of nationalisation; Julia Cook, Brian Collings, John and Betty Garner, all of whom knew the boats long before I did.

The final product comes to you courtesy of my trusty proof-readers: Pam, Mac, Sioux, Bill, and a new recruit, Sheila – welcome aboard! And, as always, my thanks to Roger, of Amherst Publishing, for turning my typescript into a real book!

A special thank-you, this time, to young Simone Yorke, who, courtesy of Grandma Lorna, posed so ably as 'Carrie' for the front cover picture, on a chilly October morning!

But the biggest thank-you I owe for this story is to you, my dear reader: So many of you, after *A Boy Off The Bank,* asked when the sequel would be published, that I thought I had better get on and write one. And that thought has grown on me, so that not only is this new volume now in print, but a third and final story will be appearing before too long: I hope to have *The New Number One* finished in time for early next year – watch this space!

Geoffrey Lewis
March 2008

Introduction

The Inland Waterways Association was inaugurated in February, 1946, at a meeting in Gower Street, in London. It was the inspiration of two like-minded men, Robert Aickman and Tom Rolt, canal enthusiasts who were distressed at the state our waterways were being allowed to fall into after six years of war; two men who first met on a narrowboat at the top of Tardebigge Locks in August 1945, while the war in the Pacific was still raging.

Over the sixty-two years since then, it has grown to become not only a huge, democratically-run organisation of people who love Britain's waterways, but an influential force in their preservation and restoration – many of the canals we can enjoy today, whether it is as boaters, anglers, walkers, naturalists, cyclists, or just casual visitors, are there to be enjoyed because of the efforts of the Inland Waterways Association.

The spark of an idea, which was to become the story of *The Boy Off The Bank*, had been with me for some years before it began to germinate, and it was during that process that it occurred to me that 2006, the year when I planned to have it ready for publication, would be the I.W.A.'s diamond jubilee. So it seemed only fitting that a book which tells of the canals in the years immediately before the founding of the Association should commemorate that significant anniversary.

This second book – in what is now to be a trilogy – *A Girl At The Tiller*, sees the end of the war and the start of nationalisation.

Geoffrey Lewis
March 2008

Prologue

Now, at last, it really was all over. After six years of conflict, the Third Reich was no more, its dictator dead by his own hand, the Rising Sun had gone down into its self-inflicted night with the ultimate persuasion of two atomic bombs, and the world was once more at peace.

August 1945: The succession of astonishing news stories from the Far East had broken as the three pairs of Fellows, Morton & Clayton Ltd's boats were making their way back to Braunston after an abortive trip to Worcester. The *Sycamore's* aging Bolinder had begun to play up again; Skipper Albert Baker had told Bill Hanney and Jack Warden to go on, to get back for whatever orders were available, while he and Michael did their best to keep the tired engine going. They had lost more than a day, but made it back eventually; Braunston depot's manager, Ben Vickers, had had to send to Saltley Dock for a spare injector, and they remained tied on the towpath near the iron bridge to await its arrival.

The end of the fighting, after so many years, brought on a strange feeling of nostalgia in Albert, as it had in so many others. With little to do, they were sitting in the cabin of their butty, the *Antrim,* the next morning, breakfast finished, with a mug of tea apiece; he looked up at Michael:

'Oi was toied joost here, furst toime we met – yew remember, boy?' Michael nodded:

‘Tha’s roight, Dad. Oi’ll never forget – Oi was so nervous!’

‘Oi was pretty grumpy wi’ yeh, wasn’ Oi?’ Michael grinned at him:

‘Not really!’ Albert drew on his pipe, blew out a cloud of smoke:

‘Oi was feelin’ so… depressed. Oi’d joost buried moy Rita – ’n Oi was worried ’bout Alex, o’ course, ’im bein’ away in the Navy…’ He chuckled quietly: ’N along cooms Bill ’Anney, wi’ this daft oidea that Oi should tek on this know-nothin’ kid off the bank ter ’elp me roon the boats! ’Ow stoopid can yeh get, that’s what Oi thought.’

‘Boot yeh took me on, any’ow?’ Albert nodded:

‘Ther’ was soomthin’ about yeh, Moikey. A… koind o’ spirit, Oi suppose. Skinny little kid, yeh was! Boot yeh had a feelin’ o’… oh, Oi dunno, copin’ wi things, soom’ow. ’N Bill said yeh’d doon well wi’ them, on the roon from Stoke Bruin…’

Ginny had been sitting quietly, listening to their memories:

‘’N then yeh got saddled with me ’n all, didn’t yeh, Dad?’ Albert smiled down at her:

‘Well, Oi couldn’t leave yeh all alone when yer Mum doied, could Oi? Yer Grandad agreed, yeh oughta be wi’ yer brother…’ The girl chuckled, then she asked:

‘Are you glad yeh did, Dad?’ Albert turned to her, shook his head:

‘Nah! Wurst thing Oi ever did in moy loife!’ But the grin on his face told its own tale – she reached over and punched his shoulder; he grabbed her hand, drew her close and took her in his arms:

‘Yew two are the best things ever ’appened to me – ’cept per’aps meetin’ Rita. ’Ow Oi’d a’ coped without yeh, ’specially when Alex was killed, Oi joost don’ know.’ Michael felt tears suddenly burning behind his eyes; he said quietly:

‘Yew saved moy loife. Oh, Bill and Billy fished me out o’ the canal, that noight – boot it was workin’ with you, ’avin’ a new Dad, soomeone Oi could love and respect… Yew gave me a loife worth livin’, Dad.’

‘’N I’d be stuck in soom dreadful orphanage soomwher’, if it wasn’ fer yew, Dad.’

‘Yeh don’ regret coomin’ on the boats, then? Yeh don’ miss yer schoolin’, toime teh play wi’ yer friends?’ Two heads shook as one:

‘No!’

‘Never!’

‘Coom ’ere, Moikey!’ The boy stood up; Albert’s eyes followed him:

‘Look at yeh, boy! So tall ’n ’andsome – no woonder yoong ’Arriet’s got an oiye fer yeh! Yer Mum would be proud o’ yeh, both o’ yeh.’ Michael slipped into the bench beside him; Albert freed one arm from Ginny, slid it around his shoulders:

‘Moy son – moy daughter! Oi’m so proud o’ the two o’ yeh…!’ Ginny wriggled closer:

‘I love you, Daddy.’

Teenage boys are not given to displays of sentiment. But:

‘Oi love yeh too, Dad.’

Chapter One

Ben Vickers pushed most of the pile of mail on his desk to one side and picked up the heavy little package. He weighed it in his hand, noted the return address – *Fellows, Morton & Clayton Ltd, Saltley Dock, Birmingham* – and smiled: *Alby'll be pleased!*

He got up from his chair and walked out of the small office, along the old, truncated arm of the canal which served as FMC's Braunston dock to the junction with the main line of the Grand Union Canal. Just to his left, near the old toll office, Alby Baker's pair were tied, the butty to the bank, the motor on its outside, taking advantage of the deeper water to accommodate its greater draft; a curl of smoke drifted from the cabin chimney into the still summer air: *Good – he's got the kettle on!* He walked up, knocked on the cabinside and stood looking out over its roof, averting his eyes from the open slide, until he heard the doors swing open.

'Ben! 'Ow're yeh doin'?' Alby's head emerged, wreathed in its usual cloud of tobacco smoke.

'Fine, Alby. I've got something for you!' He held up the package, chuckled at the delighted grin which spread across the old boatman's face.

''Bout toime, 'n all!' Vickers laughed; they both knew that Baker's pretence of grumpiness was an act:

'I only ordered it yesterday, Alby – give the Post Office some credit!' Baker chuckled too, now:

'Coomin' on fer a cuppa, then?'

'D'you need to ask?'

The Boatman stood aside for the Dock manager to step aboard and descend into the tiny cabin, and then followed him down, closing the doors behind him as he did so.

'Where're Mikey and Ginny, then?' Vickers looked around the confined space as he sat on the sidebed opposite the little range, where a polished copper kettle murmured to itself. Baker reached into the cupboard, lifted out the Measham teapot which had been his wife's pride and joy and spooned in the tealeaves:

'Gone oop the village, Ben. Teh the shop, they said – boot Oi'll bet they're chattin' with their mates! Oi 'ope young Moikey woon' be long, oi could doo wi' 'is 'elp fixin' that injector. 'N 'e needs to learn.' He poured boiling water into the pot, lifted two mugs from the shelf and set them on the lowered table-cupboard.

'He does pretty well already, doesn't he?'

'Yeah, not 'alf! 'E's a bright kid, Ben, mooch cleverer than Oi was. 'E's bin wi' me foive, foive 'n a 'alf years, now – 'n 'e's a better boater'n soom lads 'is age 'oo were born to it. 'E knows 'is way 'round them old engines, too – boot a bit more practice woon' 'urt 'im.' Vickers laughed:

'He's going to be a first-class captain himself, before long, eh, Alby?'

'Ah!' He poured milk into the mugs, added the steaming tea and waved at the sugar-bowl in invitation.

'The *Towcester* and the *Bodmin* went by yesterday, Alby, just before you got here. Heading South.'

'Oh ah? Saw 'em, did yeh?' Vickers chuckled again:

'I knew Mikey'd want to know where they are, so I had the men keep an eye out!'

'That was good o' yeh, Ben. They'll be a coople o' days ahead of oos, then? Oonless yeh're sendin' oos back teh Birnigum?' Vickers shook his head:

'No, Alby – I need you to go to Brentford and load sugar for

Sherborne Wharf. Things are getting back to normal, slowly, and we should be able to go back to running regular trips before long. I'd assume the Caplins will go to Bulls Bridge for orders, so you'll catch up with them somewhere!' Baker nodded, a smile on his face, and took a long draught of his tea. The Grand Union Company's boats ran closely similar routes to FMC, despite often loading at different points on the canals, so they would come across Henry Caplin and his family, with their pair, before many days had passed.

'Harriet's still sweet on our Mikey then, is she?' Vickers asked.

'Oh, ah! 'N 'e loikes 'er well enooff, too. They'll be gettin' in tow when the toime coomes, Oi reckon.'

'That would be good, Alby. She's a nice girl – and he's a credit to you, and the company.'

'Ah.'

Vickers drained his mug:

'I'd better be getting back to the office, Alby. Before I go…' He reached into the pocket of his jacket, pulled out two pound notes and proffered them to Baker:

'We doon' need your charity, Ben.' The boatman's tone was quiet, but a glint of steel shone in his grey eyes. Vickers burst out laughing:

'I *knew* that was what you'd say, Alby! Don't worry, it's not my money! I had a word with the fleet manager, and he's authorised me to give you two quid extra. You've been stuck here, on top of that wasted trip down the Worcester cut – and both he and the directors know that you're one of the best crews on my patch, so take it as a kind of bonus, right?'

'Well – if Mac Anderson says it's okay…' Baker took the notes, stuffed them in his own pocket, and suddenly grinned: 'We'll mebbe take a walk oop the Old Plough this evenin', after all!'

* * *

It had been a pleasant evening. Michael and Ginny had returned from the village not long after Vickers had left the boats, bearing the few items from the shop they had ostensibly gone for – more tea, a pint of milk, and some cheap stewing beef from the butcher's. Ginny had started on the dinner while her brother and the old boatman had set about replacing the injector in the *Sycamore's* Bolinder engine and then setting up the pumps so that it would run efficiently – the big old single-cylinder diesels favoured by Fellows, Morton & Clayton were solid and indestructible, but after six years of war many of them were becoming worn and tired. Finally satisfied with their efforts, man and boy had emerged into the sunshine, grinning through the oil and grime on their faces, to be faced with the eleven-year-old's refusal to let them into the cabin until they had had a thorough wash.

Ready for an early start the next day, all three of them had walked up the hill from Butcher's bridge to Braunston High Street and the Old Plough. Albert and Michael had sat talking, speculating about how their lives would change with the return to peace-time work on the waterways, while Ginny curled up in a corner with her glass of lemonade, happily listening to their banter and wondering what the future would hold for her, too. Alby had passed on the intelligence he'd received from Vickers, and laughed aloud at the eager look on Michael's face as he heard it. It was about ten o'clock when they set off to return to the boats, cheerfully tired after their day and a couple of drinks apiece.

Down the long hill, over the bridge and onto the towpath. Just by the bridge, another FMC pair was tied in the gathering gloom of the August night, two children playing on the grass, their voices shrill with laughter in the twilight. The younger, a boy of maybe six years old, suddenly turned from his older sister as they passed, and dashed in front of Albert, nearly tripping him:

'Careful, lad, yeh'll 'ave me in the cut!' Alby grabbed the boy, who looked up at him with wide eyes set in a grubby face:

'Sorry, mister, didn' see yeh!' The kid's grin showed brightly white in the dusk. He twisted out of the boatman's grasp and ran off; his sister stood nervously aside to let them by:

'We didn' mean no 'arm, mister.' Albert gave her a smile:

'Oi know that, choild. Yer folks not about?'

'They're oop the pub, the Nelson. These're our boats.' The outraged wisdom of eleven years sounded in Ginny's tone:

'Shouldn' yeh be in bed boy now?' The girl was no more than seven or eight herself; the child shrugged:

'Ma 'n Dad'll put oos down when they coome back.'

'All roight – boot yew take care, now.' Albert ushered Ginny past and followed with Michael – the little boy dashed back to his sister's side from up on the bridge, where he had been watching them.

'They're too young to be up at this toime, Dad!' Alby smiled:

'It's not our affair, Ginny, leave 'em be.'

They walked on in silence to the iron bridge by the toll house, before Ginny spoke again:

'Did yeh see how moocky they were, 'n all? 'N the state of 'er frock – dirty, 'n frayed 'round the sleeves loike that…'

''E was pretty grubby, as well, wasn' 'e, Dad?' Michael joined in. Albert stopped, turned to them:

'Yeh're roight, both o' yeh, 'n Oi ain't sayin' ootherwoise, boot it's noone of our business 'ow oother folks bring oop their kids. Now coome on – a quick cuppa 'n into bed, roight? We oughta be away sharp in the mornin'.'

Chapter Two

'I'll set 'em ahead, Dad, 'n mek breakfast on the summit.' Ginny had adopted the dungarees that had been popular with the trainee boat-girls during the war; now she lifted down the old bike they kept on the butty for lock-wheeling.

'Okay, Ginny love. We'll be roight be'ind yeh!'

A little after six the next morning, and the *Sycamore* and the *Antrim* were ready to go. Ginny set off on the bike, a windlass tucked into her belt, to cover the short distance from the Stop House to Braunston bottom lock; Albert already had the engine running. Michael loosed off the fore-end as he untied the stern, and the boats were away, Alby picking up the cross-straps as the motor pulled clear of the butty, the pair running empty, fore-ends high. Michael stepped on to the stern of the butty as it passed, slotted the heavy wooden tiller into the 'ellum to guide the boat through the haphazard chicane of moored boats along the way.

In a flight like Braunston, they would always adopt a similar habit of working – the boats themselves would be breasted, tied tightly side-by-side, controllable by one steerer, to leave two of the crew free to operate the locks; one of them on the bike, getting the locks ready for the boats, with either Albert or Michael in charge of the pair, stepping off to help the other at each lock.

At Butcher's Bridge, the boatman surveyed the pair they had seen the previous night with undisguised disapproval. In the morning light, the dishevelled state of them could be seen, the cloths untidily covering over the load, the paintwork on the cabinsides grubby, the brasswork dull. He took his pipe from his mouth, gestured with it to Michael in the hatches of the butty, who nodded his own dislike of the state of them.

Approaching the bridge which spans the canal below the bottom lock, Albert knocked out the clutch, allowing the motor boat to slow, and cast off the cross-straps. Michael steered the butty along the left side of the motor as they nosed into the bridge-hole, then leapt onto the cabintop, ran forward along the top planks to tie the fore-ends together while Albert passed the breasting-string through the butty's shackle and drew the sterns tight. A third line onto the central t-stud on the butty's stern deck, and they were ready to proceed. Michael stepped off the fore-end onto the lock-tail as Albert dropped the clutch back in, nosing the pair in past the gates which Ginny had opened as they drew near.

Once in the lock, Albert reversed the engine and stopped the pair, just touching the cill below the top gates. He climbed up, jumped from the cabintop onto the lockside as Michael and Ginny pushed the gates closed, and went to lift the paddles; as she passed him, Ginny called out:

'Did yeh see the state o' those boats, Dad?'

'Yeah – roight pair o' Rodneys, ent they?' Ginny stopped in her tracks, looked back at him:

'Oi've 'eard Bill Hanney say that before, 'bout other boaters – what's it mean, Dad?'

'Dirty booggers, who can't be bothered teh keep 'emselves or the boats clean. Give oos all a bad name, they do.'

'Oh – but whoy *Rodneys,* Dad?' Alby shrugged:

'Don' roightly know, love – it's joost an expression.'

'Ain't too many loike them about, are there? Oi mean, most all the boats yeh see are clean and smart, ent they?'

'Aye, thank God! Now can yeh see whoy Oi didn't want yeh getting' involved wi' them kiddies last noight?'

'Oh! Roight...' Alby grinned at her:

'Now boogger off 'n get that next lock ready, girl!' She laughed and hurried off as he whipped up the top paddles. Michael had already drawn the paddles on his side, and the boats quickly rose to the higher level; they swung the heavy gates open, and Alby returned to the stern of the motor to take the pair out as Michael stepped across the fore-ends onto the towpath ready to walk on to the next lock.

'Moikey!' He turned at the sound of Albert's call: ''Noother pair follerin'!' The boatman gestured over his shoulder. Michael looked ahead – no sign from Ginny, which meant there were no boats approaching, coming down the locks to meet them. He sighed under his breath – the boater's code of conduct said he ought to close the gates and set the lock back for the other pair by pulling a bottom paddle, which would slow them down. He let his own boats pass him by as they ran out of the lock, quickly dropping the paddles as he waited, then hurried to close one gate, whipping up a bottom paddle as he walked around the lock to close the second. Across the top gates, and he stepped down to run forward after the boats, to be in time to work the next lock.

But as he set off, a sudden scream, a splash, stopped him in his tracks. A child's voice, shouting in panic from behind him – he ran back to the tail of the lock, looked down. The other pair, the scruffy boats from Butcher's Bridge, were below, almost broadside across the canal; and in the water, between them and the lock, the little girl was struggling, fighting to keep her head above water against the turbulence created by the open paddle, coughing and choking. Snatching the windlass from his belt, he reversed it and struck the catch from the paddlegear with its handle. The paddle slammed down with a crash, stopping the flow of water; he dropped his windlass on the grass, and, without thinking, ran down the steps and dived into the canal.

Struggling out until he was next to the child, he put his arms around her:

'S'okay, tek it easy, Oi'm here.' She was thrashing around, coughing up muddy water, still in a state of panic – he held her tightly, his own feet planted in the soft mud on the bed of the canal, talking to her reassuringly. She slowly calmed down, looking at him from huge, terrified, green eyes, tears streaming down her cheeks: 'Coom on, let's get yew out of 'ere!'

Holding her tight, he half-swam, half-waded to the bank. Pushing his own feet deep into the mud by the copings under the bridge, he heaved her up into the arms of the lock-keeper, who had appeared on the scene at the sound of the upheaval. The man hurried her off, to where the stern of the pair had swung against the bank, handed her up into the arms of her mother, in the butty's well. Michael hauled himself out, and stood dripping on the coping stones, listening to the sounds of an altercation from the other end of the boats:

'What d'yer think yer doin', yeh stoopid little bitch?' Her father's voice, from the motor's counter.

'Tek it easy, captain, weren't 'er fault she went in.' The reasonable tones of the lock-keeper, from the bank.

'Wha' d'yer mean, weren't 'er fault? 'Oo's fault was it, then?'

'She lost 'er balance when yeh 'it the bridge-hole, mate!'

'Bollocks! It was 'er fallin' in what made me turn 'em!' The lock-keeper just stared at the man for a moment, then turned his back on him, clearly disagreeing with this version of events. He looked back over his shoulder:

'Yeh owe that yoong man ther' a vote o' thanks, any'ow, fer fishin' 'er out!'

The boatman looked at Michael, but then ignored him and set about reversing his boats, lining them up again for the bridge. The lock-keeper shrugged, and walked back to where Michael stood under the bridge, soaked to the skin:

'No accountin' fer soom folks, is ther', son? Are yew all roight?' Michael nodded:

'Oi'm foine, thanks. 'Ow's the kiddie?'

'Oh, she'll be all roight, joost scared out of 'er wits. 'S long as 'e don't tek it out on 'er.'

''E wouldn't do that?' Michael sounded incredulous.

'*'E* would. Boot 'er mam moight stop 'im, if she's loocky. Nasty bastard, 'e is. All 'is fault, too – did yer see?' Michael shook his head; the man went on: 'Yeah! Got 'em breasted wrong way, see, butty on the roight, so when 'e 'eld back fer the lock, they screwed soideways, 'n 'it the bridge. Little'un was on the planks, 'eading ter step off the fore-end under the bridge, 'n it toppled 'er off. Oi was on Nurser's yard, saw it all 'appen. Loocky fer 'er yeh were there, lad – yeh can swim, can yeh?'

'Yeah – Oi learnt, when Oi was little, 'fore Oi came on the boats.'

'Oh – yeah! You're Moikey, ain't yeh? Alby Baker's new boy?' Michael laughed:

'Yeah! Foive years 'n more, 'n Oi'm still the new boy!' The lock-keeper grinned at him:

''S 'ow we are on the cut, lad! Don't tek no offence – we're all quoite proud o' yeh, the way yeh've teken to the boatin'.'

'Thank yeh! 'N Oi'd better go 'n see what's 'appened to our boats – Dad 'n Ginny'll be woonderin' wher' Oi've got teh!'

'Tek care, lad – what yeh did ther' was very brave, 'n Oi'll say thank yeh even if they can't. 'N Oi'll be sure Ben Vickers knows about it, 'n all.'

Chapter Three

The lock-keeper turned to open the gates for the little girl's boats, a final grimace on his face for Michael's benefit. The boy gave him a grin over his shoulder as he bent to retrieve his windlass and then hurried away, water squelching in his boots; looking up, he saw his sister hurtling towards him on the old bike. She stopped in front of him with a screech of worn-out brakes and dropped the bike, jumping off it to confront him with a look of astonishment on her face:

'Moichael! What's 'appened – yeh're all wet!' He grinned at her:

'Oi *had* noticed, Ginny!' She gaped at him, and then, realising that he wasn't hurt, burst out laughing:

'Yeh fell in!' He joined in her laughter, shaking his head:

'Oi *didn't!'*

The lock-keeper had overheard this exchange; he called across to her:

'Your brother just jumped in the cut to save a kiddie!' Ginny regarded her brother with sudden awe:

'Did yeh, Moikey?' He nodded reluctantly:

'She fell in, off those Rodney boats…' he shrugged his shoulders. Ginny was still looking at him, admiration in her eyes, making him feel uncomfortable: 'Coom on, Ginny, Dad'll be woonderin' wher' we are.'

He set off along the lockside, past the top gates and up the towpath towards the second lock, not stopping to see if she was following him. He looked up at the sound of the bicycle brakes beside him, as she caught up with him and stepped off again to walk alongside him:

'What 'appened then, Moikey?'

''Keeper says yer man 'ad the butty breasted wrong side, 'n 'it the bridge-hole as 'e troied ter 'old back. The kid was on the top-planks, roonnin' forward, 'n got knocked off inteh the cut. Ther' was no-one else about, so I dropped the paddle 'n dived in teh get 'er out.'

'That was brave of yeh, Moikey!' He shrugged again:

'Couldn' joost leave 'er, could Oi?'

They walked in silence for a moment, then Ginny asked:

'Yeh say 'e 'ad the boats breasted wrong?'

'Yeah. Yeh know we alwes 'as the butty on the left, in the locks?'

'Yes – boot, isn' that joost, loike, 'ow it's doon?'

'Yeah – boot ther's a *reason* fer it! When yeh're gooin' ahead, 'n put the motor into stern gear teh slow 'em down, the blades act loike a paddlewheel, pushin' the stern teh oone soide. That meks the motor swing, see?' He used his hand to demonstrate a boat swinging left: 'Now, if yeh puts the butty this soide' his other hand, to the left of the first 'it's weight troys teh keep goin' forward, 'n that pulls the motor back in loine, stops it swingin. Boot, if yeh 'ave the butty the *oother* soide…' He swapped his hands, demonstrated the boats screwing wildly to their left. Ginny chuckled her understanding:

'They'd go all oover the place!'

'Roight! 'E went soidewes, 'n the kiddie got bounced off the planks as 'e 'it the bridge.'

'Stoopid boogger!' Michael laughed:

'That's what 'keeper called 'im!'

They were at the next lock, now; Albert stood on the lock-tail, staring down at his bedraggled son and giggling daughter, the boats standing in the full lock behind him:

'What the 'Ell have yeh bin oop to, boy?' Michael gave him a big grin:

'Tell yeh later, Dad. Oi'll get changed sharpish – yew 'n Ginny'd better get 'em ahead, them Rodneys are roight be'ind oos, 'n yeh doon't want 'em gettin' boy!'

'Okay, son.' He shook his head and turned to step onto the motor, as Ginny pedalled off to set the next, third, lock of the flight of six. Michael squeezed past him, into the motor cabin, to find some dry clothes and his spare pair of boots.

Inside the cosy warmth of the cabin, he quickly stripped off his soaked clothing, offering up a silent prayer of gratitude that it wasn't a cold winter's morning. He threw some scraps of newspaper and a handful of kindling into the stove and lit it, standing the full kettle over the open firebox to boil for a pot of tea, and then turned to rummage in the drawer below the sidebed for his spare clothes. He dressed as the kettle began to sing; clean shirt, dry trousers and socks. His spare boots, old but just about serviceable, were in a corner out of sight – he found them, clean if a trifle dusty, pulled them on, mentally noting that his best pair would need polishing once they'd dried out: Later!

By the time he had the teapot brewing, they were through the third lock, by the *Admiral Nelson* pub, and into the fourth, the boats quickly rising. He poured himself a mug, and another for Alby, as the boatman ran the pair across the next pound and into the fifth lock. Ginny would make a fresh pot as they went through the tunnel on the summit – she couldn't easily manage a cuppa whilst lock-wheeling. As Alby brought the pair to a stand in the lock, he emerged onto the counter and handed the mug to his captain, receiving a grunt of thanks in response. Albert took a quick swig, then climbed onto the cabintop and jumped up to the lockside; he and Ginny closed the bottom gates and raised the top paddles.

As the boats rose, amid the roar and turbulence of water entering the lock, Michael drained his own mug, picked up his windlass from where he'd left it on the roof, and stepped off again onto the lockside. Ginny was already away, setting the last of the flight; the two men opened the gates, and Alby walked back to step on the motor and run the pair on.

'Yeh ain't settin' back, Dad?' Michael asked. Alby shook his head:

'No – sod 'em, Moikey! 'Is fault we lost toime, waitin' fer yeh, so 'e can close up and empty 'em fer 'imself.'

'Roight-oh, Dad.'

Out of the top lock, they were almost immediately driving into Braunston Tunnel, emerging once more into daylight twenty minutes later. Ginny reappeared at the same time from the butty cabin, a plate and two mugs in her hands; stepping with practiced ease onto the cabintop, she walked forward along the top planks over the open, empty hold, and jumped down onto the fore-deck. Running on cross-straps, the butty's fore-end was tight against the motor's stern, so it was easy for her to pass over the two mugs of hot, thick soup, resurrected from last night's stew, and the slabs of bread on the plate.

'Thanks, Ginny.' Michael took them from her, put the plate on the slide in front of Alby with one of the mugs, took a deep draught from his own and sighed with satisfaction as he resumed his stance on the gunwale to one side of the motor's cabin. He turned to compliment his sister, but she had already disappeared back to the stern of the butty for her own breakfast.

On through the day: Down the seven locks of Long Buckby, along the sixteen-mile pound to Stoke Bruerne, the last half-hour of it in the darkness of Blisworth Tunnel; down Stoke's seven locks; an hour and a half to the single lock at Cosgrove, and then over the Iron Trunk aqueduct above the Great Ouse River; around the long, twisting pound, past occasional villages, to Fenny Stratford and the almost-derisory ten-inch lock which begins the climb up the Chiltern Hills. A single lock, an hour later, and then the sudden rise of Three Locks, near the village of Stoke Hammond. They tied for the night there, above the abrupt flight, and spent a little more of Alby's two-pound bonus in the pub which stands beside the locks.

'Yew did well back ther', boy.' Michael shrugged self-consciously at Alby's compliment, as the boatman went on: 'That kiddie could easily 'ave bin swept oonder the boats 'n drowned, with the paddle roonnin'.'

'Oi know, Dad. Soon as Oi saw 'er in the water Oi dropped the paddle – 'n then, 'er folks didn' seem ter be doin' anythin', so Oi 'ad ter get 'er out, didn' Oi?'

'Yew did, son, 'n oi'm proud of what yeh did. It's loocky fer 'er that yeh can swim, eh?'

'Mebbe. Yeh could 'ave got 'er out anyway, boot it's quoite deep in that lock-tail.'

'Aye.'

'Oi'm proud of yeh, too, Moikey!' Ginny leaned across the table and planted a kiss on her brother's cheek. She turned to Alby: 'Whoy don't boatee kids learn teh swim, Dad? It don' seem sensible, not to!' He laughed:

'Oi see what yeh mean, Ginny! I suppose it's not 'aving the toime, mostly. 'N, o' course, we boaters troy ter mek a point o' *not* fallin' in – 'olds the boats oop, yeh see!'

They all laughed; Alby got to his feet: 'Anoother beer, Moikey? Lemonade, Ginny?'

'Yeah, please!'

'Please, Dad.'

And with that, the incident was forgotten – or so Michael thought…

Chapter Four

Two long days followed. Taking the maximum advantage of running light, empty boats, starting early and finishing late, the second night after leaving Hammond Three saw them tied in Brentford Basin, ready to load the following day.

That afternoon, they'd passed the layby at Bull's Bridge, by the junction with the Paddington Arm, where the Grand Union Company's boats tied to await orders for loading in the London area. Michael, at the helm of the *Sycamore,* had anxiously scanned the serried row of boats, tied in their pairs stern-on to the bank, looking for the *Bodmin;* just as he spotted Henry Caplin's butty, the *Towcester* tied alongside, a slim figure in a pretty blue frock leapt up and came running along the planks, laid at gunwale height on the cross-beams on the empty boat, waving frantically. She stopped by the mast, still waving with both hands:

'Moikey! Moikey – yeh're back!' Her voice carried clearly across the water; he grinned, waved back:

'Worcester trip got called off – we're loadin' at Brentford, fer Sherb'ne Wharf!'

'We're waitin' on timber, ter go teh Northampton, loadin' tomorrer!'

'Roight – see yeh on the way, with any loock?'

'Oi 'ope so, Moikey!' The boats were past, now; Harriet had turned to follow him with her eyes: ''N no more joompin' in the cut after oother girls, all roight?'

He laughed, and blew her a kiss, chuckled anew as she blushed scarlet:

'See yeh soon, 'Arriet!'

'Bye, Moikey!' Harriet turned to wave at Ginny, leaning in the butty's hatches peeling potatoes for their dinner; Michael looked beyond his girl, to the tall figure of Henry Caplin standing on the motor's counter, his eyes protectively on his only daughter. The boatman looked up, spared a cheerful smile for the young man he was beginning to consider as a possible future son-in-law.

* * *

Bob Renwick was in his office on Brentford's dockside at his habitual 6.30am the next day. As under-manager of Fellows, Morton & Clayton's local operation, organising the loading of the boats for their journeys to the midlands was his responsibility, and he liked to be on hand by the time the boatmen were up and about and itching for their orders. He smiled to himself at the scribbled note the nightwatchman had left for him:

Sycamore and Antrim arrived nine tonight – tied near the locks. Pedrewski. He'd asked the Polish ex-cavalry officer to keep an eye open for Captain Baker's boats; now, he put his head out of the office door and hailed a passing dockhand, told him to go and rouse the steerer and his son, and ask them to report to him straight away. Sitting down again, he riffled through the papers in front of him, found what he was looking for and read it through again, the smile back on his ascetic face.

Leaving Ginny to prepare the breakfast, Albert and Michael made their way along the dockside. The call to the office was usual for a captain to receive his orders for loading, but the request for Michael to go as well left the boy feeling distinctly nervous, wondering if he'd done anything wrong, if he was to be carpeted for some unintended misdemeanour. Albert knocked at the door, and they entered to find the under-manager waiting for them; the tall, grey-haired, rather studious looking figure of Renwick stood and held out a welcoming hand:

'Mr Baker, thank you for coming over so promptly.' Albert took his hand and shook it formally:

'No trouble, Mr Renwick – yew know moy son, Moichael?'

'Of course – it's good to see you, Mikey.' The hand was proffered to Michael, who shook it rather cautiously:

'Good Morning, Mr Renwick. Yeh wanted teh see me?'

'Only to congratulate you, Mikey. Tom Forrest, the lock-keeper at Braunston Bottom, told us what you did to save that little girl the other day. I want to thank you on behalf of the company for your bravery and quick-thinking.'

'Oh – ah. Roight...' Michael felt himself blushing furiously, muttered to the desk-top: 'Oi only did what was needed, nothin' special.'

'Well, you did a grand job, and we're very proud of you.'

'Thank yeh, Mr Renwick.' He glanced up from his scrutiny of the desk, to see the under-manager smiling at him, and essayed a smile in return. Renwick turned his attention to Albert:

'Mr Baker – you're ready to load?'

'Aye, we are, Mr Renwick.'

'Good, good. We've fifty tons of sugar for you this trip, to go to Sherborne Wharf. After that – the directors are keen to get back to running the business properly, now that they're back in charge, and that means putting regular pairs, regular crews, on the regular runs. We're aware of your boats as being among the best run in the fleet...'

'Thank yeh, Mr Renwick!' Alby and Michael chorused as he went on:

'...And we want you on the City Road to Fazeley Street route, carrying whatever goods are required at each loading. Is that all right with you?'

'That'll be foine, Mr Renwick!' Albert answered with a proud smile sideways at Michael – that was one of the prestige trips operated by Fellows, Morton & Clayton, a hangover from the heyday of the steam-driven fly runs of the past.

'Good, good. You'll run empty from Sherborne Wharf to Fazeley Street Depot, then, and pick up the regular trips from there. Is your engine all right now? I know you've had some trouble with it.'

'It's foine now, thank yeh. It was joost the h'injector, got so worn yeh couldn' keep it sprayin' roight – boot we got a new oone from Saltley Dock, 'fore coomin' 'ere, 'n it's okay now.'

'That's good. Is there anything else you need? Any other problems with the boats?' Albert shook his head:

'No – nothin' teh woorry about. Butty'll need dockin' soometoime, the bottoms checkin', boot it ain't leakin' not yet, any'ow. 'N they could both do wi' a coat o' paint!'

'So could most of the fleet!' Renwick laughed; Alby joined in:

'Yeah – we've seen 'em, ain't we, Moikey?' More seriously, Renwick said:

'We will get round to them all in time. The company doesn't like to see the boats looking so shabby, any more than you boaters do!'

'Oi know that, Mr Renwick. Even if ther's soome 'oo don' seem teh care too mooch.' Renwick's ears pricked up at this:

'Oh? What makes you say that, Mr Baker?' Albert glanced at Michael, then turned his attention back to the under-manager.

'We saw oone pair, follered oos oop Braunston – cloths all awry, paintwork dirty, 'n yeh should 'ave seen the brasses!'

'Fellows's boats?'

'Oh, aye. Butty was the *Florence,* didn' see the name on the motor. It was their kiddie that Moikey fished out o' the cut.'

'Oh – I didn't realise… It just says another boater's child, here. But – yes, I know who you mean. Motor is the *Apple,* steerer is a man called Martin, Frank Martin. Following you, you said?'

'Aye, that's roight. Loaded.' Renwick shuffled through some of the papers on his desk, checked one:

'Yes – he's due here tomorrow, with tubes from Stewarts & Lloyds.'

'Aye.' Michael glanced at his Dad, decided to stick his neck out:

'Mr Renwick – whoy do yeh keep a man loike that on? The boats are a disgrace, 'n Oi 'ear as 'e treats 'is missus 'n kiddies pretty rough, too.' Renwick looked at the boy, sighed:

'He gets the job done, Michael. And God knows we're short enough of crews, right now. We took him back about two years ago – he'd lived on the bank, worked in a Birmingham factory after marrying a girl there, Joan, her name is, I think. He was in the Air Force ground crew during the war, but got injured in an accident and de-mobbed in 1943, came back on the boats.'

'Is 'e old Josh Martin's boy, then?' Alby asked.

'That's right, Mr Baker. You knew Josh, I take it?'

''S roight – good boater, old Josh was. Shame if 'is son lets 'im down loike that.'

'It is. He's been told to pull his socks up more than once, but he soon goes back to his slip-shod ways. I daresay the directors will sack him, in time, if he doesn't mend his attitude. But for now…' He shrugged his shoulders: 'As I say, we need the crews.'

'Can yeh get oos loaded 'n away today, Mr Renwick?' Renwick laughed:

'Don't want to get too close, eh? Yes, I need you to be away as soon as possible anyway, Mr Baker. They should be ready for you by now, if you'd like to put your boats on the wharf.'

'No sooner said than doone, Mr Renwick! We'll be off soon as we're loaded.'

'Thank you, Mr Baker, Michael. Have a good trip!'

Chapter Five

They hurried back to the boats and began the half-hour ritual needed to start the old Bolinder. A number of other FMC pairs were tied almost randomly around the basin; a little later, as they untied the boats ready to move onto the loading wharf, a wave came from the pair already there and partly loaded. Alerted by the young man on the motor's counter, the rest of the crew looked up from their tasks and waved their own greetings.

'Dad – it's 'Anneys, in froont of oos,' Michael called down to Albert, still tinkering in the engine-hole; he looked out, gave the other crew a quick wave before returning his attention to the engine. Michael and Ginny pulled the pair alongside the wharf, tied them in place ready to begin loading, as the stocky figure of Bill Hanney strode up:

'Moikey! Ginny! Yeh got back okay, then?'

'We did, Mr 'Anney. Bit slow, boot we made it. Mr Vickuss got oos a noo h'injector, 'n she's goin' foine, now.' Albert climbed out of the engine-hole, shook Bill Hanney's hand:

'Good teh see yeh, Bill. Yew on this sugar roon, too?'

'Yeah, we are that. Sherb'ne Wharf?'

'Yeah, oos too.'

'Foine! We'll go butty, then, shall oos?'

'If yeh can wait, Bill?'

'Oh, toime fer a cuppa 'fore we set off, Oi reckon!' He turned and hurried back to his own boats to go on supervising the loading;

the dock foreman strolled over to them, checking his lists as he did so:

'Steerer Baker? Fifty tons of sugar for Sherborne Wharf, Birmingham?'

'Yeah, that's oos.'

'Right – we'll get on loading you straight away.' He turned and beckoned to some of the dock-hands, walked off to meet them and give them their instructions.

* * *

Fifty tons of sugar, in two-hundredweight bags, takes a while to load into the holds of a pair of narrowboats, even with both dockers and the boat crews working flat out. It was almost mid-day before the two pairs were loaded and clothed up, ready for the trip to Birmingham. Bill Hanney's wife, Vi, had a big pot of tea brewed, and she and Ginny handed round the mugs as the men set to, mopping down the boats so that they would be clean and smart for the journey, Albert and Michael on their pair, Bill and his two sons, Billy and Stevie, on the *Acorn* and the *Angelus.*

Michael had been feeling more and more anxious as the time went by, not knowing if Henry Caplin had been loaded elsewhere – boats from Bull's Bridge most often loaded at Brentford, unless they were directed to Paddington or somewhere on the Regent's Canal, and there had been no sign of them. But, mid-morning, Alby had glanced across the basin, and dug him in the ribs as he hefted a sack of sugar, nearly making him drop it. He looked over in the direction of his captain's nod and saw several Grand Union pairs nosing up against some river lighters on the far side of the basin. A hand waved in greeting; he dropped the sack and waved back quickly, before lifting it again to stack it in place in the hold. Thereafter, he went about his work with a more cheerful mein.

As they turned the boats and headed back to the gauging locks to depart on their journey, he swung the *Sycamore* over close to the other boats. Henry Caplin looked up from the hold of his butty, mopped his brow and waved; Harriet's head appeared in the hatches at his shout. She gave Michael a wave and a shy smile; he called over:

'See yeh later, 'Arriet!' He looked at Henry, who was giving him an amused look, leaning on the gunwales: 'When'll yeh be away, Mr Caplin?'

'Coopl'a hours, if we're loocky, Moikey.'

'How far'll yeh go today?' The man grinned:

''S far as we can get, lad!' He laughed, seeing in the boy's face his disappointment with such an uninformative answer: 'Ooxbridge, mebbe Widewater if we get a good start!' Michael smiled his relief:

'Thanks, Mr Caplin! Oi'll mebbe see yeh later, then?'

'That'll be foine, boy!' With a last wave, he turned to his labours.

They made good time that day, helped by a good road. At every lock, pairs heading South had left them empty, saving Billy Hanney, lock-wheeling for his boats, the arduous task of draining them and opening the gates. Bill and Vi worked their pair through, leaving fifteen-year-old Stevie to help Michael turn the locks around ready for the second pair; the two boys had been firm friends since Stevie's brother and father had pulled Michael out of the canal in Wolverton, that cold dark night in January 1940, and now they both enjoyed the opportunity to work together, to share in a continuous flow of ribald banter as they wound stiff paddles and heaved on reluctant gates.

Up out of the Thames Valley they climbed: Clitheroe's Lock, Osterley lock, Hanwell six, Norwood, and so on to the long level, six miles to Cowley Lock. It was between the two junctions, Bulls Bridge, and Cowley Peachey where the Slough arm heads away West, that they met Michael's protagonists from Braunston.

The recognisably-scruffy boats coming to meet them proved to be the *Apple* and the *Florence;* at the helm of the motor, a tall, dark-complexioned man in his thirties at first tried to be inconspicuous behind his chimney as the boats drew close, but in the end showed himself and called across to Michael, at the tiller of the *Sycamore:*

'Oi should thank yeh fer the loife o' moy girl.'

'No need, Captain, anyoone would 'ave doon the same.' Michael's reply was as formal as the man's gratitude had been.

'Ar, that's as may be. Oi didn' oughta 'ave bin so rude, it was the shock, see?' Michael just waved in reply, unconvinced of the man's sincerity.

The pairs passed; as the butty glided by, Michael saw the slim fair woman at the tiller bend down and speak to someone inside, and the little girl appeared in the hatches, gazing over at him from those soulful green eyes. She gave him a tentative wave; the shyness in her smile made him think of Harriet, and he returned her wave with a wide smile of his own:

'Yew all roight?' he called to her; her nod was just as shy.

A mile past Cowley Peachey junction, to Cowley Lock; another long stretch, almost two miles to Uxbridge Lock, near the dock where Fellows, Morton & Clayton built and repaired their wooden-hulled boats; a mile to Denham Deep, at eleven feet the deepest lock on the Grand Union Canal; then the boring, dead-straight pound up to Widewater Lock. It was here that Stevie Hanney, bearing a question from his father, hung around to talk to Alby as he and Ginny ran the boats into the lock:

'Dad says wher' d'yeh want ter stop tonoight, Ooncle Alby?' Alby glanced at Michael, saw the anxious look on his face:

'Tell 'im 'ow about the Fisheries, boy Coppermill Lock?'

'Okay!' The youngster dashed off to catch up with his boats.

'Dad?' Michael's voice held an unspoken question; Alby laughed:

'We've 'ad a long day, boy, that'll do. Besoides, if yeh want to see yer gal, we'd better not be too far 'head of 'em, eh?' Michael grinned as he went to draw a top paddle:

'Thanks, Dad!' He knew very well that they would usually have pushed on until dark, on this long summer evening. Love and respect for his adoptive father swelled his heart as they worked on through the lock, as did the prospect of an hour or two in the company of Harriet Caplin – if Henry did make it to Widewater, where they were right now, he'd only have two miles, a bit less even, to cycle back...

Ginny had been preparing the meal between locks; now, she handed them a plate each as they left Widewater. They ate whilst traversing the mile-long pound to Black Jack's Lock. Michael spelled Alby at the helm of the motor, his dinner on the slide in front of him while his Dad sat in relative ease at the table-cupboard below; Ginny ate leaning in the butty's hatches, the tiller under her arm. They worked both pairs through Black Jack's, then Coppermill Lock, and tied them above a little after seven-thirty in the evening.

After a quick wash and brush-up, everyone congregated on the towpath, and Michael, anxious to get away, found himself bombarded with questions about his rescue of the little girl. The canals had always had a dependable if mysterious telegraph of their own, which inevitably meant that any event of interest would be known to all and sundry long before logic suggested the news could possibly have travelled so far. He fended their curiosity off, embarrassed at such attention, until Bill Hanney laughingly put a stop to it:

'Let the lad go, will yeh, 'e's got oother things on 'is moind! Say 'ello teh 'Enry 'n Suey fer oos, 'n give 'Arriet our loove, roight?'

'Oi will, Mr 'Anney. See yeh later, Dad, Ginny.' He picked up the bike, stepped over it and set off back the way they'd come with a last wave to them all.

Bill Hanney leant casually against the cabinside of his butty, felt in his pocket for his tobacco pouch. Glancing up at his eldest son as he rolled a cigarette, he remarked:

''Bout toime yew got yerself a regular girl, Billy.' The nineteen-year-old grinned:

'Give me toime, Dad!'

'Not found anyone yeh fancy, then, Billy?' Alby asked, carefully packing his pipe.

''E foinds too many of 'em!' His mother growled. Alby laughed as he sucked the match flame through the tobacco:

'Loike that, is it? 'E'll settle down in 'is own good toime, won't yeh, boy?'

'Reckon so, Ooncle Alby!' Billy's good humour was undimmed by his mother's disapproval.

'Moikey 'n 'Arriet seem loike they're goin' strong, don't they?' Vi asked.

'Bit yoong teh be gettin' so serious, Oi reckon.' Her husband commented.

'Oh, don't be sooch a wet blanket!' She told him.

'They're only, what, sixteen?' Bill was not to be put off his opinion. Alby chuckled:

'They're not stoopid, neither of 'em, Bill – they'll boide their toime! 'Soides, 'Enry's not daft, 'e 'n Suey mek sure soomeoone keeps an oiye on 'em!'

'Pretty girl, 'Arriet…' Billy said thoughtfully. His mother rounded on him:

'Don't yew dare, Billy 'Anney!' The boy laughed, pleased at having succeeded in winding his mother up.

Albert looked around, nodded towards the Hanneys' younger son, standing chatting with Ginny a few yards away:

''Ow 'bout yoong Stevie, 'as 'e got 'is oiye on anyoone yet?' The boy in question, sensing that he was suddenly the subject of discussion, looked up:

'What?'

''Ave yeh found a girl yeh loike yet, lad?' Alby asked him. The boy glanced at Ginny, who gave him a nervous smile, then back at Albert:

'Oi'm only fifteen, Ooncle Alby!' Albert chuckled:

'Ah, that's roight, boy!' Vi caught his eye and grinned; she too had noticed the exchange of looks between the two youngsters.

Alby gestured at Bill with his pipe:

'Coom on, let's get oos an ale apiece!' The six of them strolled back, to where the Fisheries Inn sat a little back from the towpath below the lock.

Chapter Six

Ernie Caplin sat in a corner of the bottom bar, in the Boat Inn at Stoke Bruerne, nursing his glass of lemonade. Like Alby Baker and the Hanneys, further South, they had stopped early that night, although for very different reasons – little Jack had developed a painful rash, and Gracie had wanted to see Sister Mary about it.

Grace Hanney, Bill and Vi's oldest child and only daughter, had married Ernie's elder brother two years before. Jack, three months old now, was their first child, and the apple of his father's eye, even if the baby had given him some disturbed nights along the way. Many a time Ernie had woken in the morning, in the cabin of their motor boat, to find Joe curled up on the sidebed, usually still snoring after decamping from the butty in the wee small hours. But Jack was getting better, and those occasions were fewer now – until this rash had unsettled the kiddie again. Joe had been just as keen to get it looked at as Gracie: *No surproise ther'!* Ernie smiled as he took a swig of his drink.

When they'd married, the Grand Union Company, as eager for crews in the war years as any carriers, had given the newlyweds their own pair – Ernie, twelve then, had gone along as extra crew, leaving his Mum and Dad with just his elder sister and little Sam. *Oi wonder wher' they are?* He would see his family quite often as their paths crossed in the course of their travels, even if it was usually just a quick 'hello-goodbye' in passing, the need to press on with their trips, to arrive and unload in order to get paid for the job, taking precedence over anything else. Sam was eleven now, a competent, experienced young boater – *'e's not far off bein' as good as me!* – and Harriet had reached the grand old age of sixteen. And she was really sweet on Mikey Baker – *they'll be getting' in tow, soomeday – boot they're mooch too young, yet* Ernie decided, with the wisdom of his fourteen years.

Now he sat back, took another long draught of his lemonade. He envied Mikey, and Stevie Hanney – their folks were much more sensible, in his eyes, letting the boys drink proper beer, even if they weren't allowed more than a couple of pints at a time. Joe, like his father, had stricter ideas – Ernie'd been permitted one pint of shandy tonight, in view of their early halt, but now it was back to lemonade. It was quiet in the pub – too early for many boaters to be in. Joe was up at the bar, chatting with the crew of a Faulkner's boat, from Leighton Buzzard, stuck there with a broken gearbox, and Gracie was still over in Sister Mary's cottage, by the top lock. Bored, Ernie leaned forward to listen in on the conversation.

The Faulkner's boatman had been regaling Joe with his tale of their breakdown, but now he changed the subject:

'D'yeh hear about the kiddie, took a look in Bra'nston bottom th'oother day?'

'Yeah – we coom through ther' this mornin', 'eard all about it.'

'Seems 'er Pa 'it the bridge-'ole, knocked 'er off the planks – she'd 'ave been swept oonder the boats 'n drownded fer sure, boot soome young lad dropped the paddle 'n went in after 'er!'

'Yeah…'

'That was moy little broother!' A proud voice spoke from the doorway. Joe turned and swung an arm around his wife as she came in:

''Ow's Jack, is 'e all roight?' Gracie smiled at him:

''E's *foine,* Joe! Sister Mary's given me soome liniment to roob in, 'n soome special powder to wash 'is nappies in. She says 'e'll be roight as noinepence in no toime.'

'It was your broother 'oo saved that kiddie, yeh say?' Grace turned to the other boatman:

'Moikey – yes. Well, 'e ain't *really* moy broother, boot…' She went on to describe how Michael had become part of her family when they'd rescued him from the icy canal, all those years ago, and how she had once worked with him and Alby Baker as third hand in the crew.

* * *

The subject of her proud discourse had come across the *Towcester* and the *Bodmin* tied up outside the Halfway House, just below Widewater Lock. Now he was sitting in a corner of the bar, one arm possessively around the waist of Harriet Caplin, a pint of shandy in front of him in deference to Henry Caplin's strictures. Harriet, sipping demurely at her glass of orange squash, regarded him with admiring eyes as he self-consciously answered Henry's questions about the girl's rescue. *Can't everyoone joost forget about that?* In Michael's eyes, he'd done no more than anyone would have, in the same situation, and the constant attention, the admiration for his ability to swim, was beginning to wear him down.

But at last the subject was changed, the talk turning to more usual matters of interest in the boating world – loads, routes, destinations, and perhaps above all the poor state of the canals after six years of heavy use and little maintenance. There was general agreement amongst the boatmen present that while the major routes like the Grand Union Canal were just about passable, despite the deterioration, other, less travelled roads like the Oxford or Stratford-on-Avon canals, or the old 'bottom road' out of Birmingham via Fazeley and Coventry, were in a parlous state:

'Yeh can't tek a full load down Curd'eth nowadays – bottom's too near the flamin' top, all the way teh Fazeley Turn. 'N the Coventry cut's no better, neither!'

'Soom o' them gates down ther' are in a bad way, 'n all.'

'Leakin' bad, are they?'

'Leakin'? 'Bout ready teh fall apart, they are!'

'Paddles are all 'bout wore out, too. Nigh on impossible teh shift – 'specially them on the Stratford cut, down Lap'eth.'

'When are the 'thorities gonna do soomat about it, that's what Oi want ter know!'

''Oo knows! Oi arst the guv'nor at Bull's Bridge, 'n 'e says they ain't got no money fer maintainance. So what's goona 'appen, Oi arst 'im: Not a lot, 'e says, not roight now, any'ow!'

Michael sat back, content in his girl's company, letting the grumbles of the other boatmen, Grand Union Company captains all, flow over him, offering up a silent prayer of thanks that he worked for Fellows, Morton & Clayton, and looked like spending his time on the easier, well-used waterways between London and Birmingham.

* * *

Two miles to the North, the conversation in the *Fisheries Inn* was going along remarkably parallel lines. Bill Hanney and Alby Baker had been swapping horror stories of damaged and leaking locks, shallow and even empty pounds, that they had come across in the recent past; now, their thoughts also turned to the prospects for improvement in the future:

'Moikey picked oop a noospaper th'oother day, Bill. 'E was readin' in it as this noo lot 'ave got diff'rent oideas about 'ow teh roon things.'

'Yeah, Oi've bin 'earin'. Call 'emselves the Labour Party – Oi'll bet ther' ain't oone of 'em's ever doone a decent days labour!' They laughed: 'Boot, loike yeh say, they've got their own ways o' doin' things. Least, so they reckon.'

'Want teh roon things themselves, from what Moikey says.

Tek everythin' oover, roon it fer the coontry! Loine their own pockets, more loike. Politicians – they're all the bloody same, for moy mooney.'

'Oi dunno, Alby – If they're goin' teh tek charge of it all, roads 'n railways 'n docks 'n canals, stands teh reason they'll want it all workin' properly. 'N the gov'ment's got lots o' mooney, roight? So mebbe we'll get the drudgin' doone, get all them leaky gates fixed.'

'Oi'll believe it when Oi see it, Bill. Oi 'ope yeh're roight, moind – the cut could do wi' things bein' sorted out. 'N mebbe they'll troy 'n bring more trade back 'n all, 'stead o' lettin' the railways tek it all.'

'Oi think we should give 'em a chance, Alby – can't do any 'arm, can it? Things can't get mooch worse, so let 'em troy, Oi say.'

Both took a long, gloomy pull at their pints, then Alby changed the subject:

''Ow far yeh goin' tomorrer, Bill?'

'Maffers? 'Ow d'yeh fancy the Red Lion?' Alby nodded his approval – the pub in Marsworth village was always a popular stop – then smiled:

'Tekin' it steady, then Bill?' Hanney laughed:

'Don't 'urt teh stop wher' yeh know there'll be good comp'ny 'n decent ale! We can mek Stoke Bruin easy, the nex' noight, then the *Cape,* if we press on a bit. 'N then we're there. Roight?'

'Stoke ter the *Cape*'s goin' teh be a long'un?'

'Ah, we can do it, Alby! Goin' butty loike this'll 'elp.'

'You 'n your bloody ale, Bill 'Anney!'

Another pull at their respective glasses, then:

'Yeh're on the City Road ter Warwick Bar roon after this'n, then, Alby?'

'We are that – 'ow did yew know?'

'Oi arst! We're on that roon too – when Mr Renwick told me, Oi says to 'im, what've yeh got Alby Baker on, 'n 'e says, same as yew, Mr 'Anney.'

'Prob'ly wants soomeoone sensible teh keep an oiye on yeh, Bill.'

A little later, they all emerged from the pub to find the rain sheeting down. Alby tucked Ginny under his arm, his jacket thrown over her shoulders; Bill Hanney took his own coat off and draped it around his wife, and they hurried off to return to the boats.

Stepping over into the stern well of the *Antrim,* Ginny glanced back:

'Is that Moikey?' Alby looked up, saw a bedraggled figure approaching, wheeling a bicycle; he squinted through the rain:

'It is 'n all! Yew get down in the droy, girl.' Ginny ducked into the cabin, made sure the kettle was on the range, stirred the fire into renewed life. Outside, Alby took the bike from Michael and lodged it on the butty, pushing it under one of the strings holding the top cloth in place:

'Get insoide, boy, 'n get out o' them wet things – yeh look loike yeh're soaked through!'

'Thanks, Dad. Started joost after Oi left teh coom back – towpath's too slippy teh roide, so Oi've pushed it near on two moile!' Alby chuckled, following him down into the motor cabin:

'Serves yeh roight – yeh could've 'ad a pint or two 'ere with oos!' Michael grinned at him:

'Yeah, Oi know! Boot…' He shrugged.

''Ow is 'Arriet, 'n 'er folks?'

'Foine, Dad – they've got timber on, fer Trennery's yard in Northampton.'

'Gonna be follerin' oos, then, fer a day or two. Yew get droy, son, Oi'll see if Ginny's got the tea brewed.' He left Michael to strip off his wet clothes, returning a few minutes later with two steaming mugs of tea, to find the boy already tucked under his blankets on the sidebed:

'Ther' yeh go, boy, get that down yer.'

Chapter Seven

Little Jack Caplin slept well that night, much to the relief and delight of his devoted but weary parents. Joe was up and about in good time the next morning, checking their load of coal, mopping down the cabins, setting Ernie to giving the brasses a quick polish while Grace brewed some tea and got the baby dressed. Soon after six they were into the top lock, pressing ahead to make up for the time lost the day before.

But fate was not going to play their game. They reached Leighton Lock in the early afternoon to find a small gathering of boats waiting to ascend; Joe drew his pair in to the side and scrambled off to find out what was causing the hold-up:

'Soome stoopid booger's teken oone 'o the gates out' he was told by another, rather aggravated, boatman, leaning in the hatches of his immaculate Samuel Barlow Coal Company motor.

''Ow long deh they reckon?' Joe asked.

'Oh, not long. They're about doone – boot they've 'ad teh fix the gate, so yeh'll have teh drag yer butty across teh get out. 'N put it in wrong soide, as well – it's that gate what's boogered.'

'Roight – thanks, mate.' He strolled back to his boats, annoyed but resigned. *Oh well – mebbe we can still mek Maffers, if we're loocky...*

* * *

Michael had woken that morning feeling thick-headed: *Can't be the beer, Oi didn't 'ave mooch!* As soon as he rose and began to dress, his nose and eyes started to run; by the time his Dad was dressed and had gone to start the engine, and the first tea of the day had emerged from the butty cabin, he was coughing and sneezing.

Steering the butty, on a long line now that they were loaded, while Ginny made some breakfast, he was feeling very sorry for himself. Ginny was laughingly unsympathetic:

'It's yer own fault, coyclin' off last noight! Now yeh've got soaked twoice in a few days, 'aven't yeh?'

At the first lock of the day, where they would switch to their usual duties, Albert suggested he took the motor-boat's tiller, but he refused:

'Oi'll be foine, Dad – better if Oi keep movin', Oi reckon.'

They pressed on as usual, running butty to Bill Hanney's boats again. The long climb up from the Thames valley to the top of the Chiltern Hills took them most of the day; evening saw them over the summit at Tring and starting downhill again, down the seven locks of Marsworth flight. Past the junction of the Aylesbury Arm, they tied up at last by the bridge in the village next to the Red Lion, around eight o'clock at night.

Dinner taken on the move, as usual, Alby was ready for a pint:

'D'yeh want a beer, Moikey, or would yeh rather stay 'ere 'n keep warm?' Michael looked up, surprised:

'Oi was goin' teh coycle back teh see 'Arriet…'

'Oh no yeh're not! Yeh'll mek that cold ten toimes worse if yeh do, Moichael Baker!' Ginny spoke forcefully from the cabin doors: 'Yew get off with 'Anneys, Dad, Oi'll stay 'n keep an oiye on Moikey, see 'e don't sneak out!'

'Boot…'

'Yer sister's roight, boy – stay 'ere 'n get rid o' that cold. Yeh'll be seein' yer girl soon enough.' Michael shrugged, knowing better than to argue against their combined wills; he perked up slightly when Albert said to Ginny:

'Ther's a drop o' whisky, back o' the table-cupboard in the motor. Yeh can mek 'im a 'ot toddy, that'll 'elp clear it oop.'

'Roight-oh, Dad.'

A knock sounded on the butty's cabinside, and Ginny looked around:

''Ello, Mr 'Anney – Dad'll be roight with yeh.' She stood clear of the doors to let Alby emerge, and then climbed down to join her brother inside. Michael sat on the sidebed watching her as she filled the kettle from the watercan, raked up the fire in the range and put it on to boil, and then began delving in the table-cupboard; from outside, they could hear Alby's voice fading into the distance, telling Bill and Vi about Michael's indisposition as they headed for the pub.

* * *

Henry Caplin stepped onto the roof of the *Towcester* as his boats fell in the bottom lock of Marsworth Flight. He jumped down to the counter, and loosed off the breasting straps holding the two sterns together; Harriet was on the fore-ends, untying them, as her mother and brother leant on the bottom gates, swung them open as the weight of the water came off them. Henry put the engine into gear, started the motor forward and took the towline from his daughter as the butty's bow drew level with him; she stepped across, quickly and nimbly, to join him. Sam stepped aboard from the lock tail at the same moment, leaving his mother to take charge of the *Bodmin* as the towline tightened and it too started forward out of the lock. Henry had taken it on a short tow – it was getting late, and he'd decided to stop in the village for the night.

Like the two Fellows, Morton & Clayton pairs before them, they ran past the Aylesbury Arm turn, past the Canal Company's yard, under Watery Lane Bridge and on to the next bridge. Just past it, he saw the FMC boats tied – he saw the light in his daughter's eyes, as well:

'Oi think we oughta press on, get teh Peter's Two, or the Nag's 'Ead – what d'yeh reckon, Sam?'

'Yeah, Oi think yer roight, Dad!' Harriet reached across past her father to threaten the boy with her fist:

'Dad! Doon' be so rotten!' Henry burst out laughing:

'Get ready teh tie the fore-ends, then!' He took the engine out of gear, letting the butty slide up alongside the motor; moments later, the boats were securely tied, a few yards in front of Bill Hanney's pair.

Henry and Suey disappeared into their butty cabin to smarten themselves up before heading for the Red Lion; Sam, at eleven, was only allowed to go with them to the pub on special occasions. Harriet quickly, eagerly brushed her hair and washed her face, and then stepped across the butty onto the bank, waiting for her parents. They joined her, and all three walked back towards the bridge.

Passing the *Antrim,* Suey noticed the light burning in the cabin of the *Sycamore,* tied on the outside as always. She leant over to knock on the butty's cabin-top, knowing it would be heard inside the motor also; moments later, Ginny's head appeared in the hatches:

''Ello, Mrs Caplin, Mr Caplin!'

''Ello, Ginny – Are yeh coomin teh the 'Lion?'

'Dad's already gone, with Mr 'n Mrs 'Anney. Oi'm lookin' after Moikey – 'e's got a bit of a cold.'

'Can Oi stop with them, Dad? Please?' Harriet asked; Henry looked doubtful, but Suey gave her a smile:

'That'll be all roight, loove. They're sensible kids, 'Enry' she said to her husband 'they'll not get oop teh any hanky-panky, 'specially with Ginny teh keep an oiye on 'em!'

'Whoy doon' yeh give Sam a shout, 'e can join yeh, too, rather than bein' on 'is own?'

'Yes, Dad.' Harriet dashed back to her boats, roused her brother and brought him along, as her parents headed off to join the gathering in the Red Lion.

* * *

Her elder brother was still feeling rather disgruntled. They'd made good time from Leighton, despite the other pairs running in front of them after the stoppage, but those same repairs had put them back appreciably. Clearing Peter's Two, the last locks before the Marsworth Flight, he too took his butty on a short line for the half-mile distance to the next bridge.

There were several pubs in Marsworth village, but of them all the Red Lion, beside that bridge, was the usual choice of the passing boatmen. Joe soon saw the expected row of moored pairs by the towpath on his approach to the bridge – he slowed the engine, looked back as Grace steered the butty between him and the bank, while Ernie scurried along the top-planks to snatch the fore-ends together. It was only as he stepped across to tie the sterns that he heard his younger brother's shout:

'Eh, Joe! That's Dad's pair in froont; 'n Bill 'Anney's joshers as well!' He looked up with a broad smile:

'They'll be in the 'Lion, then – coom on, let's go 'n join 'em!'

Ernie ran back the length of the boats, grinning hugely; he ducked into his motor cabin to wash his face and comb his hair while Joe and Grace freshened themselves up in the butty. All three, with little Jack, sleeping soundly, cuddled in the crook of his mother's arm, rendezvoused on the towpath moments later. Strolling past the other boats, they, in their turn, spotted the lit lamps in the *Sycamore,* paused to see who was on board:

'It's Moikey – 'e's coughin' 'n sneezin' fit ter boost!' Ginny unsympathetically informed them: 'Got 'imself soakin' wet again last noight, coyclin' off teh see 'Arriet!'

'Yeh're lookin' after 'im, then?' Joe asked, laughing.

'Yeah – 'Arriet's 'ere too, 'n Sam.' Joe raised his voice:

'Yew playin' gooseberry in ther' then, Sam?' The youngest Caplin's head appeared in the hatches:

'Joe! Gracie!' He pushed past Ginny, leapt onto the bank and threw his arms around his big brother's neck: 'Good ter see yeh, Joe!'

Grace bent to hug the boy in her ample spare arm as he turned to her:

''Ow are yeh, Sammy?' He stretched up to kiss her cheek, laughing:

'Oi'm foine, Gracie! 'Ow's Jack?'

''E's all roight, Sam.'

Harriet had emerged too, to greet her brother and sister-in-law, as eagerly if less energetically than Sam, while the two younger Caplin brothers talked furiously at each other. Hellos, good wishes and gossip were quickly exchanged, while Ginny looked on with an almost matriarchal smile on her face, until Michael put an inquisitive head out of the hatches:

''S'all roight fer soome! Oi'm banished from the pub 'cause o' this bloody cold!'

''Ow're yeh feelin', Moikey?' Grace's voice held a tone of amused compassion.

'Oh, not too bad. Better'n oi was – Oi'll be roight as rain tomorrer, with a bit o' loock.'

'Is that owin' teh yer sister's nursin', or moy little sister bein' 'ere?' Joe asked him, laughing.

'Bit o' both, maybe!' Michael admitted. 'Yew get on oover the pub – yer Mum 'n Dad are ther', with ar Dad 'n Bill 'n Vi 'Anney, 'n Billy 'n Stevie.'

'D'yeh want me teh stop with yeh, Moikey?' Grace asked him; he shook his head:

'No – it'd be good teh 'ave a chat with yeh, boot yeh doon't want young Jack pickin' oop moy germs. Oi'll see yeh in the mornin', maybe.'

'Besoides, 'Arriet's 'ere, 'n yeh've got enough gooseberries as it is, eh, Moikey?' Joe suggested. Michael gave him a sheepish grin, while Harriet blushed pink; he went on: 'Coom on, Oi'm dyin' fer a pint. Yew coomin' or stayin', Ernie?'

The fourteen-year-old hesitated, weighing his choices, but the chance of a shandy, and the thought of seeing his parents, won out: 'Oi'm coomin', Joe! See yeh later, Sam.'

Chapter Eight

'Yew get back down in the warm, Moikey!' Ginny ordered her brother, but he was in the mood for rebellion:

'It's a foine evenin', Ginny – the fresh air'll do me good. Won't it, 'Arriet?' The girl looked from brother to sister, reluctant to take sides. Ginny laughed:

'Don't let 'im put yeh on the spot, 'Arriet! All roight – boot yew stay there in the 'atches, wher' yeh've got the warmth from the stove, roight?' She spoke sternly to him.

'Yes, Ma!' Michael pretended meek subservience, and ducked, laughing, when she aimed a playful blow at his head. Harriet stepped back onto the boat, went to stand close to him; Ginny sat on the gunwale of the well-deck, and Sam hotched up to sit on the roof of the cabin:

'Is it roight, Moikey, yeh joomped in the cut teh save a little girl?' Michael lifted his eyes to Heaven, drew a deep breath:

'Does everyone 'ave teh keep goin' on about that? Oi didn't do anythin' special!'

Sam subsided, quashed, but his sister said quietly:

'It was very brave of yeh, whatever yew say, Moikey.' She reached up to draw him close, gave him a quick kiss on the cheek: ''N Oi'm proud of yeh, anyway.'

'We all are, Moikey. All roight, Oi know yeh don't want teh talk about it!' Ginny raised her hands to stop him telling her off; he relaxed, smiling:

'Okay – boot can we drop it, now?' A slightly awkward silence fell, until Sam asked:

'Wher' did yeh learn teh swim, Moikey?' Michael turned to him with a frown, feeling that this subject was only marginally removed; but he replied:

'At school, 'fore Oi came on the boats. They used teh tek oos teh the local swimming baths oonce a week.'

'Oh – 'ow about yew, Ginny, can yew swim too?' She nodded:

'Not as well as Moikey. We still 'ave a go, when we go to the baths in Birnigum, or wherever we can.'

'Yew are loocky!' Sam was gazing down at his hands, folded in his lap 'all the things yeh learned in school. Oi wish Oi could read, 'n wroite…'

'Yew could teach oos, Moikey…?'

'What?' He looked down into the soft brown eyes, saw the affection glowing in them: 'Oi don't know…'

'Whoy not, Moikey?' His sister joined the argument: ''E's been helping me teh learn more, since Oi joined 'im 'n Dad' she told the others. Sam turned around, an eager look in his eyes:

'Please, Moikey? *Please?'* Michael looked around at them, saw the appeal on two faces, the encouragement on Ginny's:

'It teks *ages* teh learn, 'n we don't see each oother that often, do we?'

'Yew could show them a bit, each toime, 'n they can practise in between, Moikey?'

'Oh – Oi suppose so…' He gave in to their combined pressure: 'Yeh'd better all coom in the cabin then. 'Ave we got soome paper, anywher', Ginny? 'N pencils?'

'Dad's got soome bits o' pencil in the ticket-drawer. 'N yeh could use the edges o' that newspaper, if we can't foind anythin' else!'

'Okay…' Vaguely embarrassed, and still reluctant, Michael led the way down into the confines of the butty cabin.

* * *

Alby Baker would have enjoyed the evening that bit more had his adopted son and daughter been with them. It often amused him how little Ginny had taken over the role of matriarch in his crew, learning from Gracie before her marriage to Joe Caplin, and would now firmly boss her brother, and even himself, about, in matters domestic. Her insistence that Michael stay home had been sensible, given the boy's obvious discomfort with his head-cold, but that didn't stop him missing their company. Especially on such a night.

He had not been entirely surprised when Henry and Suey Caplin had joined them, knowing that they were not far behind, but the arrival of Joe and Grace had come as a welcome excuse to increase the frivolity of the occasion. Given the day-to-day pressure of the boatman's job, the ongoing need to 'get 'em ahead' in order to finish the trip and unload (and get paid), the meeting of the four pairs of boats, the four interconnected families, at the same place was a rare occurrence, and a good reason for a joyful if restrained celebration.

Harriet's decision to stay on the *Antrim* with her beau had sparked off a round of cheerful banter when Suey announced it; Ernie's preference for the pub had given them all another laugh, and even prompted his father to buy him a pint of shandy in recognition of the occasion.

It was past closing time when the landlord of the Red Lion bid them all goodnight, pushing the door to with a grin as they chuckled their way out into the warm August night. Over the bridge, down onto the towpath; Grace made straight for her butty cabin, with the sleeping baby nestled on her shoulder, taking a mildly-protesting Ernie with her, as Suey knocked on the cabin-top to rouse her daughter and youngest son. A smiling but sleepy-eyed Sam appeared in the open hatch:

'Look, Mum! Look what Oi can do!'

'What've yeh got ther', Sam?' The boy held out a long thin scrap of paper, torn from the margin of a newspaper:

'Moy name, Ma – Oi can wroite moy name!' Suey gazed at the strip in surprise, then lifted her eyes to her son:

'How…?'

'Moikey showed me! 'E's been learnin' me 'n 'Arriet!' The girl had emerged too now, and Suey turned to her, a question in her eyes:

'That's roight, Mum. Look:' she held out two similar strips of paper: 'that's the alphabet, all the letters they use teh wroite with – 'n that's moy name, too!'

Michael had climbed up to stand behind her now, a cautious smile on his face. Five and a half years of living with the boat people had taught him that many of them were suspicious of folk on the bank, of their ways and their education. Sue regarded him steadily for a moment, making him feel even more nervous, then her face broke into a smile.

'Oi 'ope yeh don't moind, Mrs Caplin – they talked me into doin' it.' She laughed, and shook her head:

'O'course Oi don't moind, Moikey! Yeh're a good boy, 'n if yeh're 'elpin' moy girl 'n yoong Sam, then Oi'm grateful to yeh.'

The rest of the gathering from the pub were clustered behind Sue Caplin now; her husband spoke up:

'That goes fer me too, Moikey – Oi can see a day coomin' when we'll all be lookin' fer jobs on the bank, 'n it'll be mooch easier fer them as can read 'n wroite, Oi'm sure.' Bill Hanney turned to him, a look of scorn on his face:

'Oh, coom on, 'Enry! Oonce this noo gov'mint tek things oover, get all the drudgin' doon 'n fix things oop, we'll be busier'n ever!' He was continuing an old argument.

'Don' be so sure, Bill! Oi don' trust no gov'mint, whatever they say they'll do, 'n Oi ain't countin' no chickens. 'Ow about you, Alby?'

'Oi've said before, 'Enry, Oi'll let 'em 'ave their chance. Mebbe they'll set things roight, 'n mebbe they won't – boy then, Oi'll be getting' too old teh care any'ow!' They all laughed; through their merriment, Stevie raised his voice:

''Ow about me, Moikey? Would yeh learn me 'ow to read 'n all?'

'Yes, go on, Moikey, show Stevie as well!' Ginny had pushed past her brother to stand in the stern well, and now turned her appeal on him too.

'Well – yeah, Oi suppose Oi could... Wher' are we 'eading for tomorrer, Dad?' he asked Albert.

'Bill 'n me thought Stoke Bruin, probably. 'Ow about you, 'Enry?'

'That'll suit oos, too, Alby – we're off down teh Northampton, 'n that'll put oos roight teh get teh Trennery's the nex' day.'

'Okay then – Moikey can go on with 'is lessons, whoile we go down the Boat fer a beer, eh?' They all laughed again at the look of disappointment on the youngsters' faces; Suey took pity on them:

'Don' be so rotten! They can 'ave their learnin' when we tie oop, 'n then we'll all go fer a drink later. Roight?'

'Yes, loove – we were only teasin' 'em!' Henry put an arm around his wife's waist, gave her a quick squeeze: 'Coom on, bed, all of yeh! It's gettin' late.'

Sam clambered wearily onto the bank holding his precious strip of paper; Harriet stretched up to give Michael a quick peck on his cheek before following her brother:

'See yeh tomorrer, Moikey.' He gave her a smile and a wave as he stepped over onto the motor's counter and went down into the cabin.

As the Hanneys strolled along to their boats, Vi turned to her oldest son:

''Ow about yew, Billy? Oi'm sure Moikey'd learn yew 'n all, if yeh wanted.' But the nineteen-year-old shook his head:

'Nah, Oi'm foine as Oi am, Ma. Whoy would Oi need teh read? Dad's roight, we're goin' teh be boatin' for ever!'

Chapter Nine

Fred Morris strolled along the overgrown towpath of the abandoned canal arm, his hands in his pockets, his thoughts many miles away. Few people now came this way – most of the folk in the town avoided the sight of the dark, stagnant water, the banks of reeds and the encroaching brambles.

There hadn't been a boat along here, into Buckingham, since before the turn of the century. And, so he'd heard, they'd actually dammed off the canal near Cosgrove, where it joined the Grand Union's busy main line from London to Birmingham, sometime during the war. But to be here, even if the old navigation stood derelict, made Fred feel a little less lonely; it made him think of his grandchildren, somewhere out there, following the way of life they had both come to love, in the company of the old boatman who had become their substitute father. He saw them very rarely – the last time had been at Ethel's funeral, in November, when they had left the boats tied in Wolverton and come on the bus to see their grandmother laid to rest beside their mother in Buckingham's cemetery. *At least she saw the damned war over and done with!*

He would have to write to them later. Their exchange of letters was sporadic – he found it difficult to think of things to write to them which he thought would interest a teenager and a twelve-year-old – but Ginny's latest letter, which had arrived the day before, had been chatty and cheerful, so he would have to make the effort. He looked around, smiled to himself: *I'll tell them how pretty it is around here, with spring appearing all over, the blossom on the trees, the buds in the hedgerows!* And he must congratulate young Michael, too, the way the boy had taken on the challenge of teaching some of the other boat-children to read – it must be difficult, but his sister's pride in him had shone through in her words as she'd written of his success. One name had kept cropping up in her letters lately – one of Michael's pupils, a boy called Stevie – the smile widened on his face: *Silly girl's got a crush on him, for sure!*

They were both growing up so fast. He pictured them in his mind's eye at the funeral, dressed in their best – Michael, so tall now, so handsome with his thick sandy hair, his soft, grey-green eyes, that Fred had found himself moved almost to tears by his pride in the boy. And Ginny – pretty, blond, blue-eyed, the image of her mother at that age, in that heavy black skirt and lacy white blouse which made her look so grown-up… He'd ask about their schedule, in his letter, try to arrange to meet them one day as they passed through Wolverton again…

His loneliness forgotten, contentment filled his heart as he turned for home.

Christmas had come and gone, the first Christmas of the new peace. And Fred's first Christmas alone, after almost fifty years of marriage – not that he'd had time to be lonely then, either! A popular, easy-going character, he'd found himself cheerfully passed around his circle of friends and neighbours over the holiday, and then again at New Year. He'd received cards, and a small gift, from each of his grandchildren, and had happily berated them for spending their meagre and hard-earned money on him in his next letter, sent with his own gifts to them care of the company office at Braunston.

Yes, he must write very soon – it would be Michael's birthday in a matter of days. *Seventeen – it can't be possible, can it?*

He turned in through the front gate, let himself into the little house in Nelson Street, and stopped, puzzled, at the sight of the note lying on the doormat. He bent to pick it up, turned it over:

Mr Morris, I'm sorry I missed you. I will call again this afternoon.

Loretta Hope-Tanswell

The name meant nothing to him; he shrugged and went on through into the kitchen, where he helped himself to some bread and cheese and pickled onions for lunch.

The knock at his door came just after three o'clock. He rose from his armchair, putting down the book he had been reading, and went to answer it; on the doorstep stood a woman of around forty, smartly dressed, with a neat, fashionable hat perched on her thick wavy yellow hair, a file of papers under her arm:

'Frederick Morris? I'm Loretta Hope-Tanswell – may I come in for a moment?' Fred stood back to let her in and then ushered her into the sitting-room:

'Won't you sit down, Mrs Hope-Tanswell?' She gave him a brief, rather formal smile, and did as she was bid:

'It's *miss,* actually.'

'Oh – I beg your pardon. What can I do for you?'

'I work for the Buckinghamshire County Council, in the children's welfare department, Mr Morris.'

'Oh?' He sat back, expecting to be asked for a donation or something similar, only to be taken completely by surprise at her next statement:

'It's about your grand-daughter, Virginia.'

'I… what?' The woman gave him a look of long-suffering patience:

'Your daughter, Annette, died in 1942, I believe. She left a daughter herself, Virginia, eight years old.'

'Er… um…' The look on her face now clearly showed that she thought her interviewee must be completely senile, as she went on:

'She was supposed to be taken into Council care, but according to our records, she never arrived.' Neatly-gloved hands were crossed on top of the papers in her lap as she sat back to await his reply.

Fred found himself struggling for a suitable response. If he told her the truth, would they let Ginny be, or would they insist on snatching her away from Michael and Albert, and put her in the orphanage she had been threatened with before? He didn't need to be clairvoyant to know the answer – he prevaricated:

'She isn't here, Miss Hope-Tanswell.' The air of restrained impatience was back in her tone:

'No, I realise that, Mr Morris. Do you know where she is?'

'Well…' Inspiration struck: 'Yes and no – you see, she went to live with my son, her uncle, in Australia. And they're just moving, and I don't have their new address.'

'Oh!' This had clearly taken the woman by surprise: 'How long has she been there?'

'Over a year, now – she had been living with friends in Wolverton, but then we sent her out to Tony once it seemed safe to put her on a ship to Sydney.' The lies were coming more easily now.

'What happened to her after your daughter's funeral?' Fred found the woman's persistence beginning to irritate him:

'She stayed with us, Ethel and me, for a while. But we couldn't cope – my wife was already in a wheelchair then, that was why one of Annette's friends said they'd take her in.'

'I see – is Mrs Morris…?'

'My wife died last November.' Fred's growing annoyance was beginning to show in his stiff tone, but she seemed unaware of it:

'Oh – I'm so sorry.' Her voice held little sympathy: 'And these friends – you have their address?'

'No! They had to move, their house was damaged by a stray doodlebug – that was when we decided to send Ginny out to join Tony. I don't know where they are now.'

'I see… Is there *any* way I can confirm what you've told me, Mr Morris?'

'Are you saying that my word is insufficient for you, Miss Tanswell?'

'No – no! But you must understand, my concern is for the little girl. I have to be certain that she is safe and well cared for.' Fred, his anger beginning to get the better of him, rose from his chair:

'You may take it from me, Miss Tanswell, that Ginny is well, and safe, and happy, where she is! I'm sure you have other, much more deserving cases to pursue rather than wasting your time here!'

'It's *Hope*-Tanswell, actually. I have many other cases, but I am still supposed…'

Feeling that he had the advantage of her, Fred interrupted, striking while the iron was hot: '*Miss Tanswell!* Five years ago, I had a loving family all around me – I had a wife, a daughter and son-in-law, two grandsons and a grand-daughter – Now look at me! My daughter is dead, so is her husband – both my grandsons are gone, one dead of pneumonia, one lost, presumed dead, back in 1940 – Ginny is twelve thousand miles away – and I recently buried my wife! I do not need you or any other Council busybody coming around here, raking it all over and reminding me of what I've lost – now please go!'

'Mr Morris…'

'JUST GO!'

She looked up at him for a moment, standing over her, his fists clenched by his sides, then, clearly flustered, gathered up her papers, rose to her feet and headed for the door. He followed her, slamming it shut behind her.

Once her footsteps had clicked their way into silence, he turned away from the door, catching sight of himself in the mirror on the hall stand. The twinkle in his eye became a huge grin: *That went well, Fred!* Like most working-class men of his time, Fred Morris had a deep, ingrown suspicion of authority, especially political authority – combined with his instinctive mistrust of the lady herself, it had led him to take some satisfaction in her discomfiture. He chuckled quietly, remembering her scurrying departure, her tail between her legs.

But then his doubts returned – would she leave them alone, now? Had his quickly-improvised story convinced her, or would she, from sheer cussedness, try to investigate further? But where could she look – Australia? Maybe – he supposed it would be possible for someone, especially someone in authority, to trace Tony in Queensland, to find out if he had his young niece living with him… But surely that would be a step too far, even for that officious wench? And – what else did she know, what else could she discover? A few people – the Eastwoods, Nettie's old neighbours in Wolverton, Grannie Thompson, the children's paternal grandmother, and others – knew the truth: Would it occur to that woman to contact any of them? Possibly… He'd better try and warn them all, just in case; and Michael and Ginny, of course.

He smiled at his reflection again, rueful at his own paranoia: *Come on, Fred, get that letter written!*

Chapter Ten

A drizzly day in late March – on their regular scheduled way from City Road Basin in London to the Fazeley Street depot in Birmingham, Albert Baker and his young crew stopped off briefly, as was their habit, in Braunston. The FMC dock and boatyard there was their official base, even though their loading orders were issued by the traffic managers at the termini of their trips – the boats would, when necessary, go there for maintenance; fresh items of equipment, ropes, cloths, and so on, would be issued from there, and the boats themselves were registered as dwellings with the public health office in Daventry, the nearest large town. Perhaps more importantly, at least for Michael and Ginny, it was to the Braunston office that any letters from their grandfather would be delivered.

And it was in Braunston, a couple of weeks before Christmas, that a chance encounter had surprised and moved Michael. They had stopped there as usual – Ginny had gone to Ben Vickers' office to see if there was any mail, and Albert had headed for the stores for a replacement towline. Michael, spending his few free minutes polishing the brass rings on the motor's cabin chimney, had been roused from his labours by a shy, childish voice:

'Mr Baker?' He looked around, saw the little girl standing on the towpath: 'It's me, Mr Baker – Carrie Martin.'

'Carrie – Oh, o' course! 'Ow are yeh, Carrie?'

'Oi'm well, thank yeh. Oi've got this for yeh – fer Christmas.'

She held out a package, wrapped in brown paper. He stepped over into the butty's well, took it from her:

'Tha's very koind o' yeh, Carrie – ther's no need, though, really!' Her smile was as shy as her voice:

'Yew saved moy loife, Mr Baker. Mam 'n me, we made that for yeh – Oi 'ope yeh loike it.' He gazed at the package, touched by her gesture, turning it over in his hands:

'Oi'm sure Oi will, Carrie. Thank yeh very mooch.' Her smile became more relaxed, more natural; a cheeky glint appeared in her green eyes:

'Mam says yeh're not teh open it 'til Christmas!' He looked up again, and chuckled:

'Oi won't – Oi promise! Thank yeh again, Carrie.' The child gave him a happy grin, and turned to scurry away.

Their Christmas had been spent in Birmingham, between trips, in company with the Hanneys and a number of other Fellows's crews. Christmas Eve was an occasion of high humour and high spirits, as the first without the restrictions of the blackout for so many years – on Christmas morning, as they exchanged their usual small gifts, Michael kept the package from Carrie until last. He opened it to find a beautiful set of spider-work braces, traditional wear of the old-time boatmen, and sat gazing at them in admiration:

'Look 'ere, Dad, Ginny!' Albert raised his eyes:

'They're grand, Moikey!' Ginny held out her hand:

'Let's see!' She took them: 'From that little girl?'

'Yeah!' Ginny looked up at him, a twinkle in her eye:

'They are loovely, Moichael! Yeh'd better not tell 'Arriet wher' yeh got 'em!' He laughed:

'Mebbe not! She med 'em 'erself, with 'er Mum, that's what she said.'

* * *

Now, Ginny hurried back to the boats, an envelope clutched in her hand. They set off once more, Alby on the motor, Michael steering the butty so that she could open and read her letter in the warmth and dryness of the cabin:

Miss V. Baker
c/o Fellows Morton & Clayton Ltd
The Wharf
Braunston
Nr Daventry
Northants *March 21st 1946*

Dearest Ginny,

Thank you so much for your letter – I'm sorry it has taken me a little while to reply. It sounds as though you are all working as hard as ever; I'm sure, as you say, that it is much better to be on a regular schedule now, after all the years of going hither and yon as the demands of the wartime traffic demanded. I'm glad you're both well; I'm doing okay, managing quite well on my own, so you've no need to worry about me! Tell Michael that I'm pleased to hear how well his lessons are going – I'm so proud of him, giving his own time to help those other children like that, of you too of course, for helping and supporting him. And tell him I am so looking forward to meeting his Harriet, one day; one day soon, perhaps?

I went for a walk along the old abandoned canal here in Buckingham again this morning – it looks very pretty now, with lots of blossom coming on the trees, and flowers in the hedgerow, even if it is all rather overgrown – I suppose no-one is interested in looking after it now, since the boats can't come this way any more. It's silly, I know, but going there always makes me feel a little bit closer to you and Michael, knowing that you two are sailing along somewhere on another canal!

Now – I have to warn you about something, my dear: You remember how Mr Baker and I spirited you away after your mother died, to prevent you going into that dreadful orphanage? Well, I had a lady from the council turn up today, asking about you, where you are, what happened to you, and so on. I suppose they're trying to go back over things that didn't get resolved during the war, or something. She was very persistent, to the point of being quite annoying. I spun her a line about you going out to live with Uncle Tony in Australia, and I think she swallowed it, but I'm still concerned that she might try to check up – she seemed like the kind of busybody who won't let things lie – and, because I had to make it all up on the spur of the moment, she will probably spot the flaws in it if she does! So, both of you, please keep your eyes and ears open for anyone snooping around! I don't think there's anything to lead her to you unless she really gets her teeth into things, but I'm afraid she would want to make you leave the boats and go to the orphanage if she should find you. You're all right, Michael – you're seventeen, in a few days, and you have the right to make up your own mind, but it's you, Ginny, that I'm worried about. I know how happy you are, and I would hate to see that happiness destroyed by some interfering nosy-parker like her.

Ginny went on to read the remaining paragraphs of her grandfather's letter, the gossip about people she remembered from their previous life, the little anecdotes about his friends in Buckingham. But then her eyes strayed back to the passage about the lady from the Council, and a feeling of unease returned to trouble her. She'd thought, after four years, that the threat of a Council children's home had gone away, but now it seemed that they might try again to send her there: *I won't go, I WON'T!* She got up from her seat on the sidebed of the butty cabin, and tapped Michael's leg to be let out into the stern well; he stood clear, and she stepped up to join him.

'Moikey?'

'Yeah?'

'Grandad says ther's bin soome nosy woman from the Council snoopin' around troyin' ter foind me.'

'Troyin' teh foind yew?'

'Yeah. 'Cos Oi disappeared after Mum's funeral. They wanted me teh go inteh that 'ome, remember?'

'Yeah, 'course! What did she want now?'

'Grandad thinks they'll troy and send me there, if they can foind me. But' she giggled: 'e's told 'em Oi'm in Australia, wi' Ooncle Tony!' He turned to look at her:

'Did she believe 'im?'

''E thinks so. Boot 'e says teh keep our oiyes open, in case she 'asn't given oop.'

'We will 'n all! Yew ain't goin' in no orphanage, Ginny – we kept yeh out o' ther' before, 'n they ain't puttin' yeh ther' now!' His voice was firm, determined.

''N Oi ain't goin, either!' She grinned at him: 'We'll tell Dad later, okay?'

''Course we will. 'E won' let yeh go, neither!'

And, as Michael had surmised, Albert's reaction was as determined as his own had been:

'Ther's no way they're tekin' yeh away from me, Ginny, so joost yew stop worryin', roight? We'll tell Mr Vickers, nex' toime we're boy, so's even if she doos get that far, 'e'll give 'er the 'eave-'o!' Ginny reached up, put her arms around his neck and kissed his cheek:

'They can't split oos oop, can they, Dad?'

'Joost let 'em troy, girl!'

Chapter Eleven

Sylvie Benchfield carried the tray of dirty cups balanced on one hand as she backed through the door into the little canteen. Turning, she placed it down on the work surface between the gas stove and the grubby stone sink; dumping the cups into the bowl, she turned on the hot tap and gave a grunt of disgust as it coughed dryly and spat out some dusty, luke-warm water: *Aren't they ever going to get the geyser fixed?* She filled the kettle resignedly, put it on the stove to boil.

She'd been working for Patten's since early in the year, taken on almost grudgingly by Mr Patten Senior because he knew her grandmother rather than because he appreciated her qualifications. Which were few enough, in all conscience! She should, she knew, be grateful to have the job – able-bodied young men were in demand, especially in trades like theirs, as builder's merchants, but girls with minimal secretarial skills were not in short supply. Heaving a slow, disgruntled sigh, she leant forward and pushed open the window over the sink, gazing out into the autumn day while she waited for the kettle to boil.

Patten and Son's premises were in Alperton, in West London, her office and the canteen on the third floor of an old brick-built warehouse. Handy, for her Gran's house in Perivale, just a short bus-ride away; and not far from her old home in Greenford… Grief caught in her throat for a moment, but she quickly swallowed it. Blinking, she raised her eyes – only a street away, between two buildings, she caught a glimpse of water, the sun flashing a reflection at her like a beckoning light in the darkness, and she smiled at the memories: *How often...?*

Sylvie had been twelve when the war started. She left school at fifteen; a year in Greenford's secretarial college, and she'd got a job with a local firm of solicitors. But then, dissatisfied with her lot, she'd spotted the advert in the paper: *Young, able-bodied women needed to train to run narrowboats on the Grand Union Canal.* She rang the number from work the next day, and, that same afternoon, took a bus to Bull's Bridge and signed up, lying about her age in case they turned her down.

Those had been grand times, with Mary and Cissie! After her training, with a diminutive but strong-willed lady known as Kit, she'd settled with her regular crew on a pair of the Grand Union Company's boats, plying between London and Birmingham with frequent excursions via the Warwickshire coalfields. There had been the black times, too, when that stray bomb hit the little house in Greenford. She had cursed herself, so often – if she hadn't rushed off to play at boating, she would have been there too, died with her parents and little Jonathan, instead of having to go on alone... But Gran had taken her in, and the boat people had been so kind, so generous, when they knew. Especially that young lad, with his father and little sister – they'd met a number of times, despite them working for a different company, and it had been some time before she'd learnt that they had lost an older brother, a son, to the war. *I wonder where they are now, how they're getting on...* The father, Alby, had said to her once, that if she wanted to go on boating after the war, she should get in touch with their manager...

The kettle was boiling quietly, as if knowing that it was going to be ignored. She gazed at that distant sparkle of water: *I can't do this, Gran, I've got to go back!*

James Patten glanced up from his desk as she hurried past:

'Tea brewed, Sylv?' She looked over her shoulder:

'In a minute, Jim – I just remembered a call I have to make.'

'Okay, love. For Dad, is it?' She just smiled in reply; James Senior, while no tyrant, was known to rule his domain with strict discipline and a powerful tongue. At her desk, quickly riffling through the telephone directory, she found it:

Fellows, Morton and Clayton Ltd, New Wharf Road...

* * *

Late September, and the bronze and gold of autumn reflected in the still waters of the Braunston Summit. *'N we ain't disturbin' 'em mooch, neither!* Billy Hanney, not long past his twentieth birthday, stood feeling frustrated at the tiller of the *Acorn* – for the last twenty-four hours, their progress had been fitful at best. The linkage to the oil rod had broken, and, despite his and his father's best efforts at bodging it up, it kept letting go, so that they could only proceed, in effect, at part throttle. And with heavily-loaded boats, that meant very slowly indeed. Emerging from the tunnel into the morning sunshine, he gave a sigh of relief – just the run down the locks now, and they'd stop at the dock for repairs.

A number of other pairs, including Fellows's and Barlows boats, had overtaken them, so hopefully Mr Vickers would be ready for them, forewarned of their troubles.

At their present rate of progress, they'd soon be passed by the boats which had left City Road the day after them. An ignominious prospect – but at least they'd see Alby Baker and his youngsters again, perhaps be able to spend an evening with them wherever they happened to stop. Billy glanced around to be certain that the *Kerry,* in the charge of his mother on its long line eighty feet behind him, was okay. The old *Angelus,* their previous, wooden-hulled, butty, had been retired earlier in the year, to be replaced by a sister-boat of Alby's *Antrim.*

As they approached the top lock, Bill, grease and grime on his face and hands as well as his clothes, clambered out of the engine-hole.

'Yew tek 'em, Dad – yeh look loike yeh could do wi' a rest! Oi'll lock-wheel.' Bill gave his son a thankful smile:

'Roight-oh, Billy.' His smile widened: 'At least we moight get a point for loonch in the Plough, eh?' Billy grinned back as he handed over the tiller, settled his windlass in his belt and prepared to step off to set the lock.

Half an hour later, they tied up outside the basin, an old arm of the Oxford Canal, which was home to Fellows, Morton and Clayton's Braunston dock. Bill put the motor by the bank, the butty outside – contrary to normal practice, but it meant that the fitter would have easier access to the engine:

'Pop round 'n tell Mr Vickuss we're 'ere, will yeh, Billy? Oi'll toidy oop in ther' a bit, let the cat see the canary.'

* * *

'I'm not sure I can help you, Miss Benchfield.' Ben Vickers sat back in his chair. Sylvie had travelled up by train to see him after at last obtaining his number from the offices at City Road Basin; they'd gone over her wartime experience, and Vickers was sympathetic to her plight, and even keen to make use of her skills. But:

'You see, our boats have to have a crew of three, it's company policy – and all my boats are fully crewed at the moment. No-one is going to be too keen to take an extra hand on unless they need to – the company only pays the captain, you see, and he then has to pay anyone who crews for him. If it's his own family, they all live on his earnings, so that is how most of the boats are run. I can't put you on a pair of boats at the moment – but that isn't to say that I might not need you in a few month's time!

People leave – some of the younger ones are going to work on the bank nowadays, giving up the boats – or if a young couple marry and want their own boats, they need a third hand to make up the crew. So there are possibilities; but not right now, I'm afraid.'

'Yes, I see, Mr Vickers.' Sylvie gazed down into her lap, more disappointed than she had expected at this news, although she had acknowledged its possibility all along.

'However…' She looked up; his tone was more encouraging, now: 'If you are interested, I could use some help here in the office. My old secretary retired a few months ago, and I haven't got a replacement yet. I've been struggling on my own – and it's been a struggle, believe me! I know it isn't what you wanted, but maybe we could keep our ears to the ground, find you a place in a crew sooner or later, if you were here on the spot? What do you say?'

Sylvie looked at him in silence, weighing her options – if she gave up, went home, she'd be condemned to the typing pool for the rest of her life; but here, even if it meant the same old drudgery for a while, maybe she'd be lucky, in time. And at least she'd be near the water, get to see the boaters as they passed by, talk to them when they came in for docking or for things from the stores…

But, before she could reply, a knock sounded at the door, and a young man strode in:

'Mr Vickuss? 'Ave yeh 'eard about our… Oh, sorry teh boott in, Oi didn' know yeh were busy…' He'd seen Sylvie – now, he was gazing at her with a surprised smile on his face, and she found herself gazing back: *What a striking fellow he is!*

'It's all right, Billy, I was expecting you. If you… Billy?' The young man turned to him, the smile still on his face:

'Sorry, Mr Vickuss – yeh were sayin'?' Vickers gave him a thoughtful look:

'If you go round to the workshop, Paul's waiting for you. He knows what's wrong – take him over to the boat. Where are you tied?'

'Near the iron bridge.'

'Okay. I'll come over in a while, see how you're getting on.'

'Roight-oh, Mr Vickuss…' Billy's eyes were on Sylvie again, and she felt her heart lift as she returned his smile. Vickers felt a grin beginning to stretch his own face:

'Billy – this is Sylvie Benchfield. I think – I hope – she's going to be my new secretary.'

'*Oh* – Oi'm pleased ter meet yeh, Miss Benchfield.' He held out a hand, and she took it nervously:

'Hello, Billy. It's Sylvie, please?'

'Oh ah – roight. Billy 'Anney, Miss… Sylvie. Off the *Acorn* and the *Kerry.*'

'It's good to meet you, Billy. You've got problems, have you?'

'Yes – it's…'

'Go on, Billy, give Paul a shout' Vickers interrupted: 'get the job under way. I'll be round shortly – and maybe Miss Benchfield will come to meet your family while she's got the chance. She'll need to get to know people.'

'I'd love to, Mr Vickers.' Her eyes were still on Billy as she spoke.

Paul Merson looked up at Bill and his son, standing around the elderly Bolinder:

'Shouldn't take too long to fix it, Mr Hanney. I've got a new spindle in the workshop, we've had 'em break before – I'll just go and get it.' He climbed out onto the bank, and Billy followed him. Walking alongside him past the bridge, he took his companion by the arm:

'Yeh won' get it doone today, will yeh, Paul?' The mechanic looked around, puzzled:

'I don't see why not! It'll take a while, you won't be away until, oh, late afternoon maybe.'

'No, Paul – yeh *won't* get it fixed today, will yeh?'

'What are you at, Billy?' Suspicion echoed in the fitter's tone.

'Well – ther's soomeoone Oi want teh see again 'fore we go.'

'Oh, I *see!*' Billy's reputation was not unknown.

'It ain't loike that, Paul! She's… diff'rent.' Merson stopped, gave him a long, hard look:

'You all right, Billy Hanney?' The young boater laughed:

'Oi'm foine, mate! Never better! Boot…?'

'I think it might take me 'til the morning to fix your engine, Mr Hanney!'

'Good lad!'

Billy turned with a chuckle and headed back to his boats.

Chapter Twelve

'We'll joost about 'ave toime fer a quick 'un 'fore they close, if we 'urry, boys!' Bill Hanney dropped his fob watch back into the pocket of his waistcoat. Paul Merson had returned from the stores with the parts he needed, and was ensconced in the engine-hole of the *Acorn,* from which were issuing bangs and clatters, and the occasional swear-word.

'Mr Vickuss said 'e'd be boy in a whoile ter see 'ow we're doin', Dad,' his elder son informed him.

'Oh – better wait 'ere then, Oi s'pose.'

'Never moind, Dad, we can mek oop fer it later!' Bill looked at him, then bent to the open engine-hole doors:

'Yeh'll be doone 'fore long, won't yeh, Paul?' A dishevelled head appeared:

'Probably not 'til this evenin', Mr Hanney.'

'What? Oi'd 'oped ter be away 'fore dark!' Merson shook his head:

'I'd reckon on stayin' here tonight. It's not fittin' the new bits, see, it's getting' the old bits apart. Might take a while.'

'Oh – roight. Okay lad – do yer best, eh?' Paul nodded, with a quick grin at Billy, and ducked back out of sight. Bill called out to his wife, in the butty cabin: ''Ow 'bout a pot o' tea, Vi?'

'On it's way, Bill!' Her voice echoed from within.

'You got enough for two thirsty paper-pushers as well, Vi?' Bill and his sons turned at the sound of Ben Vickers' voice behind them:

‘’Ello, Mr Vickuss! Din’t see yeh there.’

‘Hello, Bill – how’s things?’

‘Not so bad – Paul says ’e’ll ‘ave it fixed tonoight, ’n we can get away in the mornin’.’

‘That’s fine. You’ll be a day behind, but we can’t help that, can we? Bill – this is Sylvie Benchfield. She’s going to be my new secretary, starting Monday. Sylvie – Bill Hanney, captain of the *Acorn* and the *Kerry.*’ The girl held out her hand; Bill took it with a smile:

‘Good ter meet yer, Sylvie. Mebbe Mr Vickuss’ll be lookin’ a bit less wore out in future!’ She laughed as Vickers said:

‘I’m going to be glad of her help, for sure!’

‘These two are moy boys, Billy ’n Stevie.’ She’d been aware of Billy’s eyes on her from the moment they arrived by the boats; she deliberately held out her hand to the younger boy, shook his with a smile in response to his ‘pleased ter meet yer’, before turning to his brother:

‘Billy and I met in the office earlier.’ Their eyes met, and she felt that same sudden lightness of heart.

‘Aye – um…’ He found himself uncharacteristically tongue-tied: ‘Yeh’re tekin’ the job, then?’

She nodded, smiling:

‘Yes. I’d wanted to go back on the boats, but there isn’t a place for me. This way, I’ll be near by, and Mr Vickers has said that if a crew needs someone, he’ll put me forward.’

‘Yeh’ve been boatin’ before, then?’

‘Yes – I was a trainee, during the war, on Grand Union Company boats.’ Billy grinned, delighted to have found some common ground:

‘Oone o’ the Oidle Women, were yeh?’ Sylvie laughed:

‘That’s right! I can’t tell you how much I enjoyed it. I went back on the bank, last Christmas, but I don’t like it – that’s why I called Mr Vickers. Someone I met back then gave me his name.’ A thought struck her: ‘Do you know a man called Baker, Alby

Baker? He's got a young son, and a daughter, Mikey and Ginny.'
It was Billy's turn to laugh:

''Course we do! Eh, Dad, she knows Ooncle Alby!' He turned to his father, who echoed his delighted grin.

'He's your *Uncle?'*

'Well – not really. 'E's – Mum's cousin, or sommat. A bit of a relation, any'ow. Boot we call 'im Ooncle Alby. They'll loikely be 'ere tonoight, won' they, Mr Vickuss?'

'I'd expect so, Billy, if they're on schedule.' The young man turned back to Sylvie:

'Can yeh stop, 'ave a drink with oos in the Plough, later?'

'Depends when the last train leaves, Billy. I have to go home to London tonight.'

'Oh – Oi see.' He sounded so crestfallen that she felt a crazy urge to take him in her arms and comfort him.

'I think the last train from here's about nine-thirty, Sylvie' Vickers put in 'but I don't know about connections.' She gave him a grateful glance, looked back at Billy:

'I'll stop, then. I can always get a taxi at the other end, if I have to.' His expression was that of a child promised a very special treat:

'Tha's grand, Sylvie!' They gazed into each others eyes until Vi's voice sounded from the butty's hatches:

'Yeh can eat with oos if yeh loike, girl – ther's plenty in the pot.' Sylvie turned to the boatwoman:

'I'd love to – if you're sure it's no trouble?'

'No trooble at all, choild!'

* * *

Darkness was falling as the *Sycamore* nosed out of Braunston Tunnel. Michael reached into the cabin to flick off the switch for the headlamp, turned to watch the *Antrim* follow him out into the fading daylight. They had heard of Bill Hanney's problems, the towpath telegraph doing its usual efficient job – and a blind if beneficent chance decreed that a stop overnight in Braunston would lose them no more than an hour at most, stopping a little earlier than they might otherwise have done. Although, truth to tell, there were few places to stop after that last village of Northamptonshire until you reached Shuckborough, a couple of hours on.

It was not quite eight o'clock when they tied the boats near Butcher's Bridge. Dinner had been taken earlier, on the run across the summit before the tunnel; Alby and Michael made the pair secure while Ginny ran on to see if she could find the Hanneys. Minutes later, she was back, having found them about ready to walk up to the village and the Old Plough – Michael was standing on the towpath in a clean shirt and his best trousers.

'Dad's joost 'avin' a quick shave – 'e'll be out in a mo. 'Ow's things, Mr 'Anney?'

'Not so bad, Moikey. The oil rod gave out, boot Paul's fixed it now – we'll be off in the mornin'.'

Vi stepped forward and gave the boy a quick, warm hug:

'Noice ter see yer, Moikey! Yeh're gettin' taller boy the day!' He chuckled, smiling down at her:

'It's great ter see yeh too, Mrs 'Anney!'

'We've got a surproise fer yeh:' She stood aside, pushing Stevie away:

'Hello, Mikey!' His jaw dropped, and then a huge grin split his face:

'Sylvie! 'Ow've yeh bin? It's good ter see yeh agen!' She reached out and put her arms around him, kissed him on the cheek:

'I'm grand, Mikey. God, how you've grown – how old are you, now?' His smile turned shy:

'Seventeen.' She laughed:

'Nearly old enough for me to marry you, then!' Three years before, after a long and riotous Christmas Eve in the Cape of Good Hope, in Warwick, she had threatened him with marriage, and the joke had survived ever since. Now she held him at arm's length and studied him: 'I envy the girl who does marry you, you handsome devil!'

Michael blushed scarlet, looked to Vi Hanney to rescue him; she laughed:

'Oi'll tell 'Arriet that when Oi see 'er!'

'You've got a girl, Mikey?' He nodded, smiling selfconsciously:

'Yeah. 'Arriet Caplin – 'er Dad's 'Enry, works for Grand Unions.'

'Going to marry her, are you?' Sylvie's smile had a devilish edge to it.

'Oi dunno…' Vi was giving him a stern look: 'Mebbe… Prob'ly. When we're older.'

Sylvie kissed his cheek again:

'Good for you! I hope you'll be very happy – and I expect an invitation to the wedding!'

Billy had watched this exchange with a carefully neutral expression, but now he stepped forward from behind his father:

'Coom on! Let's get oop the pub, Oi'm dyin' fer a drink. Yeh ready, Ooncle Alby?'

An arm reached out of the motor's cabin, tipped the contents of the handbowl into the canal:

''Old yer 'orses, Billy 'Anney! Oi'm joost coomin'!' Alby climbed out onto the counter, closed the cabin doors and stepped over, across the butty's stern and onto the bank. He held out his hand:

'Sylvie – it's grand teh see yeh.' She took his hand, but pulled him close and kissed him on the cheek as well:

'And you, Alby!'

'Yeh back on the boats, then, girl?'

'I am! Well, not quite…' She quickly explained the position, as the party turned and set off over the bridge and up the lane to the High Street.

Chapter Thirteen

Settled in the public bar of the Old Plough, among its black oak furnishings, with a round of drinks in front of them, Sylvie looked around at her friends, old ones and new ones:

'Come on then – tell me everything that's been happening since I left the boats!'

The conversation rambled comfortably around for the next hour, revealing all the little incidents, the amusing and the dramatic, that had overtaken them since the war ended. Michael's embarrassment returned when the tale of his rescue of Carrie Martin was retold; and concern brought a frown to Sylvie's face when he told her of the warning they had had from Grandpa Morris about the council woman's visit:

'You've heard nothing more about that since?' Alby shook his head:

'Nah! They've got better things teh be doin' – Oi reckon as she's forgotten about oos.'

'I hope so...' But the worried look was still on her face, until Billy began one of his funnier stories.

She had been keeping an eye on the clock, and just after nine she got reluctantly to her feet, doing up her coat:

'I'd better go, or I'll miss that last train.'

'Yeh could stay over – on Alby's butty,' Billy suggested, getting to his own feet: 'Yeh wouldn' moind sharin', would yeh, Ginny?' Ginny shook her head, but Sylvie refused, smiling:

'I'd love to – but my Gran would worry. And I'm supposed to go to work tomorrow – they don't know I'm leaving, yet!' She turned to Billy, her smile softening: 'I'll be back on Monday – and then I'll be here in the office, every time you come by.' Their eyes locked and held, until he said:

'Can Oi walk yeh ter the station, then?'

'I'd love you to, Billy.' His uncertain smile became a huge grin.

After the couple had departed, Vi leant back in her chair, a satisfied smile on her face as she drained her glass of stout. Placing it cheerfully on the table, she said:

'Well! That's ah Billy sorted, then!'

'What d'yer mean, loove?' She looked scornfully at her husband:

''Aven't yeh got no oiyes in yer 'ead, Bill 'Anney? Din't yer see 'ow 'e's bin lookin' at 'er, all noight?'

'Yer mean…'

''E's fallen fer that girl, good 'n 'ard!'

'Boot – 'e only met 'er today!'

'Yeah! 'N did yer see 'ow she was lookin' at 'im, 'n all?' She looked around their faces, seeking for confirmation of her observation: Alby grinned, and nodded his head:

'Oi reckon she's roight, Bill!'

Michael and Stevie both looked as surprised as Bill, but Ginny, sitting beside Stevie on the bench by the wall, smiled her agreement:

'Yeh'll only 'ave Stevie 'ere to go, then!' She slipped her arm through his, snuggled up against him; he looked down at her, uncomfortably:

'Er – oh, Oi'm only sixteen, Oi ent marryin' no-one!' Ginny gave him one of her sweetest smiles: 'Well – not yet, any'ow!'

Laughter echoed from the walls as Bill got up to fill their glasses.

* * *

Two days later they were in Birmingham, tied at the New Warwick Wharf, part of the complex that was FMC's Fazeley Street headquarters. They had run the two pairs butty, as they had so often in the past, the two crews working together to ease the load and speed the journey.

Albert and Ginny had both noticed an unaccustomed quiet in Michael, but neither spoke of it. It was Sylvie's question, about his relationship with Harriet, which had prompted his thoughtfulness – he had spent much of the trip from Braunston thinking about her, trying to look into the future. Their friendship, for that was how he thought of it, had begun quietly, slowly, during the war, largely from Harriet's prompting; but it had held strong, grown almost imperceptibly into something much deeper, over three years and more of their adolescence. Now, he made himself look at it, at her, at himself: How *did* he feel about her? *Was* he going to marry her – always assuming that Henry and Suey Caplin would let him, of course. Did he *want* to spend the rest of his life with her, bring up children with her…?

In recent months, their meetings had been sporadic, and often fleeting. Henry's boats had been working mostly on coal deliveries, from the Coventry coalfields to Apsley or Nash Mills, so with Alby's boats on their regular City Road – Fazeley Street runs, they had been sharing their route for only a part of each journey. The bike had seen some hard service, but so often they were too far apart for the two to see each other; and Michael found himself missing her company, her shy smile, the warmth of her soft brown eyes, the sound of her gentle laughter…

By the time they had unloaded the boats, and were able to relax briefly while waiting for orders, he had reached, if not conclusions, at least an understanding of his own emotions. Did he want to marry Harriet? Yes, as far as he could tell, if their shared feelings didn't change in the next few years. Would she want to marry *him?* As far as he could tell, again, yes. Was he ready to commit himself to that future? No, not yet! *We're only seventeen! Too yoong teh be getting' in tow joost yet.* And he knew that that would be Henry and Suey's view, were he to raise the subject now.

And their journey had not been without incident. The final length of the Grand Union Canal provides the only regular delay and aggravation for the working boater – those last six locks of Camp Hill, on the edge of Birmingham proper, were never widened in the rebuilding works of the 1930s, when the Second World War intervened. Remaining at seven feet across, they require the motor and butty to be worked through independently, effectively doubling the amount of effort needed to pass. Below the locks, a few hundred yards brings the boats to the New Warwick Wharf, after passing Bordesley Junction where the old line known as the Garrison turns off to the right, to lead to Salford. And it is up the Garrison where lies Fellows, Morton and Clayton's Saltley Dock, where much of their boat-building and maintenance is carried on.

The *Acorn* and the *Kerry* had passed the junction; the *Sycamore,* with the *Antrim* duly following eighty feet behind, was just approaching when an empty pair appeared, driving hard into the turn from their right. The steerer glanced over at Michael's frantic blast on his brass horn, but made no attempt to stop or to avoid what looked like an inevitable collision; the high-riding motor swept around, across the *Sycamore*'s bows, its empty butty on cross-straps tied tight to its stern. Michael hastily reversed the engine, at the same time putting his helm hard over to steer away from the other boats. Albert, standing on the gunwale of the motor, let rip with a well-chosen assessment of the other captain's parentage while desperately trying to pull in the towline, before it became entangled around their own propeller; Ginny, relatively helpless with no means of slowing the butty, steered for the bank and ran her fore-end along the towpath, trying to lose way.

As the *Sycamore*'s fore-end struck the stone-edged bank opposite the turn and bounced off, swinging out as if to take its revenge on the other butty as it swung past, Michael struggled to hold it away from an actual collision. At its tiller, a young girl gazed across at him, almost in tears as she also fought to keep clear water between them:

'Oi'm sorry, Mr Baker!' Her voice reached him over the exhaust of the Bolinder

The empty boats clattered off into the distance, rapidly overtaking Bill Hanney's pair; Michael stood, trembling with anger as well as reaction to the shock, at his tiller, the boat lying across the channel where it had come to rest. He looked around – the butty lay similarly diagonal, a horrified Ginny gaping at him. He felt Alby's hand on his shoulder:

'Yeh did well teh miss the booger, boy.'

'Stoopid bastard! What d'e think 'e was *doin',* Dad?'

'Huh! Not lookin' wher' 'e was goin', that's fer sure.'

'D'yeh see 'oo it was?'

'Yeah.' Albert's voice held a wealth of meaning: 'Them bloody Rodneys! Frank bloody Martin – Oi'll 'ave sommat ter say when we get ter Warwick Bar, yew mark moy words, boy!'

'Yew 'n me both, Dad. Oi thought that was Carrie on the butty – at least she was troyin' teh keep clear of oos.'

'Coom oop from Saltley, Oi reckon. If 'e's at the wharf when we get ther'...' Michael suddenly grinned:

'Yeah, me 'n all, Dad! Coom on, let's get on wi' it.'

He reversed the engine again to make it run forwards, and pushed in the clutch lever, watching behind as he steered to straighten the motor's progress until the towline drew tight. Easing open the throttle, he drew the butty straight also, and then took them the last few hundred yards to the depot.

Chapter Fourteen

Fifteen minutes later, they were tied under the canopy of the wharf, directly behind Bill's boats. The immediate task was to untie and remove the cloths covering the holds; by the time that was done, the heavy canvases carefully folded and stowed out of harm's way, Albert's anger had waned:

'T'ain't worth mekin' a fooss, boy. Let it go.'

'Boot Dad…'

'Oi know, son.'

Michael subsided, still annoyed – but even he knew that Albert was right. Their employers would not be happy, would certainly reprimand the other boatman if they knew their boats were being driven with such recklessness and arrogance, but reporting him would only cause bad feeling, maybe lead to further trouble with the man if he was as difficult as rumour would have him. Better to let sleeping dogs lie!

But later, after the effort of unloading the two pairs, when both crews and the dock hands were relaxing over mugs of hot, fresh tea, the incident was the topic of conversation:

'Vi says yeh had trouble wi' that empty pair, Alby?' Bill Hanney started it with his question.

'Yeah, s'roight, Bill. Coom floyin' out o' the Garrison, never moind oos startin' out o' Camp 'Ill bottom!'

'Stoopid booger nearly 'it oos!' Michael added.

'Yeah – Vi said yeh'd wound oop all over the cut, when she

looked back. He coom clatterin' past oos, too, joost as we were troyin' teh turn in 'ere.'

'Them Rodney boats it was. The *Apple.*' Billy told them.

'Yeah – Oi know, lad. The kiddie on the butty held 'er starn over – 'tween 'er and Moikey 'ere, we joost missed.'

'We saw 'em go boy 'ere – goin' fit ter boost, 'e was,' one of the wharf hands put in.

'Yeah – been oop Saltley Dock since day 'fore yestiday, they 'ave!' His mate added with a grin.

'Oh ah?' The man chuckled:

'Yeah! Coom in 'ere to unload, they did – 'n the Pooblic 'Ealth man coom boy! Found they'd got bugs in the cabins, told 'em to go 'n get 'em foomigated 'fore they loaded again.'

'Well that ain't no surprise! 'Ave yeh seen the state o' the boats?' Vi commented.

'Yeah! 'N the kids – alwes filthy, they are!' Ginny concurred.

'Aye – well: They went off ter Saltley, 'im callin' fer change boats – boot they told 'im 'e couldn' 'ave none. Kept 'em there, gassed out the cabins oone boy oone! Took 'em 'til terday to get 'em doone.'

'Oi bet 'e was livid, wa'n't 'e?' Bill asked. The wharf men laughed:

'Foorious! That ain't all of it, either – burnt 'is mattresses, they did, 'n then charged 'im fer new oones!'

'Cost 'im, as well as losin' two days work.' The other added: 'Boot it's 'is own fault – nobody loikes Rodneys. 'N yeh can oonderstand that they wouldn' want ter give 'em another pair, let 'em get *them* inter the same state, can't yeh?'

'Wher' are they off teh now, d'yer know?' Bill asked.

'Coombeswood. Orders coom through fer 'em ter go 'n load toobes, fer Brentf'd. 'N 'e don't loike that, neither! 'Ard, moocky job, them toobes. Boot:' the man shrugged his shoulders: 'if 'e kept 'is boats 'n 'is fam'ly clean 'n toidy, 'e'd 'ave a chance o' the good jobs, loike yew folks.'

'What about oos, mate?' Alby asked.

'Dunno, yet. Loads 'ave left fer today, so Oi 'spect yeh'll be loadin' termorrer. Toime fer a beer 'n a bath, tonoight!'

'That'll be great!' Everyone laughed at Ginny's sigh of relief.

It was, as the wharf men had predicted, the next morning before both pairs were reloaded for their return trip. They all took full advantage of the rest, trekking off to the local public baths for a scrub and polish; Michael and Ginny, as always, grabbing the chance of a brief swim in the main pool at the same time. Back at the boats, Michael gave Stevie a refresher lesson in reading, and made him copy out a passage from a book in a vain attempt to neaten his writing. More than a year on, and all of his pupils were making steady progress, if the intermittent nature of their teaching meant that it was of necessity rather slow – Harriet, perhaps, was the most eager and devoted of all, though Sam, as the youngest, was quickest to learn. Stevie and Ernie, who had joined the roving class as soon as he heard about it, plodded on with dogged determination rather than any degree of brilliance.

The six narrow locks of Camp Hill behind them, they hustled along the ten-mile pound to Knowle, down the five big locks and on to Hatton. Here too a good speed was kept, the water levels topped up by recent heavy rain; down the twenty-one to a late halt opposite the Cape of Good Hope in Warwick. Here, after a quick wash and shave and another half-hour lesson for Stevie, they congregated in the public bar.

Seeing Sylvie again had brought memories to the Baker crew, especially Michael:

'Yew remember that Christmas 'ere, Dad? Fust toime we met Sylvie?' Alby chuckled:

'When she arst yeh ter marry 'er? 'Course Oi do, boy!'

'When was that, Moikey?' Vi asked with a laugh – elsewhere on that occasion, the Hanneys hadn't heard the story.

'Oh, nigh on three year ago…' Michael went on to tell how

he'd come across the girl, solitary in her butty cabin, and dragged her across to the pub for the Christmas Eve, how they'd learned of her tragedy, the loss of her family a scant fortnight before. Billy in particular listened intently:

'It's so bloody unfair, ent it? Noice girl loike 'er, ter 'ave that 'appen!' He burst out when Michael stopped talking. Everyone mumbled their agreement; Vi looked at her son:

'Yeh loike 'er a lot, don't yeh, Billy?' He turned to her, his expression suddenly sheepish:

'Ther's sommat diff'rent about 'er, Ma. Sommat special – yeh know?' Vi just smiled at him; but Stevie butted in:

'Compared wi' all the oother girls yeh bin out with, yeh mean? Oi don' believe it!'

''Ow 'bout yew, yeh little ratbag! Oi seen yeh, mekin oiyes at young Ginny 'ere! Yew watch 'im, girl!' Ginny, sitting next to the youngest Hanney, laughed and said:

'Oh Oi will, Billy – Oi won' trust 'im an inch!' But she blushed pink, all the same, as Stevie put a protective arm around her shoulders.

'Yeh'll be wantin' teh mek a stop at Braunston every trip now, will yeh?' Bill asked his eldest son.

'When it's needful, Dad!' Billy said defensively, raising a laugh around the table.

'She's stayin' in Braunston, is she?' Vi asked, not expecting anyone to know – but Billy answered:

'Yeah. Mr Vickuss's offered 'er the cabin of a spare butty 'e's got laying oop the arm. She's goin' ter stay ther' in the week, go 'ome ter 'er Gran's place weekends.'

'Didn' waste yer toime on that walk ter the station, then?' Billy had the grace to turn pink himself as his father's question raised another laugh. Stevie leant forward across the table:

'Did yer give 'er a kiss, then, Billy?' He ducked as his older brother aimed a playful swipe at his head:

'Tha's noone o' yer business, Stevie 'Anney!'

Chapter Fifteen

The telephone on Ben Vickers' desk rang, drawing his attention from the depressing sight beyond his window. He reached down and picked it up:

'Mr Anderson for you, Ben.' Sylvie's voice crackled in his ear.

'Okay, put him on, Sylv.' A click on the line:

'Hello, Mr Anderson, how are you?' Mac Anderson, Southern Fleet Manager of FMC, sounded distant, a buzz tending to obscure his words:

'I'm well, thank you, Ben. You?'

'Fine, thanks. How's it looking?'

'Bad, Ben. No sign of the freeze ending as far as they can tell us. Could be days, even weeks. What's it like down your way?'

'Damned cold! Everything's frozen solid. The roads out of the village are difficult – we can't get up the hill towards Daventry at all. Even road transport's struggling.'

'Hmmm… What about the boats, the crews?'

'I know where all of my boats are, now. Most of them managed to get to something like civilisation before getting stuck. The men are coping, but it's difficult, as you'll appreciate.'

'Of course. You're getting their laying money to them?'

'Yes – I'm making the rounds of them each week. One or two are awkward, but it's worth tramping over a few fields to see the look on their faces!' Anderson laughed:

'I'll bet! No real problems?'

'Martins are the worst, with the *Apple.* Stupid bastard insisted on smashing his way on even when it was obvious they weren't going to get through. They've ended up on Rowington Bank.'

'Damn! That's a bleak place to be at a time like this, Ben.'

'Certainly is. But they're not too far from the village – and it seems that his missus, Joan, has got on the right side of the village Inn-keeper. She tells me they all go down there every night for a warm by the fire, and he's given her the odd bucket of coal for the range, as well.'

'Oh, that's good. They may be a grubby lot, but we don't want them suffering.'

'No, indeed. I've been keeping an eye on one or two other pairs in the area, as well – just to be sure they're okay.'

'That's fine, Ben – I'd hope other company's men would do the same for ours.'

'I'm sure they are! There's one thing that worries me a bit – there's a story going around that a number one's stuck out on the Oxford summit somewhere, miles from anywhere. No-one seems to be sure, and I've no idea who it might be, but I've had a go at finding them a couple of times. No luck, though.'

'That's bad, if it's true, Ben.' Both men shared a concern for the family – a self-employed boatman would have no company, no-one to look after for him, to get money or supplies to him. And, indeed, no laying money, no source of income at all while the boats were frozen in: 'By all means keep looking, Ben – but if you can confirm the story, it would be good: You might be on a wild goose chase. And always remember, our own men come first.'

'Of course. But if they are there, I can't let them starve.'

'Good God no! Help them, if you find them, and the company'll pay.'

'Thank you, Mr Anderson. About the only boater I know who's not sorry about all this is young Billy Hanney!'

'Oh?'

'Bill's boats are stuck on the puddle banks, about a mile and a half away from here. Billy's been walking down every day – and I'm afraid he's going to take my new secretary with him when they go!'

'Is that right?' Vickers laughed:

'Those two have been sweet on each other since the day they met, here in my office – he's twenty now, and so is she, and I reckon we'll be having a wedding before much longer. I got so sick of the sight of him, since this freeze started, that I've been giving him odd jobs to do around here, helping the craftsmen on the dock. Means that I get some of my letters typed as well. Mr Anderson?'

'Yes, Ben?'

'Can I give them a pair of boats, if and when it happens?'

'Hmmm… I'd like to – Bill's a good skipper, and his son's got all the makings. I think we should. But trade's been going down and down, Ben. It was on the decline before the war, and the only reason it hasn't been obvious lately is that we've been so short of crews. This damned freeze is going to make it worse – we've already lost a couple of contracts to the roads since it started, and more will go if it carries on longer. The day's coming when we'll be losing men, laying them off, you mark my words.'

'The men are all hopeful of this idea of nationalisation – they're saying once the government take over, put everything right, the trade'll come back.'

'I wouldn't pin too many hopes on that, Ben. The Government is near as bankrupt as the rest of us, they haven't got any more money for maintenance than the Canal Companies – and I'm afraid the political pressure is to put everything on the roads, they're saying that's the future of transport. We're too old and outdated!'

'I hope you're wrong, Mr Anderson.'

'You're not alone there, Ben!'

* * *

Loretta Hope-Tanswell rose from her desk and went to gaze out of the window. Trampled, dirty snow covered the courtyard of the Council Offices; occasional figures hurried in or out, huddled in thick coats and scarves, hats drawn low over their brows, purposeful but of indeterminate gender. The bitter weather had held for weeks now – and the forecasters seemed incapable of telling when it would end. A self-appointed prophet of doom had written in the local paper that week, claiming that this was the beginning of the next ice age. *And some stupid people will believe him, as well!*

She turned and sat back down, scanning the papers scattered across the desk. A feeling of self-satisfaction rose in her – so many cases brought to a conclusion! When you thought of the chaos she had taken over – all those poor children that had gone missing during the war years!

Of course, there were those she had had to write off, the ones she had failed to find; they were either somewhere beyond her ken, or dead. But some had been traced, reunited with their families; others had been found, living with the most unsuitable people, sometimes not even relatives!

They had mostly ended up in the Council's orphanages, where they would receive a proper up-bringing, a decent education. Ungrateful little brats, some of them – a few had even had the nerve to run away!

But… A small pile of files on the corner of the desk attracted her attention. Her collection of mysteries! Only half a dozen now – but those half-dozen troubled her. They represented a blot on her record, evidence of failures which she hated to admit to. They were cases where she had failed to trace the missing child, but felt that the truth should be within her grasp; some of them cases where she thought the truth had been deliberately withheld from her – and that rankled!

She reached for them, drew them to her; maybe now, with the weather preventing some of her other work from progressing, she should take another look at them. She leafed through them and selected one file that particularly annoyed her…

That arrogant old fellow! It had been nearly a year ago – the way he had brow-beaten her, verbally thrown her out of his house: It had quite unnerved her at the time, and ever since it had brought a swell of anger in her throat just to think of it. He'd been lying to her! She was certain of it, certain that the child was *not* abroad, as he'd claimed, certain that he knew full well where she was. And equally certain that, whatever *he* thought, *she* was the one who knew what was best for the little orphan girl. She gazed at the name at the top of the file: *Virginia Thompson.*

Opening the file, she quickly cast her eyes over the papers within, reminding herself of the facts. A strange case, altogether – the father had been killed in a bar-room brawl; the mother had died in Buckingham Hospital two years later, of pneumonia. Pneumonia contracted whilst nursing the elder, Mongol, brother – and there had been another brother, of course… The eldest, he had disappeared in January 1940, in weather not unlike this, never to be found. The authorities at the time had concluded that he'd run away of his own accord, and that he was most likely dead – but no body had ever been found. The report suggested that he may well have drowned in the river, in which case, with the high water following the thaw a few days later, his body could well have been swept many miles away, even out to sea. So, there were actually *two* mysteries, here: Where was the little girl? And what had *really* happened to her big brother…? Yes, she thought, now is a good time to go back over this one! *The truth is there somewhere – and I'm going to find it!*

* * *

'Ain't this bloody frost ever goin' ter give oover?' Alby Baker leant in the hatches of the *Sycamore* as Michael buttoned up his donkey jacket, tucking his muffler well in to keep out the biting wind.

'Boogered if Oi know, Dad. Forecast says not – not yet, any road oop.'

'Hnh! Booger all they know, 'n all!' Alby growled his disapproval of both weather and forecasters; Michael gave him a sympathetic smile:

'It'll go in its own good toime, Dad. Ain't mooch we c'n do about it!'

'Hnh! 'Ave a good day, boy.'

'Yew tek care o' yourself, Dad. Oi'll see yeh later.' He settled his cap on his head and stepped off the counter and onto the bank. The 'beep-beep' of a car horn sounded from the bridge, and he hurried away with a last wave.

Seven in the morning, and the dawn barely lightening the February sky. Four weeks now, and no sign of a let-up. Alby gave a last grunt and ducked down again into the warmth of the cabin; in the butty next door, Ginny was brewing fresh tea and toasting bread in front of the range for their breakfast.

They had been lucky – Stoke Bruerne was among the best places to be if you were frozen in with no prospect of moving in the near future. At least there was civilisation – a good pub, a local shop, pleasant people! They'd battled their way through, along the sixteen-mile, on a day when the frost refused to lift, breaking through ever-thickening ice until the cutting at Blisworth provided a welcome respite. But emerging from the tunnel into the evening darkness of Stoke, they'd found several other pairs already ice-bound above the locks, and had to give up the unequal struggle. Now, the boats were stranded, trapped in ice more than a foot thick, not even tied up but simply held there, close to the bank, the *Antrim* more or less alongside the motor.

Friends and acquaintances were scattered the length and breadth of the Southern canals. They'd heard from Bill Hanney, finally stopped after two days of slow, arduous travel, much to his disgust but Billy's delight, as Vickers had told the Fleet Manager – he was happy to be within such easy reach of Sylvie. Now, a month on, both he and his father were adding a little to their weekly 'laying money' by helping on the dock or in the stores, sweeping up behind the painters and craftsmen – even if Billy's earnings mostly went on entertaining his girl. After five months of frequent stops at Braunston, a quick passing word if their schedule meant that they could not stay overnight, it was quite clear to everyone that the two were crazy about each other. Vi was keeping a watching brief, a gleam of proud satisfaction in her eyes: *'E'll be arskin' the question any day now!*

* * *

'Coom on, Josh, fer croyin' out loud get a move on!' Frank Martin stood shivering on the towpath in the gathering dusk, his threadbare donkey jacket pulled tightly around his shoulders. The high bank above Rowington village, north of Hatton locks, is completely exposed, and the great thickness of ice was what had stopped the boats in their tracks. Now the *Apple* and the *Florence* were stuck fast, held where they'd been stopped by the ice, some forty feet apart and in the middle of the channel. The ice was thick enough to support a man's weight now, which at least meant that they could get out and down to the village, and Joan's abilities at persuasion had gained them a limited level of credit at the little shop, and an invitation to warm themselves at the pub's fire every evening. Which was where they were heading, if only Josh would co-operate:

'Oi don' *wanna* go out!'

'Let me do yer coat oop for yeh, Josh' his big sister bent to the buttons with an encouraging smile: 'it'll be noice 'n warm in the poob – 'n mebbe the man'll let oos play dominoes again, eh?' The little boy gave her a sullen look, but let her button him up.

'Go on then, both o' yeh – let me shoot the door, keep the 'eat in!' Their mother chivvied them out, quickly closed the cabin doors behind her. Scrambling carefully down the bank, they tramped about a mile through the frozen snow to the village, hastened on by the thought of the roaring fire that awaited them in the public bar. Loaded with more steel tubes, they had little fuel on the boats, and later, when they returned, would be forced to sleep all huddled together in the one cross-bed for warmth, despite the publican's generosity.

* * *

Joe and Grace Caplin were as lucky as the Baker crew – they'd been at Sutton's Stop, near Coventry, awaiting orders to load from the Warwickshire coalfields, when the frosts had struck. The little community of Hawkesbury Junction offered similar facilities to Stoke Bruerne – and, like Stoke, was made up of people who understood the way of life, the difficulties under such conditions, of the boating families. Shopkeepers and landlords who would cheerfully offer supplies and ale 'on tick', knowing that they would be paid without question when the boaters were working again; mothers who would give of their own meagre provisions to ensure that the boat-children wouldn't go hungry, fathers who would slip the odd 'liberated' rabbit or pheasant into the hatches of a boat. Biggest problem they faced was keeping young Jack, nearing two and toddling everywhere, amused and out of trouble, a task not made any easier for Grace by the growing bulk of her second pregnancy. Ernie, just turned sixteen, was eking out his cash by helping in the Greyhound in the evenings, and running errands during the day for anyone who would pay a shilling, and Joe had been taken on by the local coal merchant to help with loading and deliveries to the homes of Foleshill and the other Northern suburbs of the city.

His parents hadn't been so lucky. Loaded with sand from Leighton Buzzard destined for road-building in the Tyseley area of Birmingham, they'd battled their way down the steep drop of

Hammond Three Locks, between Leighton and Bletchley, only to be forced to admit defeat near the next bridge. The village of Stoke Hammond lay less than a mile from the canal at Talbot's Bridge, but it was still a long slog through deeply-drifted snow to its shops and pub, whose incumbents were sympathetic but less compliant than those of the truly canal-side communities. With an incombustible cargo, and no other boats anywhere near, Henry and Suey were hard put to it to keep themselves warm – he and Sam would cut wood from the towpath hedge or nearby trees to supplement their meagre stock of coal, and all four of them had taken to the butty cabin to halve the fuel required. Harriet had been the most downcast of them all – until a knock had sounded on the cabinside one Saturday afternoon:

'Anyoone aloive in ther'?' A familiar voice had sounded; she had looked up from the children's book she was trying to read, incredulous joy on her face:

'Moikey!' Leaping up, she threw open the hatch and looked out; he burst out laughing at her expression:

''Ello, 'Arriet!'

''Ow did yew get 'ere?' She still couldn't believe what she was seeing.

''Itch-'iked. Down the Watling Street, then 'cross from Bletchley.'

Harriet quickly clambered out to join him on the towpath and threw her arms around him. He held her close, kissed her eagerly:

''Ey, yew put moy daughter down, boy!' The laughter in Henry Caplin's voice, the grin on his face, gave the lie to his words.

'Sorry, Mr Caplin!' Michael grinned back: ''Ow've yeh all bin?'

'Oh, we're managin', son.'

'Oi've got soom coal 'ere. For yeh. Thought yeh moight need it.' Henry beamed at him:

'Moikey, yeh're a good lad!'

'Well – Oi 'eard as 'ow yeh were stoock out 'ere, 'n... We 'ad a message from Joey, said as 'ow 'e'd got work with a coalman in Coventry, fer as long as the frost lasts. So Oi did the same, got work with the man in Towcester. 'E picks me oop in the mornin', drops me back at noight – 'n the mooney 'elps a lot, stops Dad usin' 'is savin's whoile we're froze oop.' He gestured at the bag by his side: ''S only 'alf-'undredweight, that's all Oi could manage.'

'Good fer yew, Moikey! Coom on in the warm, boy – yeh'll stop over tonoight? The Missus'll loight the range in the motor for yeh.'

'Well, Oi…'

'Yeh'll never get back 'fore dark, now. Stop 'ere 'n go back in the mornin'. Besoides, 'Arriet'll be grumpy fer days if yeh don't stay a whoile now yeh're 'ere!'

'*Dad!*' Harriet rounded on her father. Michael laughed:

'Okay, Mr Caplin – thank yeh!'

''N what do we owe yeh fer the coal?'

'Nothin'! Moy boss give it ter me when Oi told 'im 'ow yeh were fixed.'

'Yew be sure 'n thank 'im fer oos, when yeh get back, then, boy.'

Michael had duly made his way back to Stoke Bruerne the following day in a very cheerful frame of mind. But the continuing drudgery of working for the coalman, the prolonged anxiety about the weather, soon had him back in that state of worried resignation which was shared by all of the boaters trapped by the ice; most of the men had found some kind of casual employment, wherever they might be, to help provide for their families. And, as Michael heaved sacks of coal, wielded a shovel on the back of a lorry, a self-important spinster sat in her Buckingham office, plotting her next move…

Chapter Sixteen

Mandy Wheeler cocked her ear, stopped pushing the carpet sweeper over the rug in the sitting room: Yes, there it was again! She hurried to open the front door.

'Good afternoon – Mrs Wheeler?'

'Yes?' She surveyed the rather prim-looking woman on her doorstep.

'My name is Loretta Hope-Tanswell, and I am from the Children's Welfare Department of the Council. May I come in for a moment?' Mandy looked puzzled:

'We don't have any children, Mrs…?'

'Hope-Tanswell – *Miss.* I know – it's about your neighbours, in number 108.'

'The Andrews's? They haven't any children, either, at least not yet! They've only just got married!'

'No – the people who were there a few years ago, the Thompsons.'

'Oh – I see. Oh, please, come in out of the cold won't you?'

She led the way into the sitting room, hurriedly pushing the carpet sweeper against the wall and waving to one of the easy chairs. The Council woman sat down and opened a file of papers she was carrying:

'You knew the Thompsons, Reginald and Annette, and their children?'

'Oh, not well! We'd only moved here just before the war, you see. David – my husband – is a foreman upholsterer for the Railway. And they… left, the next summer.'

'Can you tell me what you remember?'

'Well, let me see… They seemed settled enough, although… I don't like to speak ill of the dead, but – *he* was a pretty unpleasant type! Used to drink much too much, and… Oh, he'd be polite enough, if you met him out, but… He used to lose his temper, very easily, I can remember hearing him shouting and swearing at times! And… He used to hit her sometimes, you could see the bruises! And that poor little boy…'

'That would be Michael, the eldest, would it?' Mandy sat forward, a look of horror on her face:

'Yes! You would see him sometimes – the bruises on his face, on his arms… How can a father do that to his child?' Loretta shook her head in sympathy as she went on: 'He ran away you know, in the end.'

'Did they ever find him?'

'Oh, no! He's dead, or so they reckon, drowned in the river most likely. They never found him, poor little mite! Although…'

'Yes?'

'Well – it sounds silly, but I remember there was a story… Only a rumour, you understand…'

'Yes?' Loretta prompted her, holding back her impatience.

'Well… I did hear somewhere that he'd ended up on a boat…'

'A boat?'

'Yes – on the canal, you know. He was supposed to be living with a family on a boat…'

'A family of canal bargees?' Mandy laughed:

'Yes! I know it's ridiculous, but that was what someone told me, in the butcher's, I think it was. Silly, but you know how people come up with these things!' Loretta smiled, and asked:

'What happened after that?' Mandy's tone became conspiratorial:

'Well, *He* died! Got in a fight, in the Craufurd, one evening after work – my David was there! Some of the other men were making fun of him, taunting him, saying it was his fault that the little boy had run away and drowned himself. He lost his temper, of course – and in the struggle, he fell over, smashed his head on the corner of the fireplace. They took him to hospital, but he died the next day. Nettie – Annette – moved back to her parents' house after that. In Buckingham, I think. You ought to talk to Janet Eastwood – she lives the other side, in 106 – they knew them much better, and I think she kept in touch after they moved.'

Loretta closed her file and looked up with a smile:

'Thank you, Mrs Wheeler, I will do what you suggest. You've been very helpful.'

'Oh, not at all! You're welcome, I'm sure!' Mandy ushered her to the door, closed it behind her with the satisfied smile of the vindicated gossip.

But Loretta was feeling much less self-satisfied when she left the Eastwoods' home half an hour later. Janet had been on Fred Morris' list of those to be forewarned of her interest, and had instantly pooh-poohed the idea of Michael having gone to the canal:

'Oh, that's just stupid! I know that story went around not long after he'd vanished, but you know how folk try to make a mystery out of the simplest things. The police think he's dead, and I'm sure they know best.'

And she had confirmed for Loretta how Nettie had died after nursing Andrew through his pneumonia, and that the last she had heard of Ginny, she was living with friends somewhere; and no, she didn't know where.

Back in her office, Loretta thumbed through her notes again. The only hint of a different story from the one that Morris fellow had given her was the strange tale of the boy ending up on a barge. If that was her only lead, she'd try following it up – but maybe another visit to the old man himself, first...

* * *

A couple of weeks went by; Loretta found herself engaged upon other matters, supposedly of greater importance, concerning the support of less privileged children in the awful weather, which had been foisted upon her by her colleagues and superiors. But eventually she was able to put these aside and get back, once more, on the distant scent of the elusive Virginia.

It was the day of the thaw. Gazing out of his front room window, Fred Morris offered up a prayer of thanks – and not only on his own behalf: *Michael and Ginny will be so relieved! And Alby, too.* The BBC weather man on the wireless last night had promised the change they had all been waiting for, and his promise had come to pass; outside, the blanket of frozen snow which had long obliterated the garden was rapidly shrinking, hedges and bushes, plants and grass gradually reappearing. The icy-clear skies had vanished behind a thick veil of dark cloud, and a steady drizzle was helping to wash away the evidence of the long freeze, the temperatures almost miraculously raised to a point that seemed summery compared with what had gone before.

Fred had just finished a letter to Ginny:

I'll post this to Braunston, my darling, as the weather men are saying the thaw is here at last – you'll be on the move any time, I imagine. I'm sure your Dad must be happy – do give him my warmest wishes...

Turning from the window, he sought out an envelope, slipped the folded pages inside and sealed it down. Glancing out at the weather again, he thought: *I'll go to the post office tomorrow – maybe it'll be nicer in the morning.* He placed the envelope on the mantelpiece, propped against one of Ethel's brass candlesticks, where he couldn't fail to see it, and went through to the kitchen to make a pot of tea. He was just pouring the water when the doorbell sounded; tutting his annoyance, he strode down the hall and opened the door.

Loretta carefully put on her most beneficent smile:

'Good afternoon, Mr Morris. Loretta Hope-Tanswell – I called on you once before.' Fred hadn't needed the reminder:

'Good afternoon.'

'I'm afraid we didn't see eye to eye on my last visit, Mr Morris – may I talk to you for a minute or two?' Fred hesitated; maybe he had been a little hasty, after all, the woman was probably only doing her job…

'Won't you come in? I've just made some tea – would you join me in a cup?'

'That's very kind, thank you.' She followed him into the sitting-room.

'Please take a seat – I'll be back in a moment.' He left her to go and get the tea-tray; she looked around, was about to sit down when the envelope on the mantelpiece caught her eye. She took a step closer, read the address:

Miss V. Baker
c/o Fellows, Morton & Clayton Ltd
The Wharf
Braunston
Nr Daventry
Northants.

Her eyes narrowed thoughtfully; then they fell on a small framed photograph next to the letter, a picture of a young boy, about ten or eleven, smart in his school uniform. A tall, almost skinny lad, with a bright smile and a shock of light-coloured hair.

At the sound of Fred's footsteps returning, she quickly sat down in the nearest armchair, looked up as he entered the room, the innocent smile back in place.

'Milk?'

'Yes, please. No sugar.' He poured, handed a cup to her:

'Now – what can I do for you this time, Miss Hope-Tanswell?'

'Well – I am hoping you might just confirm for me the whereabouts of your granddaughter, Mr Morris?'

'I thought I had done that?' Fred felt his ire stirring.

'I know, Mr Morris – but I am supposed to make sure of the welfare of the children who come to our notice. I'm sure you understand.' He held her eyes and his temper:

'Yes – very well. As I told you before, she is living with her uncle, my son, in Australia, and has been now for, oh, over two years.'

'Can you give me their address?' He looked at her, trying to hang on to the idea that she was not the ogre that his instincts were telling him she was, that she was, indeed, only doing a job. But his instincts won out:

'No, I don't think I can. Please understand – my Granddaughter has been through an awful lot. She has lost her entire family – her brothers, her father, her mother; now, she has a new life, in a new country, and she does not need to be reminded of the past. All I can offer you is my personal assurance that she is safe, well and happy where she is. I am afraid that will have to be enough for you.'

'But, Mr Morris – I have to keep records, to show that we have done our job, and I cannot complete…'

'Miss Hope-Tanswell! I have given you all I am going to. You are welcome to cite me in your records if you wish. But I will not have Virginia's happiness disturbed by you or anyone else – is that quite clear?'

'If I was to give you my promise that no-one will try to contact her…'

'No! Forgive me, but I think I have told you all that I want to. Now, if you've finished your tea?'

Loretta hurriedly drained her cup and rose; he ushered her out with a little more ceremony than the last time, but still she was seething with anger as she stalked off down the street: *Damn him! He* is *lying, I know he is!* But a slow smile spread across her face as she thought of the address on that letter: The name of Fellows, Morton & Clayton meant nothing to her, but the address was obviously on the canal – and the girl's initial: V? Virginia? But why *Baker?* Could it be her?

Chapter Seventeen

At Stoke Bruerne, the first boats had begun working down the locks during the morning. With the little radiated heat from the buildings of the village keeping the temperature fractionally higher than the surrounding countryside, the ice had begun to melt as the thaw set in overnight. Every boatman, and a number of the locals, had gone out at first light to start breaking it up – Major Gardner, whose farmhouse stood by the second lock, had sent a number of his men out with whatever heavy implements they could find to start ice-breaking down the flight.

When it came to their turn to go, Alby and Michael ran the *Sycamore* into the top lock. With so much floating ice in the water it was impossible to use the full width of the locks, or to get the gates fully open, and every pair had had to work through singly, doubling the time and effort it took to pass the seven locks. It was well into the afternoon by the time they cleared the flight; standing on the lock-tail as the *Antrim* fell within the chamber, Alby surveyed the scene before him with some concern:

'What d'yer reckon, Moikey?' he called across to Michael, standing by the other paddlegear.

'Dunno, Dad.'

About a couple of hundred yards from where they stood, what looked strangely like a horizontal waterfall was pouring across the canal. At this point the River Tove usually passes beneath the artificial channel in a culvert, but after the swift and dramatic thaw, its waters had risen so that they were streaming into the canal over an old concrete spillway. The level of the canal was already considerably higher than normal, and, as they watched, it seemed to be rising visibly.

'Oi've never seen it loike this, Dad.' Alby shook his head:

'Oi 'ave – once or twoice. Trooble is, it'll be follerin' oos all the way ter Cosgrove. Oh, soom'll run off oover the wire-'oles along the way, boot they ain't big enooff ter get rid of it all – rest'll be goin' oover the lockgates down ther'. 'N with that mooch water oop ar arses… It'll be tricky, boy.'

'Shall oos stay 'ere, then?'

'Nah – 'f we do that, we'll joost as loike be sat on the towpath boy mornin'. Oi've seen boats stoock in the 'edge down 'ere, when it's been bad. Nah – we'll go. Boot we'll 'ave ter breast 'em oop, yeh'll never steer the butty with that coorrent be'ind it. We'll get down Cosgrove, toy below the lock – won' tek oos long ter get ther', neither!' He chuckled: 'Go get the motor, Moikey, back 'er oop ter the gates, 'n we'll pull the butty out, toy 'er on the soide.'

The *Antrim* sat in the bottom of the lock, Ginny, at the helm, looking up at them. Michael walked down to the *Sycamore,* held to the old transhipment wharf below the lock with the centre line while they had dropped the butty, and backed it up to the lockgates as Albert heaved them as far open as they would go with broken ice packed behind them. He turned from the motor's counter, reached for the butty's fore-end line, and began to drag it out of the lock and alongside, walking down the top planks with the rope. Albert hauled on the stern line, bringing the butty stern into position beside the motor; they tied the lines off as tightly as they could, attached the breasting string diagonally between the sterns, and prepared to set off:

'Oi'll tek 'em fer now, Moikey. Yew tek oover when we're past Yardley Wharf, it should be a bit easier boy then, 'cos we'll 'ave lost soom o' this water oover the wire-'oles.'

'H'okay, Dad.' Michael went to go down into the cabin, but Albert grabbed his shoulder to stop him:

'Stay oop 'ere, Moikey. Yew too, Ginny' he called across to the girl.

'Oi was goin' ter start the dinner, Dad?'

'No, girl, yew stay out o' the cabin.' He gestured at the water pouring into the canal in front of them: 'This ain't goin' ter be no picnic, roight? If anythin' 'appens, Oi don' want yew trapped insoide, h'okay?'

The two youngsters exchanged worried looks – was it really that dangerous?

Albert slammed in the clutch and wound up the throttle; the boats surged forward, picking up speed as they approached the spillway and its encroaching torrent. He pulled out the oil-rod, giving the engine even more power; they drove past the flood at the best speed they could achieve in the distance, but even then the surge of water threw them towards the towpath as it struck the fore-ends. Albert heaved the tiller over to compensate, yelling to Ginny to do the same with the butty's 'ellum; and then the torrent was pushing against the sterns, driving them in the opposite direction. Again, they fought with the tillers to maintain a straight course, the breasted boats swerving wildly to the right until they were past the spillway, and the sideways thrust of the water was behind them.

Albert gave a sigh of relief as Ginny turned frightened eyes on him; he gave her a grin:

'Well, we got past that all roight! Joost six moile ter go wi' the coorrent be'ind oos!'

'Can Oi go down now, Dad, get started on dinner?' Alby hesitated, surveying the scene around him:

'H'okay, Ginny. Boot - if Oi yell, yeh coom oop straight away, roight? Moikey – yew get on the butty, stand boy ter 'elp steer if Oi need yeh.'

'Roight, Dad.'

Places were exchanged; Ginny vanished into the butty cabin, began sorting out vegetables and their last scrag-ends of mutton for a stew, while Michael stepped, very carefully, over into the stern well and leant on the massive wooden tiller. Albert slowed the engine as much as he dared – it was necessary to keep the boats driving forwards through the water to maintain steering control, but with the current pushing hard from behind, they were covering ground at an alarming rate.

As they passed through Bozenham Mill Bridge, the water was lapping over the towpath; along the wide curves to Grafton Regis, it disappeared altogether, and Alby was steering by following the hedge-line. Through Grafton Bridge, and the weir on the right-hand turn into Grafton Straight threatened to drag them against its ancient brickwork, so much water was pouring over to return to the now-lower level of the Tove. They shot the bridge in the middle of the straight like a greyhound out of the traps, feeling the boats drop as they cleared the surge of water held back by the narrows of the bridge-hole. The straight ends in a sharp turn to the left, into another bridge; as they turned, Michael felt the weight of the current take hold of the sterns and push them sideways. He glanced across at Albert, to see him leaning groggily on the tiller, his face pale and grey as he struggled to hold the line:

'Yew all roight, Dad?' He shouted across. Albert held on, trying to force the boats into line, but they hit the side of the bridge; the fore-ends bounced across, glanced off the other side, and then the stern hit as well. The boats rocked crazily; but then, with the current driving them on, they were through and travelling straight in the centre of the channel once more.

'Tek oover, Moikey!' Alby called over to him. Michael clambered across onto the motor and took the tiller:

'Yew all roight, Dad?' he repeated; Alby shook his head:

'Don' feel so good, boy. Yew know what ter do?'

'Oi've been watchin' – Oi'll manage.' Alby nodded, and squeezed past him to go down into the cabin.

Ginny had looked out as they'd ricocheted through the bridge; now, she stepped out into the butty's well and took hold of the tiller to assist her brother should he need it. He glanced across at her as she called out:

'What's oop with Dad?'

'Dunno – joost toired, mebbe. It's been a 'Ell of a day.'

'Yeah... Dinner's cookin', be ready fer when we get ter Cosgrove.'

They raced on – past the derelict wharf at Yardley Gobion, backed by its sway-roofed farmhouse, under two more bridges, each passed without incident but at terrifying speed, and then round the long curve to Isworth Farm. Another bridge, and this time a layer of blacking from the motor hull was left on the brickwork as they scraped through; under the shade of Acre Wood, and so to Thrupp Wharf, with its old stone-built pub next to the bridge. Still the towpath was below water, still Michael was steering by keeping a distance from the hedge, but the level seemed to be dropping slowly, the weight of water driving them on easing a little as much of it spilled over into the adjoining fields. Less ice was to be seen now, the still-rising temperatures gradually melting what was floating.

The next weir took a little more pressure off, but still the water was pushing them along. Darkness had fallen as they neared Cosgrove, and Michael was debating what to do – they needed to get down the lock, his Dad had said, but with the level up like this the water would be pouring over the gates. They would have to get the top gates open, and then trust to luck that they could empty the lock sufficiently to get out again once they were in. He gave a mental shrug: *If it cooms ter it, we'll 'ave ter sit in the lock all noight!* At least they should be safe there, with the boats held in its confines while the water streamed past.

Loaded boats would normally take about an hour and a half to cover the six mile distance. That night, they were sweeping into

Cosgrove village in less than an hour, under the ornate Solomon's Bridge, over the embankment and the horse-tunnel, and around the long bend which leads to the lock. As they passed the narrows of the dismantled swing-bridge, Ginny leapt off with her windlass and ran for the lock, only to heave a great sigh of relief when she saw it standing open ready for them. She waved Michael on; he ran the boats in, slamming the engine into reverse at the last moment and winding up the throttle. Even so, they hit the bottom gates a resounding blow; he snatched out the clutch, let the water running over the bottom gates hold the boats in place as he stepped off and heaved the offside gate shut. Ginny closed the other, and they hurried to raise the bottom paddles. The level in the lock fell slowly – so much water was now pouring in over the top gates that it seemed the lock would fail to empty completely. After several minutes, in which time they would usually be well on their way, the lock was almost drained; but still they could not open the gates, with a few inches of water against them. Michael looked over at Ginny in frustration; she threw her weight against the gate once more, then shook her head.

''Old on, kids, Oi'm a-coomin'!' Albert climbed out of the motor cabin and made his way along the top planks. He picked up the rope attached to the boat's mast and threw it to Michael: ''itch that oover the 'and-rail!' He shouted, and then, jumping across to the butty, he did the same with the other mast-line. Michael had to think for a moment – his Dad had shown them how do this… He tried a couple of times before he remembered, then he hitched the rope around the rail in a simple loop so that when pulled back, it would tighten on itself. He stepped across the gates, did the same with Ginny's rope, then waved to Alby, who was now back at the tiller.

Alby reversed the engine, slipped in the clutch, and the boats pulled back in the lock. The ropes tightened, held; with Michael and Ginny adding their weight on the balance beams, the gates slowly creaked open, the excess head of water rushing out through the widening gap. Ginny gave a breathless 'hurray!', and pushed her gate fully open as Michael did the same with his. They stepped down on to the cabin tops as the boats slid past beneath them, smiling in their relief; the special hitch in the ropes released itself as the pull on them came in the other direction, the lines dropping neatly onto the cloths. Five minutes later they were tied up, the boats still breasted, against the towpath of the embankment a hundred feet below the lock.

'Oi'm joost wore out, boy, nothin' ter worry about. Oi felt a bit queer fer a whoile – prob'ly the woorry of it, s'mooch as anythin'.' Michael had joined Alby in the cabin while Ginny dished up the dinner next door.

'If yeh're sure, Dad... Mebbe yeh should stop 'n see Sister Mary nex' toime we're in Stoke Bruin?' Alby wrinkled his nose:

'Nah, no need ter bother the Sister, Oi'm foine! Wher's that stew, Oi'd loike ter know?'

''Ere y'are, Dad!' Ginny stood in the hatches, handed a plate down to him: ''N yours, Moikey.' Moments later, she joined them, her own plate in hand.

* * *

'Coom 'long be'oind oos, it'll 'elp smash it oop!' Early afternoon, by Talbot's Bridge - the cheery call from one of the men on the ice-boat prompted a nod and a wave from Henry Caplin. He'd thought about trying to start on their own, but decided that the great thickness of the ice would be too much to break until it had softened a good deal more. The sight of the ice-breaker, heaving and cracking its way along the pound, had been a more than welcome sight.

Sam had been the first to hear it, at about the time Alby and Michael had been contemplating the flooded Cosgrove pound – the rumble of a big diesel and the crumps and bangs of the ice as it split asunder beneath the weight of the ice-boat. Henry had quickly started their engine and used a long shaft to break the ice as best he could around the boats; by that time, the ice-boat had appeared around the bend, pushing slowly along, rocked enthusiastically from side to side by a crew of about a dozen men, all holding tightly to the raised rail which ran down the centre of the open deck.

''Ow's it bin?' Henry called across to them, straining to be heard over the noise.

'Bloody 'ard goin! We coom from Grove this mornin' – boot it's getting' easier all the toime! We'll 'ave yeh through Fenny tonoight.'

'Roight-oh, mate!'

As the ice-boat pulled past, they heaved the boats out into the open channel behind it and set off, the butty kept close on a twenty-foot line. It was very slow going – but at least they were moving again! After so many weeks of enforced idleness, any progress was a relief. They'd managed, for food and fuel, but with no margin for error – had the freeze gone on another week they would have been in real difficulty. Even as it was, it was only thanks to Michael's bag of coal and the friendliness of a nearby farmer that they'd had enough to survive.

Talbot's Lock; night fell as they forced their way along the two-mile pound to Fenny Stratford, where the ice-breaker turned back. Henry kept going – the ice was thinning and softening rapidly in the suddenly-mild temperatures, and now the steel-hulled Grand Union boats could break their own passage. Even so, it was late when they reached the long bank over the River Ouse, crossed the Iron Trunk aqueduct and tied below Cosgrove Lock. Usually, at this point, they would work up the single lock and stop in the village – but not this time:

'Booger me, look at that water coomin' over the gates!' Suey nodded, concern on her face:

'Shall oos be able to get on termorrer, 'Enry?' He shrugged his shoulders:

'Mebbe – Oi 'ope so! It'll be the Tove, over its banks; with a bit o' loock it'll be gone down agen boy mornin'. We'll stop 'ere – 'ave we got a shillin' or two fer a drink in the 'Mow?'

'Joost about.'

'That's good – them's Alby Baker's boats in froont! 'Arriet'll be wantin' ter see Moikey – 'n Oi need an ale!'

Chapter Eighteen

Ginny had held her patience and her questions until they had eaten; but then she asked:

'So what 'appened back ther', Dad?' Albert smiled reassuringly:

'Oh, Oi joost got a bit toired, girl. Nothin' ter woorry about.' But Ginny was not so easily put off:

'A bit toired? Yeh looked really ill in that bridge-'ole! Coom on, Dad, yeh can' kid me!'

'Oh – well, h'okay, it did feel a bit poorly. Boot it's nothin', Oi'm sure. Joost a foonny turn.'

'Huh! Yeh're goin' ter Sister Mary nex' toime we're in Stoke!'

'Now, Ginny, Oi've said ter Moikey already, ther's no need ter bother 'er. Oi'm foine, really Oi am!'

'HAH! Foine, yeh reckon? Yeh couldn' 'ardly stand oop, back ther'! Yeh're goin' teh talk ter the Sister, yeh 'ear?'

'Oh, Ginny!' He looked at his adopted daughter, saw the determination in her face, and gave in: 'H'okay, h'okay! Boot we ain't mekin' a special stop, we've lost too mooch toime wi' this freeze-oop. Oi'll go see 'er nex' toime we're stopped ther', all roight?'

'Oh – all roight. Boot yew promise, yeh'll go then?'

'Oi promise!' He turned to Michael: 'She's wuss than a woife, yer rooddy sister!'

Ginny joined in their laughter as she gathered up the plates. Climbing out onto the counter, she stepped across to the butty where a kettle was simmering on the range ready for the washing-up. A squib of washing-up liquid, some hot water from the kettle, into the handbowl; stepping up into the hatches again, she went to add some cold water from the can in front of the chimney.

‘’Ey, Ginny!’ She looked up, to see Sam Caplin’s grinning face through the darkness:

‘’Ello, Sam! Yeh’re ’ere, then?’

‘Got ’ere a few minutes back. Mum ’n Dad are coomin’, ’n ’Arriet – they sent me ter give yeh a knock, say are yeh coomin’ ter the ’Mow fer a drink?’

‘Oi speck so – s’long as Dad’s got enooff mooney in ’is pocket.’

‘Roight – Oi’ll give ’em a shout.’ He hurried off, and she returned to her washing-up.

* * *

‘Oi don’ want ter do *that* again in a ’urry, tha’s fer sure!’ Michael had been regaling the gathered boaters in the Barley Mow with the tale of their hair-raising journey from the bottom of Stoke locks. The Caplins were there, Harriet comfortably nestled in the crook of his arm where they sat in one of the benches; a number of other pairs were tied nearby, mostly headed North but waiting for the high water to subside, their crews partaking of a relaxed, if frugal through lack of spare cash, evening in the public bar.

‘Yeh’re very brave, Moikey, boot…’ He looked down into the warm brown eyes, saw the concern in them ‘what if soomethin’ ’ad *’appened* to yeh?’ He gave her a confident smile:

‘Nothin’ ’appened, ’Arriet.’ He bent his head down and kissed her cheek, caught the encouraging look in her mother’s eyes.

The door of the pub swung open; Michael looked up, as did the gathered crowd, to see a man he knew vaguely, a Barlow’s captain, standing in the doorway. From the bar, someone called out:

'Eh oop Chippy! What're yeh 'avin', mate?' But the man said nothing, didn't move. Then he drew a deep breath and stepped inside, closing the door behind him. The buzz of conversation slowly ceased as all eyes turned to him; there was something in his manner, his silence, that drew their attention:

''Ave yeh 'eard?' He spoke at last.

''Eard? 'Eard what, mate?' The same voice from the bar, but with a note of trepidation now.

'They got the oice-boat 'round the H'Oxford soomit terday. Found the *Charity* froze in 'bout two moile from Cabbage Turn.'

Michael looked at Alby with raised eyebrows, but it was Henry Caplin who leant forward and spoke quietly:

'Len Beechey's boat – 'e's a noomber one, still works with a 'orse, mostly down the H'Oxford cut.'

'We met 'im once, back in the war, Moikey' Alby added 'with a load o' coal fer Jimmy Canvin, coomin' ere ter Dinzinger.'

Michael nodded, remembering a small, skinny man with a hooked nose, a buxom wife and several children. The rest of the bar was quiet, waiting for Chippy to go on; the man raised a hand and took off his battered cap, wiped his forehead on the back of his sleeve:

'The old 'orse was laid in the 'edge, froze stiff…' He stopped, drew breath.

'What about…?' a voice asked quietly; Chippy shook his head:

'In the cabin. All of 'em – Len, Rose – 'n the four kiddies. There weren't a scrap o' food in ther'; 'n not a knob o' coal. Boat was empt, goin' back ter load. They'd burnt the stool, 'n the coalbox.'

'*All* of 'em?' someone asked; Chippy just shook his head again. Silence echoed around the bar-room, to be broken by a quiet sob from Harriet:

'Oh, *Moikey!'* she whispered, horrified; her hand tightened on his arm, and then she buried her face in his jacket. He held her close as the man went on:

'T'ent all. They follered Len's tracks 'cross the fields. Ther's a farm, 'bout two moile away, e'd gone ther', wi' oone o' the kids. They knocked on the door, 'n the man coom out, give 'em soom cock 'n bull story that 'e'd bin desp'rate short 'imself, couldn' spare nothing fer no-one else. 'E joost turned 'em away.' He paused, drew breath again: 'E'll be short now, all roight – they foired 'is ricks fer 'im.'

Gasps broke the ensuing silence. Chippy spoke again:

'T'ent roight – boot Oi know 'ow they felt. 'E joost turned 'em away, let 'em die o' cold 'n 'unger.'

The hush that held the room now was impenetrable as his audience tried to take in the horror of what had happened to a family all of them knew. First to move was the landlord – he drew off a pint of his best bitter and poured a generous tot of whisky which he placed beside it:

'Here, Chippy – you need a drink. It ain't easy carryin' news like that.'

'Bloody roight Oi do!' He made his way to the bar, delving in a pocket for some change, but the landlord waved him away:

'That's on me, mate.' He looked around his gathered customers: 'And there's a drink for every boater here, on the house. Len and Rose 'ave often been in here when they've been this way.'

Chippy took a long pull at his pint, and then downed the whisky in one gulp.

'What're they doin' with 'em, Chippy?' Henry Caplin asked. The man set his glass down:

'Oice-boat's towin' 'em ter top o' Napton. Oi 'ear as the H'Oxford Comp'ny's goin' ter coffin 'em, 'n ther's a yoong feller with a single motor 'oo was stoock ther' through the freeze – 'e's goin' ter carry 'em ter Braunston fer buryin'.'

'Don' know when that'll be yet?'

'Nah. Nex' week, Oi'd guess – word'll get 'round.'

'We've got ter be ther', Dad.' Michael's quiet words were

greeted with a chorus of assent. The voice that had first greeted Chippy rose over it:

'We should *all* be ther', everyoone as can!'

'S'roight! We should give 'em the best send-orf we can!'

Glasses were raised, emptied; the landlord was kept busy for some minutes refilling them, before he raised his own and spoke over the subdued mumble of conversation:

'To Len and Rose, and the children!'

'Aye – let 'em rest now, in peace.' Chippy confirmed.

Chapter Nineteen

Braunston had been a popular stop for the boatmen ever since its first canal, the Oxford, came through that way, but it had really come into prominence as a hub of the waterway system with the opening of the Grand Junction Canal in 1800. Boatyards and docks, offices and facilities of a number of carrying companies grew up around the junction of the two canals, in the valley below the hilltop on which stood an old windmill, and the elegant, crochetted spire of Braunston's church.

Over the hundred and fifty years since, the village had seen many gatherings of boaters and their families: Christenings and weddings, with the relatives coming together for the celebrations; funerals, when friends and acquaintances would inevitably want to join with the family to celebrate the life of the departed soul. But the numbers of people arriving at the end of March 1947, crowding the available mooring space until there was barely room to pass, was almost without precedent. Pairs, loaded and empty, crammed the entire length from the junction itself with its twin cast-iron towpath bridges, all the way to the bottom of the locks, three-quarters of a mile away. Family, friends, even a few who had barely known Len Beechey but chose to show their dismay at the tragedy; all were giving valuable time to be present.

It was ten days after the sudden and spectacular thaw. The floods which had ravaged the country, causing chaos for so many even beyond the world of the canals, had subsided, and things were beginning to return to normal.

In his office, Ben Vickers glanced up at the clock. He'd have time to walk up to the Plough, get a sandwich and a quick bracer before the ceremony; he stood up and took his best jacket from the back of the chair, slipped it around his shoulders, picked up his hat from the top of the filing cabinet. Plonking it on his head, he thought ruefully: *Back to square one, Ben!*

On the day of the thaw, his prediction had come true, and he had been a participant in a little scene which had touched him deeply. A knock had come at his door, and Sylvie had ushered Billy Hanney in, staying at his side as Vickers had looked up from the papers on his desk:

'Hello, Billy – what can I do for you?'

'Well – it's loike this, Mr Vickuss…' Billy had been fiddling with the cap held in his hands, obviously nervous.

'Go on, Billy?'

'Well, yeh see… Sylvie 'ere 'asn't got no Dad, nor a Mum. 'N Oi don't know 'oo else ter ask…' Vickers felt the grin taking over his face as he guessed the young man's dilemma:

'She's got a grandma, Billy.'

'Ar – boot she's in Loonon, moiles away from oos. So, Oi thought… D'yeh think, Mr Vickuss, as 'ow it'd be all roight if Oi asked 'er teh marry me?'

'I've already told my Gran, Ben, and she's all for it.' Sylvie spoke up for the first time. Vickers nodded; he got slowly to his feet:

'I don't know, Billy. This is my secretary you want to take away from me…'

He put a tone of reluctance in his voice, and was delighted to see the expression of anguish growing on Billy's face, until he could no longer keep up the pretence. He burst out laughing, stepped around his desk and held out his hand: 'Billy! I'm so pleased for you both – let me be the first to congratulate you!'

Billy's face cleared, a look of delight taking over his features:

'Yeh mean it, Mr Vickuss?'

'Of course, Billy! It's not for me to say yea or nay, anyhow – I hope you'll be very happy together.'

Billy, a huge grin on his face now, took his hand and shook it vigorously:

'Thank yeh, Mr Vickuss!'

Vickers turned to Sylvie, reached out to her and drew her close, kissed her on the cheek:

'I shall miss you, around here, Sylv.' She smiled at him:

'Thank you, Ben.' She turned and reached for her handbag, delved inside for a moment, then looked up at him again: 'This was my mother's; Gran gave it to me last weekend when I told her.' She opened a small jewel box, showed him the simple gold ring within, a single diamond set in a plain clasp. He took it from her, looked at it for a moment and then handed it to Billy:

'It's beautiful, Sylvie. Go on, Billy, put it on her finger, then!' The young boatman lifted the ring carefully out of the box; Sylvie held out her left hand, and he slipped it over her finger, then he embraced her, kissed her, as Vickers asked:

'When will you get married, do you think?' Billy looked up reluctantly:

'We thought mebbe in the soommer, 'bout July.'

'So I can keep my secretary for a few more months then, can I? Go on now, you'd better go and tell your folks, Billy!' They had left, hand in hand, under his satisfied gaze: *All I've got to do now is find them a pair of boats! And a third hand...*

Now, as he headed for Butcher's Bridge and the lane up to the village high street, another less palatable thought crossed his mind: *I must have a word with Alby, before that damned woman shows up...*

* * *

Alby Baker and his crew had arrived that morning and found it difficult to tie the boats anywhere. Running South again, from Fazeley Street, they'd ended up breasted outside another FMC pair not far from bottom lock, under the shadow of the old pumping-engine chimney.

Dressed in their best, they'd walked back along the towpath to Butcher's Bridge to where they'd spotted Henry Caplin's Grand Union pair; Michael had knocked on the side of the *Bodmin,* and Harriet had emerged to join them:

'Ma 'n Dad, 'n Sam, will be along ter join oos 'fore it starts, Mr Baker' she told Alby as she slipped her arm through Michael's.

In the church, the six coffins were arranged side by side on trestles, in front of the altar rail – since first light, people had been coming and going, boaters and villagers alike, each pausing to offer a prayer or a thought for the souls of the family, but it was quiet, almost deserted, as the four of them walked softly in. They went up the central aisle; Alby hung back, his arm protectively around Ginny, his hand on her shoulder, his head bowed, as she gazed in sorrowful silence at the plain pine coffins, each with its simple brass plaque on the lid. Michael and Harriet walked up to them, his arm about her waist; she paused in front of each, resting the tips of her fingers on the smooth wood as she read the inscription, then passing on to the next. At the last, and smallest, she stood longest, gazing down; at last, she raised her tearful eyes to Michael's:

'Four year old, Moikey – she was joost four year old…' She put her arms tightly around him, crying quietly into his shoulder. He looked back along the row again:

Leonard Beechey, 1904-1947
Rose Beechey, 1906-1947
Anne Beechey, 1934-1947
Arthur Beechey, 1936-1947

Lenny Beechey, 1938-1947
Rosie Beechey, 1943-1947

He had to swallow hard to hold back his own tears; then Harriet raised her head again:

'Yeh've got ter promise me, Moikey…'

'What is it, 'Arriet?'

'Yeh've got ter promise me, nothin' loike this can ever 'appen teh our kiddies.' He looked at her in amazement, smiling through his sadness:

'*Our* kiddies, 'Arriet?' Realising the import of her words, she blushed scarlet, and hid her face in his coat again. Gently, Michael eased her away until he could look into her eyes:

'Are yeh sure about that, 'Arriet?' She held his gaze for a moment, then nodded, her slow, shy smile spreading over her face:

'Oi am, Moichael.' He drew her close again, kissed her on the forehead:

'Oi'd better talk ter yer father, then, 'ad Oi?' Her eyes were sparkling now:

'Mebbe yeh 'ad, Moichael!' He felt like laughing out loud, but restrained himself in consideration of their surroundings, the occasion:

'Oi loove yew, 'Arriet Caplin!' She gazed into his eyes and whispered in return:

'Oi loove yew too!' She looked around quickly, then stretched up to kiss him briefly: 'Let's go outsoide, Moikey!'

They turned, to be confronted with the grinning faces of Albert and Ginny, and stopped in their tracks:

'Did yew 'ear, Dad?' Alby chuckled quietly:

'Enooff, boy, enooff!' Ginny was gazing up at her brother:

'Oh, Moikey!'

Out in the churchyard, away from the tragedy within, Ginny threw her arms around him:

'Moikey! Oi'm so 'appy for yeh!' Now he laughed without restraint and hugged her tightly, as Alby put his arms around Harriet and gave her a kiss on the cheek:

'Looks loike Oi'll 'ave a daughter-in-law soometoime soon, then?' She nodded shyly:

''Arriet Baker – what d'yeh think o' that?'

'Woonderful, girl!' Her expression became serious:

'Not joost yet, though. Moikey's got ter talk ter moy Dad – 'n Oi'm only seventeen, we'll 'ave ter wait a bit, Oi s'pose.' He nodded:

'Yer Dad'll want yeh ter be sure, 'Arriet. A year or two, mebbe?' She smiled:

'No longer'n that, or 'e'll be in trooble!' Alby laughed now, as Michael let go of his sister and took Harriet in his arms. They kissed, long and eagerly, as Alby and Ginny looked on approvingly.

'I hate to break up this happy scene, Alby!' The boatman turned at the sound of Ben Vickers' voice:

''Ello, Ben! Moikey's joost proposed ter 'Arriet!'

'And she's accepted?'

'Ar!' Vickers shook his head in mock disbelief:

'Tch! Silly girl. Fancy marrying a boatee!' Harriet turned to him, a look of fury on her face; he burst out laughing: 'You're very pretty when you're angry, Harriet!' She subsided with a grin as Michael said:

'It was more loike 'er proposin' ter *me,* really…' he explained what had happened inside the church.

Once he'd congratulated them, Vickers turned to his more sober news:

'Listen – you remember the warning you had from your Grandfather, last year? We all thought that woman had given up – but she's popped up again, I'm afraid. I had her on the phone in the week. At first, I thought she was just the local public health office, from Daventry – they call every now and then, check up on a couple of pairs to make sure the regulations are being followed. She said she was from the council – not *which* council, or I'd have twigged – and I'd mentioned today's funerals, that a lot of boats would be here, before… It was only when she started asking questions about did I have a crew called Baker, and was there a young girl, that I realised who she must be. How she got onto you here, I've no idea; but she's going to be here this afternoon, and she wants to see you.' He held up his hands as they all started to talk at once: 'I can't refuse her without good reason – if you come to my office straight after the service, we'll do our best to put her off the scent, okay?' Michael and Ginny both started to protest again, but Alby hushed them:

'We'll be there, Ben. Boot she ain't tekin' Ginny, coom what may!' Vickers shook his head:

'I don't see how she can *prove* that Ginny is the girl she's looking for – I'm sure your Grandad won't have told her, will he?' Both youngsters shook their heads:

'Never!' Michael confirmed.

'Well, then – we'll have to convince her otherwise, right?'

'Roight!' Harriet joined in the chorus.

Chapter Twenty

Once the six coffins were lowered into the ground, Harriet had hurried away to join her own boats. In the thronging crowds, no opportunity had presented itself for Michael to talk to Henry and Suey, but he knew that Harriet would forewarn them, and that he would have the chance to make his request to them in the coming weeks.

'Oi ain't waitin' mooch longer. We've lost enoff toime terday as it is, Ben – if she ain't 'ere in foive minutes, we're off.' The sombre pomp of the funeral over, Albert Baker and his crew were standing around in Ben Vickers' office. Ginny backed him up:

'Tha's roight, Dad – Oi'm 'opin' we can get ter Stoke Bruin tonoight.' Vickers looked at his watch:

'You could still do it, Ginny – it's only just after three. If you don't mind stopping late!'

'Depends on 'ow long this wench takes ter be put off.' Alby pointed out.

'We'll get rid of her as quickly as we can. Is it important, Ginny?' Alby grunted:

'She's got it in 'er 'ead that Oi should see the Sister.'

'Oh – why's that?'

'It's nothin', Ben – Oi 'ad a bit of a foonny turn a week or two back.'

'When we were racin' the flood 'long the Cosgrove pound,

Mr Vickers – 'e was teken bad, went really pale 'n shaky fer a bit!' Ginny expressed her concern.

'Oi was joost toired – and it was the strain of it, 'n all. It was nothin' ter get woorried about.' Vickers put a hand on his old friend's shoulder:

'Probably not, Alby – but you take Ginny's advice, have a word with Sister Mary, okay? I don't want one of my best crews laid up.'

'Oi will, Ben – if only ter stop 'er naggin' at me!'

As they all laughed, a knock sounded and the office door opened:

'There was no-one in the outer office, so I came through. Mr Vickers?' The well-groomed woman in the black coat with a silver fox-fur collar walked over to the manager and held out her hand.

'Good afternoon?' He took her hand, shook it briefly.

'Loretta Hope-Tanswell, from Buckingham County Council. I spoke to you on the telephone.'

'Yes, indeed.' He indicated Alby: 'This is Albert Baker, captain of the *Sycamore* and the *Antrim.'* She turned her head to regard the boatman, and inclined it slightly in greeting:

'Mr Baker.' She made no attempt to shake his hand. Alby looked at her for a moment, taking in her prim features and long yellow hair tucked beneath its pill-box hat, then he nodded quickly in return. Her eyes found Ginny:

'And you must be Virginia?' Ginny looked at her with open hostility:

'Ginny. Ginny *Baker.'*

'Yes – well, of course.'

'What can we do for yeh, Missus Tanswell?' Alby asked. She recoiled slightly:

'Miss, and it's *Hope*-Tanswell. Hyphenated. I work for the Children's Welfare Department of the council, and it is my job to clear up the backlog of cases that we have left after the war years.'

''N 'ow does that 'ave anythin' ter do with me 'n moy children?'

'We shall see, Mr Baker.' She turned to Ginny again: 'How old are you, my dear?' Ginny's expression hadn't changed:

'Twelve.'

'And you live with your – your *father* – on the boats?'

'O' course!'

'Don't you go to school?'

'Soometoimes! When we're stopped in Brentf'd, or Birnigum, waitin' ter load.'

'Can you read and write?'

'Yes!'

'Oh – very good.' Loretta's praise sounded condescending.

'Moikey 'elps me, as well!'

'Oh?' She turned her attention to Michael: 'So you're Michael. Virginia's brother?'

'O' course.' His tone was as terse as his sister's, his expression as hostile.

'And how old are you, Michael?'

'Eighteen.'

'You work on the boats as well?'

'O' course!'

'But you can read and write, too?'

'Yes!'

'Despite very limited schooling?'

'Moikey went ter school 'til 'e was…' Ginny let her annoyance get the better of her, until she realised what she had said. Loretta closed in, almost licking her lips:

'Until when, my dear?' Ginny tried to cover her tracks:

''E lived on the bank, 'til 'e was ten. With… With our aunt. So's 'e could go ter school.'

'Oh? Where was that, Michael?'

'Er…' Alby jumped in to try and save the situation:

'Listen, Miss – Oi can't see 'ow this is of any interest ter yew or the council. They're *moy* children, 'n no concern o' the council's. They're also moy *crew,* 'n we've got a job ter do. We've been 'ere all day fer Len Beechey's burying, 'n now we needs ter get goin'. So if yeh'll excuse Oos?'

'Not so fast, Mr Baker…'

'I can assure you these youngsters are of no possible interest to Buckingham Council, Miss Hope-Tanswell. I know them well; I've known Albert Baker most of my life, and I can vouch for them.' Vickers added his bit. Loretta bridled under their pressure, not to be put off:

'Mr Vickers! It is my belief that the wool has been pulled over our eyes – yours, possibly, and mine, certainly!' She turned to Ginny again: 'I believe that you are in fact Virginia *Thompson,* who was supposed to be taken into council care after your mother died in Buckingham in 1942. You are the right age; and you fit the description I have of Virginia at eight years old.' She looked at Michael: 'And I think that *you* are Michael Thompson! You are indeed Virginia's elder brother – but you disappeared from your home in Wolverton in 1940. You, too, are the right age – and you look much as I would expect Michael to look now from an old photograph I have seen.' She looked around at their dismayed faces, a look of triumph on her own.

Alby burst out angrily:

'Tha's *roobbish!* Oi don' know wher' yeh get sooch crazy oideas – they're *moy* kids, 'n they don' belong in no bloody orphanage!' She smiled sweetly at him:

'Oh, we couldn't put *Michael* in the home, now – he's over sixteen, and his own responsibility. But Virginia should be in care – for her own good, you understand, so that she can be brought up correctly, and get a proper education. She came from a good family – and now I find her living with a disreputable bargee. No offence, but you must see my point.'

'Alby!' Vickers spoke sharply – he'd seen Albert's anger rising, and didn't want a nasty scene to ensue. The boatman bit his tongue with some difficulty, contented himself with glaring at the woman with fury in his eyes. She went on unperturbed:

'I realise you will not surrender the girl to me freely, Mr Baker. I will be back in due course, with the support of the law.' She looked at Vickers: 'I will contact you, Mr Vickers, when that is to happen, and arrange for Mr Baker and the girl to be here.' She patted her hat into place and turned to the door: 'For now, good day to you all.'

She walked out, leaving them all speechless.

Ginny was the first to regain her voice:

'Oh, Dad! Oi'm sorry – she got me so angry, 'n Oi wasn' thinkin' what Oi was sayin'!' He put his arms around her:

'Don' fret yerself, choild. She 'ad me pretty bloody mad, 'n all. Bargee, indeed!'

'Disreputable bargee, Dad.' Michael reminded him with a smile.

'Aye, that 'n all!'

'What're we goin' ter *do,* Dad? Oi'm not goin' ter 'er 'ome!'

'Bloody roight yeh're not! We'll think o' soomat.'

'Leave it to us, Ginny – and try not to worry, all right?' Vickers added his words of comfort: 'We'll find a way of stopping her, you'll see.'

Ginny gave him a pale smile, but her eyes expressed her doubts and her fears. They all stood around in an awkward silence, shaken, disturbed by the woman's attitude and her obvious determination to shatter their settled lives. Albert continued to hold Ginny in his arms, trying to comfort her without the help of words that didn't want to come; Ben Vickers stood leaning on his desk, a look of puzzled anger on his face, and Michael gazed thoughtfully out of the window.

At last Albert broke the unspoken impasse:

''S no good, we got ter get movin'. We're be'iond enooff as 'tis.' Ginny looked up at him:

'Dad…?'

'Loike Ben says, troy not ter woorry, loove. We'll sort it out, yeh'll see.' Vickers sighed:

'We will, Ginny, somehow. You get on your way now.'

'Okay.' She sounded small and lost despite the thin smile she put on as she let Alby lead her out of the office. Michael roused from his reverie, and stayed behind for a few minutes to talk to Vickers; his thoughtful expression had gained an air of hope by the time he followed them back to the boats.

Chapter Twenty-One

They didn't make Stoke Bruerne that night but tied instead at the bottom of Long Buckby locks, sixteen miles and four hours short of Ginny's target.

When Michael had joined them, tucking his windlass into his belt to go and set the bottom lock of Braunston flight, he was feeling totally exhausted. They'd done little physical work that day, but his feelings had taken a severe battering: The gathering gloom of the impending funeral had suddenly been replaced by inexpressible elation in the churchyard, leaving him the almost irreconcilable blend of sorrow as he'd watched the burial of an entire boating family and joy at having his girl at his side. And then, to cap it all, the shock and distress engendered by the council woman's visit, her eagerly stated intention to take his sister away from him…

His words with Ben Vickers had left him believing that they could save Ginny from the orphanage, in spite of his fear of Loretta's power. But seven years on the boats had cultivated in him the same mistrust and suspicion of land-based authority that was common among the boating people, and, despite himself, he was still assailed by the idea that she would be able to pull some kind of unexpected stroke and snatch Ginny away from them.

It was mid-morning of the next day when they stopped outside the old mill building to await their turn to start down Stoke Bruerne locks. Ginny scanned the lockside – usually, they would see Sister

Mary bustling about, enquiring after the health of passing boaters, often winding a paddle or pushing a gate; but not today. She slipped away to try and find her, but returned, looking disgruntled, with the news that the good Sister was away caring for an elderly lady of the village who had been taken ill during the cold weather. Albert greeted this news cheerfully:

'Never moind, loove, we'll see 'er anoother toime. Besoides, ther's nothin' wrong wi' me now – we really didn' ought teh bother 'er...' Michael managed not to laugh at the look of relief on Alby's face, or the stern expression that grew on Ginny's at his words.

* * *

Three days later they were unloading in City Road Basin when the local traffic manager walked up to Alby:

'Mr Baker?' Alby looked around from the stack of boxes he'd been lifting out into Michael's hands:

'Aye?'

'When your boats are empty, can you go to Regent's Canal Dock and load there? We've a ship-load of steel to get to Tyseley as quickly as possible.'

'Loime'ouse? Yeh're tekin' oos off the Fazeley Street roon, then, are yeh?' The boatman's expression showed his displeasure at losing the prestigious regular trip.

'It's not that – this is a rush job, Alby. The *Acorn* and *Kerry* are on their way, and I'll need at least one more pair to join you on top of the ones already there. But – you must have seen for yourself, the traffic between here and Birmingham has been going down steadily for a long time now. The directors want us to use the available boats more efficiently, and that means sending them wherever they're needed. It's better for you, as well, if we keep you working rather than have you sitting here for a couple of days waiting for a load, surely.'

'Aye – mebbe so. We'll go soon as we've empt 'n swept out.'

'Good – I'll ask them to load you in the morning. But, Alby, remember – you mustn't touch the cargo until it's all been loaded.'

'Oh, aye?'

'It's the dockers – we've had trouble there before. The Union nearly had them all out on strike a while back, just because one captain grabbed a bundle of timber which was swinging close to his cabin. Leave it to the men they put in the boat to drop it and stack it – you can always retrim it later, once you're out of the docks. Okay?'

'If you say so,' Alby growled, clearly unhappy at this instruction – it was usually the captain's responsibility to see that his cargo was safely stacked and unable to shift, and leaving that task to others, possibly less trustworthy, went against the grain: If a cargo shifted with the boats on the move, they could become dangerously unstable.

By the middle of the evening they were in Limehouse Basin, tied to the long jetty, their holds empty and uncovered ready for the steel to be dropped in by the dockside crane. They ate in the butty cabin – Ginny had remained largely quiet, withdrawn, since they left Braunston, but it had come as some consolation to her to find the Hanney's boats already tied in the basin, to see Stevie's cheeky grin over the *Acorn's* cabintop as they turned and drew in to the jetty. A number of other boats were also there, some clearly loaded, clothed up ready to depart the next day, and two other empty pairs; a look of distaste had crossed Albert's face as he saw the dirty paintwork and dull brasses of the *Apple.*

Dinner over, they had all emerged to stand on the jetty in the bright evening darkness, Alby puffing at his pipe. A hale from their neighbours, and Bill and Stevie Hanney strolled along to join them:

''Ow do, Alby, Moikey. 'Ello, Ginny.'

'Evenin', Bill.'

'What's this about soome busybody troyin' ter tek yeh away, Ginny?' Bill asked as his son smiled a greeting at the girl. Ginny smiled back, then turned to him:

'It's this wench from Bookin'am Council…' she went on to tell them about the meeting in Vickers' office: '…'n Oi don' know what we're goin' ter do…' The retelling had left her near to tears; Stevie stepped forward and put his arm around her, to be rewarded with a nervous smile.

'Everythin'll be all roight, yeh'll see, Ginny.' Michael reassured her.

'Boot…' He gave her a knowing smile, trying to look more confident than he felt:

'Mr Vickuss's got an oidea, 'e'll work it out.'

'Tha's roight, Ginny – yer Dad 'n 'im'll sort it out, never fear. Yeh ain't goin' nowher',' Stevie agreed: 'Coom on, let's go fer a walk.'

The three youngsters wandered away, chatting amongst themselves; Bill raised his eyebrows questioningly at Alby, only to receive a shrug of the shoulders in reply:

'Oi don' know what they're at, Bill. Boot Oi 'ope Moikey's roight!'

'Yeah, oos 'n all. Did Oi 'ear as 'e's proposed ter 'Arriet?' Alby laughed, and then regaled him with the tale of events at Braunston.

'Oi'm sorry we couldn' be ther', Alby. Len 'n Rose were h'okay; 'n those poor kiddies…'

'Yeah – bloody shame. Yeh're loadin' ahead of oos termorrer?' He changed the subject.

'Yeah – boot them Rodneys are fust in the queue.'

'Martins?'

'Yeah. 'S long as 'e don' boogger it oop fer oos all!'

''Ow d'yer mean, Bill?'

'Huh! Stoopid sod 'ad a go at one o' the dockers a whoile back. They'd put two men in 'is 'old on the motor, 'n they was droppin' soom timber in on the crane. Started swingin' 'n got 'im frit that it'd 'it the cabin, so 'e put a 'and to it. Tain't allowed, see, 'cause o' the bloody union rules, 'n the two dockers told 'im if 'e did it agen they'd black 'im, refuse ter load 'im. Stoopid Boogger 'ad a go back, 'n they was all ready ter go on stroike 'til Fellers's agent coom along 'n calmed 'em down.'

''Im, was it? Ole Charley at City Road said soomat about it, tol' me not ter tooch the stooff 'til it was in the boats.' Bill laughed:

'Don' yew neither, not oonless yeh want ter be goin' back empt!'

'They really that bloody-moinded?'

'Ah – 'n then soom!'

'Best oos watch what we says, then, eh!'

Along the jetty, Stevie was almost jumping up and down with delight at the news of Michael's unofficial engagement. He'd wrung his friend's hand until it almost fell off, and then turned and hugged Ginny until she complained that she couldn't breathe:

''N any'ow, Dad'll skin yeh if 'e sees!' Stevie let her go reluctantly, as Michael told him that he was hoping to see Harriet's parents some time soon, to ask their permission. They strolled on past the line of boats, taking no notice of the sound of two young children playing in an empty hold until a voice suddenly said:

''Ello, Mr Baker!' Michael turned to see a familiar shy smile over the gunwale:

''Ello, Carrie – 'ow are yeh?'

'Oi'm foine, Mr Baker. Oi 'aven' seen yeh fer ages!' He gave the girl a smile in return:

'We've been 'tween City Road 'n Birnigum fer a long toime. Yew loadin' termorrer?'

'Yes – then oop ter Tyseley.'

'Oos 'n all. Mebbe we'll see yeh there?'

'Oi 'ope so, Mr Baker!'

'Aye – well – 'bye, Carrie.'

'Bye-bye!' But she stood and watched as they walked away again. Stevie chuckled:

'Got yerself a spare girl then, 'ave yeh?' Michael threw a playful punch at him:

'Boogger off, Stevie 'Anney! She's been talkin' teh me ever since… yeh know.'

Stevie laughed again: 'Oi still reckon she's got a crush on yeh!'

'Don' be daft! She can' be more'n noine year old!' Michael protested. Stevie shook his head, tutting:

'Oi still think Oi oughtta tell 'Arriet when Oi sees 'er…'

Chapter Twenty-Two

The next morning the call came to start loading from the ship direct into the boats. The other waiting crews watched as Frank Martin manoeuvred his pair, singled out, alongside the vessel which towered over them all. Two dockers clambered down into the hold of the butty, waved a signal, and the dockside crane burst into life with a great blast of black smoke from its exhaust stack. The slings dropped into the ship's hold, and soon rose again bearing several long billets; the jib swung out, and then the steel was dropping at an alarming rate towards the vulnerable-looking narrowboat trapped beneath. The two men grabbed it as it came to an abrupt halt, inches above their heads, swinging crazily, and held it steady as the craneman lowered it into the bottom of the boat's hold. It landed with an audible crash; the boat rocked wildly, settling with a dramatic tilt to one side.

''Ey, tek it easy will yeh?' Martin was standing in the well, keeping an eye on proceedings; he had had to grab the slide to stop himself being thrown overboard as the billets landed. Neither docker replied, but one of them turned to him with a warning look. Joan Martin put her head out of the hatches, caught the man's expression:

'Coom insoide, Frank, 'ave a coop o' tea.' Martin was glaring at the docker, but she tugged at his sleeve: 'Coom on – we don' want no more trooble.'

He followed her down into the cabin, obviously angry but

reluctant to take further issue with the loaders, realising that his job would be on the line if he caused another dispute.

'They'll be a coopl'a hours loadin' 'im, Alby. Vi 'n me's goin' teh the shops.' Bill Hanney and his wife stood with the *Sycamore's* crew.

'Oi'll coom with yeh – Oi need soom 'bacca.' He turned to Ginny: 'Anythin' yeh want from the shops?'

'Yeh could get soom 'taters 'n carrots, Dad, 'n a point o' milk. 'N soom stewin' beef if we've got the points…' She rummaged in the ticket drawer, found the ration books: 'Joost about! See if yeh can squeeze a bit extra, Dad, it'll do anoother day then.'

'Roight-oh. Shan' be long.'

The adults wandered away towards the gate into the street; Michael and Ginny returned to idly watching the loading as Stevie strolled up:

''Ow's it goin'?'

'Joost started.' Michael told him as Ginny moved to stand by his side; he slid his arm around her shoulder, gave her a quick squeeze before letting go again:

''Lo, Ginny.'

''Ello, Stevie.' Her smile was accompanied with a distinct flush of her cheeks: 'Wher's Billy?' Stevie grinned:

'Gorn off teh foind a telephone. 'E wants ter ring Sylvie.' He glanced around: 'Wher's Martins?' He asked.

'Butty cabin.' Michael replied.

'Booggered if Oi'd be down in the cabin durin' that!' He gestured at the loading going on as another bundle of billets dropped perilously into the boat.

'Me neither.' Stevie chuckled:

''Least yer spare girlfriend's safe on the bank!' He pointed along the jetty to where Carrie and her little brother were playing together. The girl, sensing their attention, looked up and waved to Michael; he waved back, raising another snigger from Stevie, and turned to take a playful swing at his friend's head. Stevie ducked, laughing aloud; then both of them looked up to see what was happening as Ginny let loose a terrified scream.

The next bundle of billets was descending into the boat; but one of the slings had slipped. The whole bundle began to slide out of the slings; the two dockers dived overboard into the water as it crashed down into the butty, all its weight on the same side as the last drop. The boat heeled, bounced; a second crash sounded as the steel already on board shifted – the dockers were swimming frantically away, people on the jetty and the dockside staring, horrified, as the *Florence* slowly turned turtle and disappeared.

'Mummy!' They spun around at the sound of Carrie's anguished yell. Michael began to run to the children; Ginny and Stevie exchanged glances and followed suit. The little girl was standing as if frozen, her eyes fixed on at the spot where her home had vanished; Michael grabbed her into his arms, held her face into his jacket to stop her seeing. Ginny knelt in front of Josh, who was just staring, his mouth open, at the ripples on the water; she took him by the shoulders, shook him, and when he made no response followed her brother's example, gathered him into her arms and held him tight.

The next instant, the stunned silence was broken. The petrified stillness of the onlookers gave way to pandemonium; faces lined the rail of the ship to see what had happened, and people on the bank scurried to and fro with apparent purposelessness as some went to help the two swimming dockers while others headed for telephones to summon assistance or sought to find ways of reaching the couple in the sunken boat.

Michael looked over at his sister:

'Ginny – get these two down in yer cabin, keep an oiye on 'em. We'll go 'n see what's ter be doon.' Ginny nodded, gently led Josh to her butty and eased him down inside; Michael followed with Carrie, and handed the girl over as she emerged again and reached for her.

'Coom on, Stevie!' The two ran along the jetty to where one of the dockers was standing, water streaming from his clothing, surrounded by a gang of his fellows:

'Can we get ter the folks in the boat?' He asked urgently; one of the men shook his head:

'Nao, mate. It's bloody deep in 'ere, there ain't no chance o' gettin' down to 'em 'til the diver gets 'ere.'

'So what can we do?' Stevie sounded horrified. The man gazed at him for a moment, then shook his head again, a look of remorse on his face as he said quietly:

'Nothin', mate. I'm sorry 'bou' yer friends, but there ain't nothin' anyone can do. Yeh won't get daown there withou' divin' kit. If they didn' ge' ou' on their aown… I'm real sorry.'

The two boys stared at him, unwilling to believe him but knowing in their hearts that he was right. Even so:

'Oi've got ter troy!' Michael threw off his jacket, kicked off his boots, and dived into the water before anyone could stop him. The dockers all stared, astonished; the one who had told them of the hopelessness of it shook his head again, tutting in mixed disapproval and admiration:

'Wastin' 'is time!'

But they all watched as he swam out to where the *Florence* had disappeared, jack-knifed and dived below the surface. Moments later, he reappeared; Stevie gave a sigh of relief as his friend swam back to the jetty. Two of the men helped him out; he stood there as the water drained from his clothes:

'Yeh're roight, mate, it's no use' he addressed the pessimist. 'Yeh can't see boogger all down ther'. 'Ow deep *is* it?' The man gave a wry laugh:

'Deep enough ter flaowt that bastard' he pointed at the ship 'an' then some!' They all stood looking at each other, feeling distraught and helpless; a couple of the dockers led their wet colleague away towards the office buildings.

'What's 'appened? What's goin' on?' Michael and Stevie

turned as Bill Hanney ran up to them, followed by Albert: ‘We joost got back ’n soomeoone said ther’d been a sinkin’!’

‘The *Florence,* Dad.’ Stevie told him: ‘Load shifted, ’n it joost rolled over ’n went.’ Bill’s jaw dropped in astonishment:

‘Anyoone in it?’ His expression became one of horror as his son nodded:

‘Yeah. Martin ’n ’is missus were in the cabin.’

‘In the cabin? That’s the last place ter be whoile that’s goin’ on!’ Alby exclaimed in disbelief. Stevie just shrugged.

Vi had staggered up, laden with two bags of shopping, in time to hear the last exchange:

‘They didn’ get out?’ Stevie shook his head.

‘Oh, no!’ She looked around: ‘What about the kiddies?’

‘Ginny’s got ’em down in ’er cabin.’ Michael told her.

‘Did… Did they see?’ She asked warily; her eyes closed in pain as he nodded.

‘Moikey troied ter save ’em, doived in ’n swum down.’ Stevie said.

‘Yeh did?’ Bill turned to him in surprise: ‘It’s too deep, ’n the water’s full o’ moock, yeh’d never get to ’em!’

‘So Oi found out.’ Michael said ruefully.

‘What’s ter be doon?’ Vi asked. One of the remaining dockers answered her:

‘They’ll get the diver down soon as they can. Salvage crew’ll get the boat up, recover the bodies in a day or two.’ There was sympathy in his eyes as he went on: ‘Friends o’ yours, were they?’

‘Not ’specially.’ Bill sounded distracted: ‘We knew ’em, o’ course.’

‘What about the kiddies?’ Vi asked.

‘We told yeh, they’re safe!’ Stevie protested.

‘No, yeh stoopid boogger – what’s ter ’appen to ’em?’

‘Ah…’ Bill and Alby exchanged looks; Vi glanced from one to the other.

‘’Ave they got any oother family?’ Alby asked.

‘Don’ think so.’ Vi replied: ‘Old Josh’s gone, ’n ’is missus. ’N Oi ’eard soomewher’ that ’er folks were killed in the war.’

‘No Ooncles or Aunties, on the cut?’

‘Not as Oi knows of.’

‘Ah…’ Looks were exchanged again.

‘Let’s go see ’ow they are, fust off.’ Vi turned and led the way to the *Antrim.*

Chapter Twenty-Three

Peter Robinson ran a hand through his hair in a gesture of worried uncertainty as he walked from the dockside. A self-employed shipping agent, with his offices adjacent to Regent's Canal Dock, Robinson also acted as the local representative of Fellows, Morton & Clayton Ltd. He'd hurried down to the jetty when the news of the tragedy had reached him, and done his best to organise the company's interests in its aftermath. He'd found the men standing around helplessly, looking shocked, angry and frustrated with their inaction; and Vi, with another boatwoman from one of the loaded pairs waiting to leave, comforting the children in Ginny's cabin. He'd sent the waiting boats on their way, knowing that they could do nothing to help by staying; he'd looked in on the children, asked about their future, and agreed, at Vi's question, to go and contact Saltley to find out if there were any relatives who might be able to take them in. And he needed to arrange with the dock authorities to continue the loading as soon as it was possible, and find out what moves were already afoot to reach the capsized butty and retrieve its victims.

In his absence, a last empty pair had arrived for the ship-load of steel; Jack Warden and his wife had expressed their horror at the news, having learnt of the disaster from the departing boats as they'd passed them on the Regent's Canal. Now they joined in the discussion about the fate of the newly-orphaned children:

'We can' tek 'em, Jack!' Maggie Warden had told her husband:

'We ain' got the room.' He'd shaken his head, a look of relief on his face:

'She's roight – not wi' foive of ar own.'

''N noomber six on the way!' His wife reminded him, patting her stomach.

'That's roight. Besoides…' he looked around the gathered boaters: 'No-one's goin' ter want 'em, are they?' Bill nodded slowly:

'Yeah…'

'What do yeh mean?' Ginny was looking puzzled; she'd left Vi with the children, and come out to get away from the fragile atmosphere in the cabin. Bill and Alby exchanged glances:

'Well… They're Rodneys, roight? People won' want ter tek in Rodney kids, will they?'

'You mean they'd let them…' Ginny shook her head, scandalised into silence, looking around the assembled faces.

'Ginny –' Alby's tone was conciliatory: 'You remember what yew thought of 'em, furst toime yeh saw 'em? At Braunston, that toime?' She blushed, and stammered:

'Well – yes, boot… All roight, they're dirty, 'n badly dressed – boot that ain't their fault! We can soon clean 'em oop!'

'It's not joost that – it's, well, what's their 'abits? They ain't been brought oop ter look after 'emselves roight, nor the boats. Yeh see what Oi mean?'

'Yeh don' want 'em ter join *oos?'* Michael asked her; she stared at him for a moment, angry and confused:

'Oh! *Oi* don' know!' She turned and strode back to the *Antrim,* disappeared back into the cabin.

'Yeh could tek 'em, Alby – yeh've got the room, 'n with only three of yeh…' There was a twinkle of mischief in Jack's eyes; Albert didn't reply, but looked daggers at him. Maggie shared her husband's sense of humour:

''Ow 'bout yew, Bill? Wi' yoong Billy getting' sploiced soon, yeh'll mebbe need anoother 'and!'

‘We still got Stevie, thank yeh, Maggie!’ Bill sounded less than happy at the idea.

‘Eh, Bill – is Mr Vickuss givin’ Billy ’is own pair?’ Jack asked.

‘Yeah, soon as they’re wed. ’E’s goin’ ter foind ’em an extra ’and… Oh no! Two little kiddies’d be no good to ’em!’ Bill sought to forestall the next suggestion, but Jack shook his head:

‘T’weren’t what Oi meant, Bill. ’Ow ’bout ar Kim?’

‘Your boy? ’Ow old is ’e now?’

‘Fifteen. ’E could do wi’ gettin’ soome h’experience with anoother crew, ’n we still got the oother kids.’

‘Yeah… Oi’ll put it ter Billy, see what ’e says.’

‘Wher’ is ’e?’

‘Oh, off in the town soomewher’. ’E went ter ring Sylvie, ’n ’e ain’t coome back yet – ’e’ll be ’avin’ a drink wi’ the local lads.’

‘H’okay, Bill, yew ’ave a word. ’F’e’s ’appy, yew tip me the wink ’n Oi’ll send Kim along soon as ’e’s needed.’

‘’E’ll be ’appy, will ’e?’

‘Oh, ah!’ Maggie told him: ‘’e’s been itchin’ ter get away fer ages – ’e’ll joomp at the chance!’

‘’S a deal, then Jack.’ Bill held out his hand; Jack and then Maggie took it, gave it one firm shake apiece: ’Oi’m sure as Billy’ll tek ’im – ’e knows as ’e’s’ a good lad.’

Vi had emerged from Ginny’s cabin and walked along to join them in time to hear the end of the conversation:

‘That’s foine, Bill – boot what are we goin’ ter do wi’ those kiddies o’ Martins?’ Her husband turned to her:

‘’Old yer ’orses, Vi – let’s see if Mr Robinson can foind any relations ’oo’ll ’ave ’em.’

‘Let’s ’ope so, eh, Bill?’ She looked around: ‘Oi’m goin’ ter ’ave a brew-oop – anyoone fer a coopa?’ There was a general murmur of assent; she nodded: ‘Coom on teh the *Acorn* then, the kettle should be ’ot. Oh, Moikey – can yeh go ’n join yer sister? The little girl’s been arskin’ fer yeh.’

He turned wary eyes on her:

'Boot what'm Oi goin' ter *say* to 'er?' Vi gave him a smile, patted his shoulder:

'Yew'll be h'okay, Moikey, yeh're a broight boy.'

Minutes later, as Vi was handing around mugs of hot, sweet tea, Peter Robinson returned. He gave her a grateful smile as she handed him a cup, and took a long draught from it before speaking:

'They're going to move the ship to a new berth' he gestured across the dock 'and start again on the loading in the morning. The Port of London diving team are on their way, should be here any time – they'll go down to the *Florence,* see if they can get Frank and Joan out of the cabin. And then the salvage crew will set about retrieving the boat and the load.'

'Yeh want oos ready fer the mornin' then?' Albert asked.

'Yes – Bill first, then your pair, then you, Jack. That should clear the ship, with any luck.'

'What about the kiddies?' Vi asked. He shook his head:

'According to the manager at Saltley Dock, they've got no relatives on the boats. And there're no aunts or uncles on their mother's side – she was an only child, and her parents were killed in the bombing.'

'Didn't Martins 'ave a daughter as well as Frank?' Albert asked.

'That's roight – Oi'm sure ther' was a sister.' Vi confirmed.

'Aye – boot she married that feller on the bank, din't she? Oop Tyseley way.' Bill reminded them.

'Oh, ah! That she did, Bill. Don' suppose they'd want a coopl'a boatee kids, then, will they?'

'I'll call Saltley again, ask if they can find her' Robinson suggested. 'They're her niece and nephew, after all – maybe she can take them. Otherwise, it's the orphanage, I imagine.' Albert had been looking thoughtful:

'Oi'm not tekin' 'em in – boot, Oi s'pose we could get 'em ter Braunston on ar way. Ben Vickuss'll know what ter do, 'e can send 'em on ter Saltley, mebbe.'

'That seems loike sense, Alby' Vi agreed.

'We can roon all three pairs butty, that way we can all 'elp keep an oiye on 'em.' Jack suggested.

'Aye – good oidea.' Bill concurred: 'We'll go oop froont, you coom be'oind, Jack, that way Alby's boats'll be in the middle, 'n loike yeh say we can all watch out fer the kiddies.'

'We're loadin' in that order any'ow.' Alby pointed out.

'Oh – aye!'

'I think you're right' Robinson agreed: 'I know it sounds as though I'm passing the buck, but the decision should be made by their own dock manager, or someone with authority in the company. I'm only a hired representative, after all. So if you're happy to do that, Albert?'

'That's settled, then. 'N it'll not 'urt Ginny's conscience, Oi reckon, if we do soomat ter 'elp them kiddies!'

Michael had stepped into the well of their butty, almost fearful of facing the two orphaned children. He had no idea of how to deal with such immediate, shocking tragedy, of what he could say or do – his mind went back to the death of Jack Hanney, Bill and Vi's youngest, who had drowned in Bascote locks many years before. He'd only been eleven himself; but he'd found himself the constant companion of a shattered, bereft Stevie for weeks after, the only person the younger boy could find solace with. He shook his head – that had been ages ago! – and let himself into the cabin.

Ginny looked up, gave him a smile and put a finger to her lips. She was sitting on the edge of the lowered cross-bed, the little boy's head cradled in her lap – grubby, unkempt, he was clad in a ragged shirt and frayed short trousers, and he appeared to be asleep, curled up on the bed, a thumb stuck in his mouth for comfort, tear-stains clear on his dirty face. On the table-cupboard lid stood two bowls of soup, one empty where she had apparently been feeding the boy, the other barely touched. He looked around;

the little girl was sitting, hunched in the corner of the side-bed beside the door where he stood, gazing up at him, her eyes wide and scared. She clutched a tattered rag doll to her chest; her dress, too, was frayed and dirty. He edged past and sat down next to her:

‘’Ello, Carrie.’ He spoke softly; her eyes had followed him as he’d come in:

‘M-Mr Baker…’ Her voice trembled.

‘Moy name’s Moichael – Moikey. Roight? Mr Baker’s moy Dad.’ She gave him the faintest of smiles, which as quickly vanished.

‘Moy M-Mam? ’N Dad?’ Her eyes were full of fear now, knowing the answer but needing to ask the question anyway. His heart went out to the scared child; he felt her grief burning behind his own eyes as he shook his head slowly:

‘Oh, Carrie…’ She stared at him for a moment, and then, with a hopeless sob, reached out to him; he took her in his arms as she leant towards him, held her as she buried her face in the shoulder of his jacket, felt the tears running down his own face, her little body shaking as the torrent of her grief soaked into his clothing. He looked over at his sister; Ginny was stroking the little boy’s hair:

‘She’s just sat there, ever since it happened’ she whispered. He nodded, looked down at the child in his arms, bent his head to murmur meaningless words of comfort.

Chapter Twenty-Four

Twenty minutes later, Albert stepped onto the stern of his butty and leant in through the hatches. Michael still cradled the girl in his arms; the first rush of her pain had subsided into a quiet snuffling of anguish, her face still hidden in his shoulder. Her brother still lay with his head in Ginny's lap, but now his eyes were open, staring somewhere beyond the cosy cabin as she continued stroking the tousled, grubby hair on his forehead.

'Moichael.' Michael looked up at the sound of his name; Ginny glanced up too, then returned her attention to the child in her lap. Albert beckoned him; he eased out of Carrie's embrace:

'Oi won't be long, Carrie' he promised her softly, but she clung to him, to the comfort of his presence. He took her chin in his hand, made her look up into his face:

'Oi'll be back 'fore yeh know it – Oi promise. Dad wants me – h'okay?' She gazed into his eyes for a moment, then nodded; he slipped out past her, a reassuring smile on his face.

'What is it, Dad?' Albert had waited in the stern well for him.

'They're stayin' with oos fer a day or two. We'll tek 'em ter Braunston, leave 'em wi' Ben Vickuss; 'e can either get 'em ter Saltley, or whatever the coomp'ny's decoided ter do with 'em.'

'They were Saltley boats, weren't they?'

'S'roight. It's Saltley's problem ter look after 'em if no-one'll 'ave 'em – ther's an auntie, but she lives on the bank 'n Vi reckons she won' tek 'em.'

'Roight-oh, Dad. They'll sleep wi' Ginny in the butty?'

'Aye. We'll 'ave ter get 'em cleaned oop a bit furst – she was roight, there!'

'What about the trip, Dad?'

'They're movin' the ship 'cross the basin, 'n they'll load oos tomorrer. Bill furst, then oos, then Jack. 'N we're goin' butty, all three pairs.'

'Roight. Oi'd better get back insoide, mek sure she's okay.'

''Ow are they, the kiddies?'

Michael just shrugged, shook his head. 'Poor little beggars!' Alby turned away as he stepped back down into the cabin.

Below, he sat down next to the little girl again; she gazed at him, her green eyes wide and sorrowful, but dry now as he put his arm around her.

'What's 'appenin'?' Ginny asked quietly.

'We're tekin' 'em ter Braunston. Then it's oop ter Mr Vickuss 'n the Saltley people.'

'What about their things? Clothes, 'n the loike?'

He looked at her – he hadn't thought of that – then turned to the girl:

'Carrie?'

'Yes, M-Moichael?'

'Wher' are yer things, yours 'n Josh's?'

'In – in the motor. That's wher' we live.'

'H'okay.' He gave her a gentle smile: 'Will you coom wi' me, 'elp me get soome things, clean clothes 'n that?' She nodded, her eyes still full of sadness:

'H'okay. Is it true – we're goin' wi yew?'

'As far as Braunston, yes. After that, we'll see.' There was a flicker of hope in her eyes as she asked:

'Can we – could we *stay* wi' yew? Fer always?'

'Oh, Carrie!' He gave her shoulders a gentle squeeze: 'Oi don't know… Coom on, let's go 'n get those things.'

He eased her to her feet, led her out of the cabin, the rag doll still clutched tightly to her chest.

* * *

The next four days were difficult for all of them. When Michael had led Carrie from the *Antrim,* he'd found the diving boat in place over the spot where the *Florence* had foundered, the men working in a grim silence to recover the bodies of her parents. The *Apple* was back alongside the jetty, returned there by the dockers; he'd managed to get her there and back, with most of her own and her brother's spare clothing, without her realising just what was going on a bare hundred yards away, and heaved a sigh of relief as he handed her back down to Ginny. Vi had come to join her; between them, they got the two children out of their clothes and thoroughly washed down, then dressed them in the best of their extra clothing, all of which was as threadbare as the things they had been wearing.

The men, Michael and Stevie included, had stood around, discussing the tragedy, reaching no new conclusions at all, while the Warden children played under the watchful eye of their eldest sibling.

In the late afternoon of that clear, bright spring day, Maggie Warden had emerged from her cabin carrying a huge cauldron of beef stew – she had purloined extra supplies from the other pairs, and set about preparing enough food for all of them, and now they sat around, on cabin-tops or gunwales, tucking into steaming plates and slabs of fresh bread. And at last, Vi and Ginny had appeared to claim their share, weary and damp from their exertions.

''Ow're the kiddies?' Jack had asked.

'Oh, not seh bad' Vi said with a sigh: ''E's asleep on the cross-bed; she's sittin' with 'er dolly. Poor little mites!'

''Ave they eaten anythin'?' Maggie asked.

'Ginny give 'em soome soup a whoile ago. Oi doubt if they'll want anythin' else.'

Movement from within caught their attention – no-one spoke as Carrie appeared in the hatches, climbed out and stepped off onto the jetty. She looked around, and then walked tentatively up to Michael and slipped her arm around his waist, looking up at him. He felt his heart give a lurch, but put his own arm about her thin shoulders, smiled down at her:

'That's a pretty dress, Carrie.' He said softly; she nodded:

'It's moy best 'un, fer Soondays.' Her voice was barely more than a whisper, hoarse after her tears. He offered her a piece of bread; she took it, and nibbled at it half-heartedly.

As the evening drew on, the younger Warden children were put to bed and Kim came to join the grown-ups. Billy had returned from his foray into the town, and the two began to talk about working together after his wedding later in the year. Dusk saw the light failing, the bright spring colours washing out of the day; several times, Vi or Ginny tried to get Carrie to go back into the cabin and settle down for the night, but each time she just shook her head and clung more tightly to Michael, until at last he took her down himself and settled her beside her brother. She was still gazing up at him as he turned to leave her; on impulse, he bent to kiss her forehead:

'Sleep toight, Carrie.' She nodded, and turned over, drawing the blanket close around her.

The next day saw them loaded: Vi, Ginny and Maggie kept watch on Carrie and Josh as well as the other children, while the men kept a very close eye on the dockers as they dropped the billets of steel into their boats. The reckless abandon of the previous day was gone; the operation was carried out with noticeably greater care, the steel landing more gently as well as more accurately in the boats' bottoms. By the end of the day, all three pairs were loaded and clothed up, ready for an early start the next morning; again, a communal meal was shared on the dockside – and again, no-one felt like going to one of the local pubs for a drink.

Three days of travel saw them all tied once again in Stoke Bruerne. Along the way Maggie had sorted out a handful of extra clothes for the two orphans, raiding her own children's meagre wardrobes to do so; Carrie gave her a nervous smile and a quiet 'thank yeh, missus Warden'. And she had begun to take an interest in what was going on, even taking the butty tiller for a few minutes at a time, when Ginny urged her into it. But her greatest delight had come on the last day when Michael had taken her on the motor with him on the eleven-mile Fenny pound, while Alby was tinkering and cleaning in the engine-room. She'd stood on the gunwale, gazing at him with frank admiration, and actually chuckled with pleasure as he'd stood her on the stool in the hatches and allowed her to steer the boat for a while. And each evening, when they had stopped for the night, she would go to Michael again, and refuse to leave his side until he took her off to her bed.

Josh had still spoken barely a word since the tragedy, seeming lost in his sorrow and pining for his parents; the only one he would respond to was Vi, whose ample embrace he would relax into whenever the opportunity arose, slipping his arms around her and clinging on almost ferociously. Michael had gone searching in the cupboard under his sidebed, found and retrieved the wooden toy fighter-plane that Albert had carved for him during that first summer he'd been on the boats – the little boy had taken it cautiously, his brown eyes wide:

'Dad made that fer me, when Oi was little. Yew can 'ave it now, Josh.' The little fingers had tightened around it, and the faintest trace of a smile had flickered around his lips.

Conversation, whenever the children were around, had been stilted and cautious. But gradually, everyone began to relax, even if certain subjects were, by unspoken agreement, taboo until after they had settled for the night. That night, as the adults had headed to the Boat Inn for a late drink and Michael was settling Carrie once again, Kim and Stevie sat with Ginny in the stern well of the

Kerry. The two boys were chatting, teasing each other, fooling around; but Ginny sat quiet and thoughtful until Michael reappeared and came to sit beside her. She glanced up, but dropped her eyes back into her lap without a word; he looked at her, worried:

'What's oop, Ginny?'

'She 'asn't said a word all noight!' Kim told him.

'That's roight.' Stevie confirmed, his own expression concerned: 'Coom on, Ginny, boock oop!' But she just shook her head:

'Oi'm foine – really!' Michael put a hand on her shoulder, shook her gently:

'No yeh're not – coom on, what's the trooble?' She looked up at him, her eyes fearful:

'Oh, Moikey – we'll be in Braunston tomorrer!'

'Yeah?' He sounded puzzled.

'What if *she's* there?'

'Who?' Kim asked; but light had dawned on Michael:

'She won' be, Ginny! Mr Vickuss said 'e'd warn oos, din't 'e?'

'Boot if she *is*… 'N she's got a p'liceman with 'er…'

''Eh, coom on! Oi told yeh, we've got a plan, Mr Vickuss 'n me – if she doos show oop, we're goin' teh beat 'er – yew ain't goin' ter no orphanage, oonderstand?'

'S'roight, Ginny – she'll 'ave me to deal with if'n she troys anythin'!' Stevie confirmed. She gave him a quick smile:

'Thanks, Stevie.' She reached out to him, and he took her hand with a confident grin, pretended to bend over it and kiss it. She snatched it back from him, laughing:

'Don' be seh silly, Stevie 'Anney!'

'That's better! Coom on, let's see if we can get a beer out o' moy Dad!'

'Carrie down fer the noight, Moikey?'

'Aye, she's settled. 'N Josh's asleep too.' he told her.

'H'okay then!' She let Stevie take her hand again, lift her to her feet and lead her into the pub; Kim and Michael followed, chuckling.

Chapter Twenty-Five

In the bar that night, the mood was still rather subdued. News of the sinking in Limehouse dock had travelled well ahead of them, and they had once more to tell the tale and field the questions of the other boaters gathered there. Billy and Stevie settled into a corner together, and, to judge from their bursts of laughter, were engaged on some ribald banter of their own; Kim Warden was sent back by his mother after a small glass of shandy to keep an eye on his younger brothers and sisters and the two orphans tucked up in the *Antrim.* After a while, their curiosity satisfied, the other patrons turned to their own affairs and the three crews were able to relax and consider the day to come:

'We should be in Braunston by loonchtoime.' Alby stated the obvious, setting the discussion in motion.

'Ah. Mr Vickuss knows we're coomin'?' Bill asked.

''E'll 'ave 'eard boy now.'

'Yeah, reckon so.'

'Yeh goin' ter 'and the kiddies over to 'im?' Jack asked.

'Well – we'll see what 'e's found out. 'Bout their relations.'

'Yeah – mebbe ther'll be soomeoone as can tek 'em.' Bill agreed.

'If ther' ain't?' Maggie asked. Bill shrugged:

'They're Saltley's problem, really. Martins were a Saltley crew – Mr Vickuss'll send 'em on, Oi suppose.'

'It'll be the poor-'ouse for 'em.' Vi put in, her eyes on the coals glowing in the grate. Her husband turned to look at her, aware of more in her tone than her words suggested; after a pause, he said cautiously:

'Prob'ly, Vi.'

'Ah.' She looked up as if to speak, but then turned her gaze back to the fire.

There was a brief lull in the conversation, before Alby said, business-like:

'Yew moight as well keep goin', Jack. No need fer yew teh stop; we'll only be an hour, mebbe, be'ind yeh.'

'Nah – Oi'll tek a breather! Yeh'll not be long, will yeh, 'n Oi could do wi' a new strap fer the motor. Oi'll wait for yeh – s'alwes better roonin' butty if we can, 'elpin' each oother along!'

Michael and Ginny had listened to this exchange without comment; Michael put the thoughtful expression on his sister's face down to her earlier fears of encountering her would-be nemesis once more, as she left to check on the sleeping children.

* * *

The next morning, not much after six o'clock, the three pairs were about ready to depart. Jack Warden, Bill Hanney and Albert were down in their respective engine-holes, blow-lamps aflame, pre-heating the plugs of their Bolinders; brasses were being polished, spare lines quickly scrubbed or neatly coiled, and much strong, sweet tea being drunk. Michael had just replaced the freshly-filled water cans on the butty's cabintop when a small arm crept around his waist:

'Moichael?' He looked around, reached out to ruffle the little girl's hair with a smile:

'Yes, Carrie?'

'Can Oi coom wi' yew agen terday? On the motor?' Her tattered dolly was clutched tightly in her other arm.

'Yeah, sure - if Dad says as it's okay.' Alby looked up from his labours with a grin:

'Oi'm ter be sent ter the butty terday, am Oi?' he called across. The child's face fell:

'Oi din't mean…' But he laughed:

'S'okay, choild! Oi'm only teasin' yeh – yew go with Moikey if yeh want, 'long the sixteen-moile any'ow. Oi'll tek me ease wi' Ginny fer a whoile, 'n we'll sort ourselves out agen at the bottom o' Bugby.' Now, she was beaming:

'Thank yeh, Mr Baker!' The arm around Michael's waist tightened with her excitement.

'Look out – 'ere goes!' Albert pushed out the pin in the engine's flywheel, laid his booted foot on it and thrust down with all his weight; the flywheel turned over and a spurt of dense smoke burst from the chimney with a loud 'Boof!' The engine turned over slowly, fired again; and again, and then settled to spinning over with its habitual 'tonk – tonk – tonk'. He reached over his head, wound back the throttle shaft until the familiar off-beat tickover of the old Bolinder was echoing from the surrounding buildings.

He wiped his hands on an oily piece of rag and climbed out, crossing the stern of the butty onto the towpath. Ginny lifted the heavy wooden tiller and set it into place in the butty's 'ellum; little Josh watched her silently from the open hatches, clutching the toy aeroplane. Within moments, similar sounds were issuing from the other two motor boats; Bill Hanney emerged from his own engine-hole and strolled back to them, Vi at his side:

'Ready ter go, then, Alby?'

'Any toime, Bill.'

'Roight, then!' He turned to walk back to his boats, signalling to a waiting Billy and Stevie to untie the lines.

''Old on a mo, Bill!' Vi was still standing by the stern, looking at the little boy: ''Ow would yeh loike ter coom wi' me terday, Josh? Joost fer a change, eh, as far as Braunston?' His dark eyes grew even bigger than usual:

'Can Oi?'

'Yeh don' moind, Ginny?' Vi asked; she shook her head:

'No, 'course not! Do 'im good ter be with soomeoone else, Oi 'spect.'

'Coom on then, boy!' He hesitated for a moment, then scrambled eagerly over the gunwales and stood looking up at Vi; then he flung his arms around her thighs:

''Ey, yeh'll 'ave me over, boy! Coom on, tek moy 'and.' He let go and took hold of the hand she held out to him, followed her happily as she led him back to the *Kerry.* He glanced back once, caught Ginny's eye and gave her a little wave, the first real smile they'd seen lighting up his round face.

Michael watched him, momentarily transported back more than seven years. He remembered his own feelings, how cheerfully, comfortingly real and reliable the ample boatwoman had seemed to his bereft and lonely ten-year-old self – and felt a tear burning behind his smile.

Moments later, they were under way, and, in a few minutes, heading into the long dark of Blisworth Tunnel. As the *Kerry* vanished into the blackness, little Josh turned and waved to his sister from the stern well; she waved back as Michael told her:

'Down in the cabin, Carrie.' She looked at him appealingly, but he remained adamant despite his smile: 'Joost through the toonnel. Yeh can coom out agen after.'

'H'okay.' She slipped past him, down the step, and he heard the rasp of a match as she lit the oil-lamp. Pulling the hatch back a little to keep its light out of his eyes, he settled to steer the pair through the damp darkness.

Eighty feet behind, Albert similarly settled himself, leaning on the curved wooden tiller of the butty, while below him Ginny busied herself scraping vegetables for that night's dinner. He soon found himself enjoying his unusual task; thinking back, he realised it had been some ten years at least since he'd steered the butty – that had always been his wife's job. More recently, Grace Hanney had taken it over, before her marriage to Joe Caplin; and then it had passed to Ginny. All through the tunnel, for twenty-five minutes, he mused on the past, the unlikely chain of events that had led him to be here now, still boating, still leading the life he loved; he remained lost in his thoughts, a smile on his weather-beaten face, when they emerged once more into the open air

There is something very relaxing about handling a butty on a long line – you are so far behind the motor boat that its engine becomes quite unobtrusive, and the only sounds are the lapping of water against the hull, the cheeping and chittering of birds in the fields and the buzzing of insects in the spring sunshine. Albert shifted his position slightly, felt through his pockets for his pipe and tobacco; he filled and lit it, and settled again, puffing contentedly, the heavy tiller tucked under his arm.

An hour later, approaching Bugbrooke, cruising alongside the railway lines, Ginny tapped his leg to signal her wish to emerge from the cabin. She stepped out and settled herself on the gunwale beside him:

'All roight, Dad?' Alby nodded happily:

'Ah. Oi'd forgotten 'ow noice it is, steerin' a butty.' Ginny chuckled:

'Yeah – Oi loove it! Whoy d'yeh think Oi don' let you or Moikey tek a turn?' She looked around: 'So quoiet, ain't it? Restful.' Alby nodded to the boat in front:

'She's h'enjoyin' 'erself!' Ginny looked: Around the gentle curve, under the bridge and out onto the embankment, Carrie stood on her stool in the motor boat's hatches, the polished brass tiller casually under her arm. At her side, Michael stood on the gunwale; he glanced back, waved when he saw his sister watching, and the little girl, seeing him, turned and waved quickly too – even at that distance they could see the smile on her face.

'She's not a bad kid, eh, Dad?' Ginny said.

'Ah – mebbe. Boot Oi ent so sure of 'im.'

''Ow d'yeh mean?'

'Well – 'e's'too quoiet. Ent said 'ardly a word in days.'

'Oh, Dad! 'E's joost lost 'is Mum 'n 'is Dad – 'e ent goin' ter be full o' the joys o' spring, is 'e?'

'No, boot – if 'e was 'ollerin' 'n croyin', it'd be roight. Oi don' loike this quoiet – it's almost loike 'e ent there, 'alf the toime.'

'Oh, 'e'll get over it, Dad.'

'Oi 'ope so – fer 'is sake.'

They rode on in silence for a while – past the old wharf and into the short, silted cutting which follows, where Michael took the tiller back from the child, then around the series of turns which lead towards Nether Heyford. On the long straight, where the old red-brick manor house gazes down on the canal, Ginny spoke again:

'Dad?'

'Yes, loove?'

'When… When Moikey first coom along, what did yeh really think? When Vi 'n Bill brought 'im to yeh?' He laughed:

'Loike Oi've told yeh before, Oi thought it was a crazy oidea!'

'Boot yeh took 'im?' He looked at her for a moment, thoughtfully, guessing where this might be leading:

'Ah, well – Oi was desp'rate ter stay on the boats, 'n Oi couldn' do that on me own. 'N when Vi said as Oi could 'ave their Gracie ter 'elp as well, Oi thought, well, we'll manage, even if 'e's no good. Boot 'e turned out joost foine.'

''N what about me, Dad?'

'Well – boy then, Oi was thinkin' of 'im as – as moy son, yeh see. 'N you were 'is sister – 'n Oi couldn' see yeh go to no children's 'ome, could Oi? No more'n yeh Grandad.'

Silence fell again for a few minutes. They ran around the long bend past the old abandoned lime furnaces, past Heyford Wharf, into the length known as Heyford Deeps. Ginny watched as Carrie, on the motor's tiller again now, threaded the boat through the narrows of an old swingbridge.

'Oi reckon *she* would want ter stay on the boats, Dad.'

'T'ent oop ter oos, Ginny.' She hesitated, but then plunged on:

'Whoy not, Dad?' He turned, held her eyes for a moment:

'Oh, Ginny! We've said before – they're *Rodney* kids! They… don' belong on decent boats!'

'Look, Dad.' She pointed ahead, to where the child was steering the pair with a casual ease despite her tender years: 'She's *diff'rent* now – clean 'n toidy, 'n she looks quoite pretty in the new frock Mrs Warden gave 'er. 'N they're *boatees,* Dad – more'n Oi was, or Moikey, when yeh took oos on.'

'Oh, Ginny… We don' need no more 'elp on the boats, do we? We're a good crew, as we are, eh?'

''Ow can yeh see 'er sent off ter soom orphanage wher' no-one'll care about 'er, when yeh're troyin' ter stop *me* goin'?'

'Dammit, Ginny! Yeh're moy *daughter!'* She laughed, shook her head:

'Oi wasn't alwes, was Oi?'

'Oh – fer goodness sake…'

'Well, Dad?'

'Oi don' know…'

'If we…'

'That'll do, Ginny – stop it, roight now!'

'Boot, Dad…'

'Fer 'Eaven's sake give it a rest! Oi'll *think* about it, all roight? No promises, moind.'

'Yes Dad.' Ginny's voice was soft, like the twinkle in her eye.

Chapter Twenty-Six

'I've nothing new to tell you, I'm afraid.' Ben Vickers surveyed the faces crowded into his office.

The three pairs of boats were tied on the towpath outside the old toll house; Billy Hanney and Kim Warden had hurried away almost before they were secured to collect Sylvie, and she and her beau had strolled off, arm in arm, while Billy explained that Kim would be crewing with them in the future. Stevie Hanney had been left in charge of his own and Alby's boats, while his parents and the Baker crew had taken the two orphan children to the office.

'They've no fam'ly ter tek 'em, then?' Bill asked; Vickers shook his head:

'No. The aunt, Frank's older sister, says she hasn't the room – she married that railwayman, up at Tyseley, and they've kiddies of their own. And there's no-one else.'

'Oh – roight.'

'They'll be 'eaded fer the poor-'ouse, then?' Vi said. Josh, standing in front of her, her hands on his thin shoulders, looked up at her; Carrie's eyes widened in disappointment as she looked around at Michael.

'There's an orphanage in Salford that'll take them, I understand.' Ben told her.

'Ah...' Vi glanced at her husband: 'That'll be no good fer this'n. Look at 'im – 'e was alwes a cheeky little beggar, boot now 'e's 'ardly said two words tergether since it 'appened. 'E'll not coom good in some 'ome wi' no-one as cares about 'im.'

'What are you saying, Vi?' Vickers asked; Bill just looked at her, his expression a mixture of affection and resignation, as she said:

'Well – Oi s'pose we could tek 'em, if no-one else will'

'Dad?' Ginny's voice had a stern edge.

'Be easier fer yeh if yeh 'ad 'im on 'is own.' Albert's voice was low, his eyes downcast. Everyone stared at him; he looked up, shrugged his shoulders:

'Oi guess we could keep 'er, mebbe...'

'Dad!' Ginny was beaming at him now.

'It's a shame to separate them, though, don't you think?' Vickers put in; Vi answered him:

'Oi dunno, Mr Vickuss. Mebbe best fer 'em, 'ave a new start, on their own. Carrie'd rather be wi' Moichael, that's fer sure!' The girl in question was staring at her, open-mouthed; she turned to Michael, gazed up at him:

'Yeh mean it? Oi can *stay* wi' yew?' He smiled:

'Sounds loike it, Carrie.'

'Oh, Moikey!' Her voice was shrill with excitement; she threw her arms around his waist, held him tightly: 'Thank yew!' He laughed:

'Don' thank me! Oi didn' know what Dad 'n Ginny were plottin'!' She released him, stepped back, and turned to Albert. She looked at him shyly, spoke quietly:

'Thank yeh, Mr Baker...' He looked back at her, a smile playing around his eyes:

'Coom 'ere, choild.' She went to him and he held her, a hand on each shoulder: 'If yeh're in moy crew, yeh do as Oi tell yeh, roight? 'N yeh keep yerself clean 'n smart, 'n the boats 'n all.' She nodded, still gazing up at him; then she flung her arms round him, tears shining in her eyes:

'Oi will, Oi promise!'

'Nothin' ter croy fer, girl' he grumbled – but his own arms went around her, held her, as Michael looked on astounded, and Ginny beamed.

Josh had watched this scene, his own eyes wide, the carved toy Spitfire clenched in his hands. Now, he turned his face up to Vi again:

'Oi'm goona be wi yew?' His voice was a whisper.

'If yeh want to, lad.' He stood unmoving; Bill reached out a hand, ruffled his thick dark hair. The boy glanced at him, his eyes bright for the first time in days; then he turned back to Vi, buried his face in her skirts as she drew him close.

* * *

Late the following day, the boats were all tied at Tyseley Wharf, ready to be unloaded the next morning. After the emotional scenes in the office Albert had grabbed a few words with the depot manager:

'Yeh've 'eard nothin' from that bloody woman, Ben?' Vickers shook his head:

'Not a thing, Alby. I suppose there's a chance she'll let it drop – but I wouldn't want to bank on it.'

'Me neither, Ben. Bent on causin' trooble, Oi reckon. Yeh'll warn oos if she's coomin'?'

'Of course! She'll have to call me to know when you'll be here, and I'll make sure you know right away.' Albert nodded:

'Roight then, Ben. D'yeh reckon we can stop 'er?' Vickers smiled:

'I think so, Alby! You leave that to me – and tell Ginny not to worry, okay?'

'H'okay! We'll be seein' yeh, Ben.'

* * *

From Tyseley, their triumvirate was split up, the three pairs sent their separate ways. Jack Warden to Coombeswood, for steel tubes; Hanneys to Sherborne Wharf, and the *Sycamore* and the *Antrim* to Fazeley Street for a mixed cargo. They loaded late in the day, and Albert, eager to make up time, worked them until well after sunset; they tied at last by the Boat Inn in Catherine de Barnes, out beyond Solihull.

Their sojourn in the pub was brief – a new child on the boats meant a new regime. Ginny insisted that Carrie should be in bed by around nine o'clock:

'She's only noine year old, Dad! Yew 'n Gracie alwes 'ad me in bed early when Oi was 'er age!' Albert backed her up; and the little girl, true to her promise, did as he told her and snuggled down without argument under her blanket on the butty's sidebed.

Early away the next morning, they were descending Hatton twenty-one locks by lunchtime, Michael running the breasted boats, Albert setting ahead on the bicycle, and the two girls working each lock as they came to it. All was going smoothly – but then, at the last lock but one, Michael arrived with the boats to find Alby sitting on the bottom balance beam, bent over, breathing deeply. He stepped off, leaving the motor ticking over against the bottom gate, and hurried over to him, as the girls heaved the top gates closed:

'Dad? Yew h'okay?' Alby looked up, nodded:

'Oi'm foine, boy. Joost got a bit short o' wind, fer a mo.' He stood up, but then winced, and reached across to hold his left arm, a grimace on his lined face: 'Moost 'a twisted me arm soome'ow.'

Ginny had run up to them now:

'What's oop, Dad?' He waved her away:

'Oi'm foine! Joost 'urt me arm a bit – nothin' ter woorry 'bout.' He turned, picked up the bike, stepped over it and set off to the last lock.

'Moikey?'

'Yeah…' He turned his worried frown on his sister: 'We'd best mek sure 'e sees Sister Mary, at Stoke Bruin, this trip. 'E looked real toired there, fer a minute.'

''E's all roight, d'yeh think?'

''E'll be foine – but best ter check, eh?'

'Yeah – roight y'are, Moikey. We'll mek 'im go, eh?'

'We will, Gin.' He turned to Carrie, standing listening beside him, smiled at the concern on her face: 'Don' woorry – 'e's bin workin' too 'ard, Oi 'spect! Now coom on – get these paddles oop!' She nodded and hurried to do as he directed; Ginny followed suit, a little more slowly, her concern, too, still evident in her expression.

They made Braunston again that night, tying near the bottom of the locks and grabbing a quick drink in the Admiral Nelson. Both Michael and Ginny had their eyes on their Dad, watching for any more signs of distress or fatigue – but now he seemed as fit as usual, carelessly brushing off their attention:

'Ther's nothin' wrong wi' me! Oi'm joost getting' old, Oi s'pose – can't roon about loike a kid any more, eh?'

'Yeh're goin' ter see Sister Mary tomorrer, whether yeh loike it or not!' Ginny insisted.

'Ah, pschaw! Ther's no need…'

'Dad…' the warning tone was again in her voice.

'Oh, all roight! Joost ter mek yeh 'appy, then!' He reached across to ruffle Carrie's hair, smiling away the frown on her face, before Ginny took her back to the boats, leaving him with Michael for a last beer.

* * *

'You'd better come inside for a minute, Albert. You too, Ginny – you can make sure he tells me everything!'

Around one o'clock the next day, they'd tied up in Stoke Bruerne and quickly found the good Sister, bustling around the lockside as was her usual habit, keeping an almost matriarchal eye on the crew of a Grand Union pair rising in the lock. Ginny had hurried Albert over to her, and insisted that he ask her to take a look at him; Michael and Carrie had stayed with the boats, tucking in to bread and soup for lunch.

Inside the bright, spotless surgery, Sister Mary had sat them both down and listened intently as Albert, frequently prodded by Ginny, had told her the full story of his two 'funny turns':

''N what about yer arm, Dad?' Ginny's stage-whisper prompted him yet again.

'Oh, that's nothin'!'

'Come on, Albert – what about your arm?' The Sister asked.

'Oh – well, when Oi was sittin' on the beam, Oi noticed me arm achin' a bit.' He pointed to his left upper arm: 'Moost 'a bent it awkward or soomat – loike Oi say, that's nothin'.' But the creases of her frown deepened at this news:

'Ginny – you run along back to your boats, dear. I want to give your Dad a quick examination, and talk to him on his own. I'll send him along in a little while.'

'H'okay, Sister.' She got up and left them together, walking deep in thought back to the boats, tied near the narrows of the old Rectory Bridge.

Michael and Carrie, sitting in the stern well of the *Antrim,* looked up as she approached:

'What'd the Sister say, Gin?' he asked.

'She's givin' 'im a look over, says she'll send 'im 'ome in a minute.'

'Oh – didn' say nothin''?'

'No – boot she was lookin' kinda worried, Oi thought.' He didn't reply, but a frown of concern crossed his face as he handed her a mug of soup, offered a slab of bread on a plate.

They slurped and munched in silence; some five minutes later, Sister Mary appeared, walking along the towpath, talking earnestly to a rather subdued-looking Albert. When they reached the boats he leant forwards against the cabinside, his elbows on the top cants, and she perched on the gunwale:

'Michael – Ginny: I have to talk to you; and you have to do as I tell you, you understand?' They exchanged glances; Michael replied for them both:

'Yes, Sister.'

'Very good.' She paused, as if for breath, then went on: 'I believe – I'm *certain* – your father has had a couple of heart attacks…' She raised her hands in reassurance at their gasps of horror: '*Very mild* heart attacks, nothing to be too worried about. At least, not as long as he does as he's told!' She cast a very meaningful look in Albert's direction, and he had the grace to look sheepish.

'Boot that's…' She raised a hand again to hush Michael:

'Don't worry, there's no reason why your Dad can't go on for years and years! But *he's got to take things easy,* you understand?'

They both nodded uncertainly:

'Y-yes, Sister…' Carrie was looking on, a scared look on her own face, as Ginny replied.

'Right, then. He *mustn't* go tiring himself, heaving on the gates and winding paddles – you two will have to do most of that, and let him run the boats. And no heavy shovelling, loading or unloading. And keep an eye on him, don't let him get over-tired, whatever you're doing. You understand?'

'Yes, Sister' they chorused.

'Now – I've got a little bottle of tablets here, look. If he does have another attack he's to take one, straight away, right? That will help to make his heart settle down again, stop anything serious happening. Keep them somewhere where you can find them quickly' she glanced up at Albert 'any one of you, all right?' Ginny took the little bottle from her:

'I'll put them in 'is ticket-drawer, roight ter 'and, so's we'll all know wher' they are, 'ow's that, Sister?'

'That's good. As I say, don't let this scare you too much, it's more of a warning than anything really dangerous – but you – and he – have got to listen to that warning.'

'We'll look after 'im, Sister' Ginny told her: 'It'll not be too bad – ther's four of oos agen, now!' She beckoned Carrie forward; the child stood up, and Sister Mary smiled at her, spoke gently to her:

'You're Frank and Joan's little girl, aren't you? I was so sad when I heard about your parents, my dear!' Carrie just nodded, the mention of her family bringing the glitter of tears to her eyes.

'Oh my dear!' The Sister reached out, stroked the child's cheek in sympathy: 'I didn't mean to upset you! You're with Mr Baker and Mikey and Ginny now, are you?' She nodded again, a hesitant smile returning to her face. Albert spoke from above them:

'Aye, Sister, she's our'n now. 'N a good kid she is, too.'

'She is that!' Michael slipped an arm around her waist, and she smiled down at him. 'She can steer the motor, even if she does need to stand on the stool to see over the cabin!'

'Oh, that's very good!' Sister Mary beamed at her.

'Aye – mebbe Oi'll spend more toime on the butty, now, eh?' Albert suggested: 'Leave the motor to Moikey 'n 'er. That'll be easier work fer me, p'raps.' The Sister turned to look up at him:

'That would be very good, Alby! The peace and quiet's just what you need.'

'Ah – well, we'll do that then, shall oos? Oi don' fancy turnin' oop me toes joost yet!'

Chapter Twenty-Seven

'Now coom on, we've wasted enooff toime 'ere!'

'Dad!' Ginny sounded ashamed at his lack of tact, but Sister Mary laughed:

'Go on, Albert, you've got a job to do! Mikey – are you coming to set the lock?'

'Yes, Sister – Dad can roon the boats down.'

'I'll walk back with you, then.'

They set off, Sister Mary slipping her arm companionably through his, as Ginny and Carrie untied the pair, already breasted, the engine still running.

'You will take care of your father, won't you, Mikey?'

'Don't worry, Sister – we don't want ter lose 'im! Is 'e really goin' ter be h'okay?'

'As long as he takes it easy, he will. Make him rest, when you can, that will help reduce the risk of another attack.'

'Roight… Can 'e still 'ave a drink? 'E'll be unbearable if 'e don' get 'is point o' beer!'

'Don't let him get too drunk, Mikey! But yes, a beer or two won't hurt him.' She glanced at the young man: 'I hear you're getting married?' He looked at his feet, blushing slightly:

'Yeah – not joost yet, though. In a year or two, mebbe.'

'To Harriet?'

'Tha's roight. She's said as she'll 'ave me – well, it was koind of 'er oidea – boot Oi 'aven't spoken to 'er Dad yet.'

'Oh, Henry will be fine with it, I'm sure! I know he likes you, Mikey. Congratulations to you both – give Harriet my love when you see her, won't you?' He chuckled:

'Yeh'll most loikely see 'er 'fore Oi do!'

'Well, I'll give her *your* love, then, shall I?' They shared a laugh, and then she asked:

'What's happened to little Carrie's brother? I didn't like to ask back there, and upset the child any more.' Michael smiled:

'Oh, 'e's with 'Anneys. They've no fam'ly anywher', so Vi said they'd tek 'im sooner'n let 'im go in a 'ome.'

'And you're keeping Carrie? She's had a real soft spot for you ever since…'

'Since Oi pulled 'er out o' the cut, yeah!' His resigned tone was belied by a wide grin: 'Oi thought people 'ad forgot about that boy now.'

The top gates of the lock still stood open, ready for the boats; they stopped beside them, waiting for Albert to bring the pair along. Michael went on:

'Wasn't moy oidea, though. Dad 'n Ginny 'ad plotted ter keep 'er – well, Oi think it was Ginny pushin' 'im inter it. Boot Oi ain't sorry – she's a decent koind o' kid, 'n she can steer a boat well enooff.'

'Look after her, Mikey, she thinks the world of you. And she deserves some kindness after what's happened.'

'Aye, we will, Sister.' She turned away with a last smile at him as Albert nosed the boats into the lock. The two girls stepped off to close the gates; Michael lifted the bike down, ready to go on ahead, before pulling one of the bottom paddles. Then he was up and away, leaving Ginny and Carrie to work the lock.

Down the seven, along the six-mile pound to Cosgrove – down the single lock, then three hours around the pound to Fenny, and the start of the rise up the Chilterns. Up Talbot's Lock; up Stoke Hammond three, onto the pound which leads to Linslade and

Leighton Buzzard. They had met and passed a number of other pairs, mostly Grand Union Company boats; in the turns approaching Old Linslade, with twilight deepening into night, another deep-loaded fore-end appeared in a bridge-hole.

Michael, in charge of the *Sycamore,* held over to the outside of the bend; the other steerer turned inside him, the taut towline following him through the bridge. Michael felt his heart give a leap: *It's Caplins!* Henry gave him a cheerful wave as the two motor boats passed; Michael waved back, called across:

'Mr Caplin! Wher' yeh goin' ternoight? Oi need ter see yeh!' Henry laughed:

'Oi know yeh do, boy, she's told me! Three Locks, we'll be.'

'Oi'll roide back ter talk teh yeh, then?'

'We'll see yeh ther', Moikey!'

They passed; then the butty was gliding alongside him, Harriet waving and smiling from the hatches:

'Moikey! 'Ow are yeh?'

'Foine, 'Arriet! Oi'm coomin' teh see yeh, later!'

'Yeh'll talk ter Dad, will yeh?'

'Oi will!' They were close, her butty's stern passing his cabin; Harriet's smile became shyly carefree, her voice softer:

'Oi loove yeh, Moikey Baker.' She reached out towards him as they passed; he stretched his arm out to touch her hand:

'Oi loove yew, too, 'Arriet Caplin.' Then she was turning to look back at him, waving furiously:

'See yeh later, Moikey!' He blew her a kiss before turning to guide his boats through the bridge.

Carrie had watched all of this, standing on the gunwale of the *Sycamore* beside him; now she asked:

'She's yer girlfriend, is she?'

'Tha's roight, Carrie. 'Arriet 'n me, we're goin' ter get married, oone day.'

'Oh…' He glanced at her, but she was looking ahead, apparently unconcerned with his future plans.

A mile or so further, through another bridge, he signalled Albert on the butty to run up alongside, against the towpath.

'Stoppin' 'ere tonoight, Moikey?' They were outside The Globe Inn.

'If yeh don' moind, Dad?'

'Foine boy me, lad. Yeh're goin' teh see 'Arriet?'

'Yeah – 'n 'er Dad. Oi've yet ter ask 'im if 'e'll 'ave me.' He chuckled:

'Good loock, boy!'

They breasted the boats, tied them to the bank; with their meal taken earlier on the pound, it was a quick wash and change for all of them, and then Michael grabbed the bike to set off back the way they'd come for the two-mile ride to the Three Locks pub. Alby watched him go, a proud smile on his face, and then turned to the girls:

'Coom on – let's 'ave a quick 'un. Two lemonades 'n a point o' best, eh?'

* * *

It was a pleasant spring evening when Michael came across the Grand Union pair tied below the three locks. Harriet had already changed into her best frock, and ran to greet him as he stepped off the old bike:

'Moikey!' She threw her arms around him, kissed him soundly before he could get a word out. A guffaw of laughter sounded from the hatches of the *Bodmin:*

'Yew put moy daughter down, young Baker!' Michael turned to Henry, grinned at the broad smile on his face, the twinkle in his eyes:

'Oi will if she'll let me, Mr Caplin!' She reached up and gave him a gently playful slap on his cheek, and Henry gave another bark of laughter as Sam emerged from the butty cabin, brandishing a sheet of paper:

'Moikey, look 'ere! Oi've bin practisin' since we saw yeh last!' Michael turned to him, took the paper:

''Ey, that's good, Sam! Yer wroitin's coomin' on well – copied this, did yeh?'

'Yeah – out o' that magazine yeh gave me. 'N Oi've bin readin' from it 'n all, ter 'Arriet, 'fore we goes ter sleep every noight!'

''As she bin practisin' too?'

'Oh, yeah – boot not as mooch as me! We goin' ter 'ave a lesson now?' Michael laughed:

'Not ternoight, Sam! Oi've got ter talk teh yer Dad. Nex' toime, eh?'

'Oh – Oh, yeah! Roight…'

'Coom on Moikey – let's yew 'n me go 'n get oos a beer' Henry suggested 'Suey'll bring th' oothers along in a whoile.'

Henry bought the drinks and they went outside again to stand by the lock in the bright, clear darkness. Michael felt suddenly nervous, unsure how to broach the subject, but Henry took a long pull at his pint, and turned to look at him:

'Yeh want ter marry moy girl then, Moichael?' Michael looked back at the tall boatman, took a sip from his own glass to steady his voice:

'Oi do, sir. If yeh'll allow me.'

'Ah. Does she want ter marry *yew?'*

'Oi – Oi think so…' Henry's laugher echoed across the lock:

'Oi *know* she does, boy! She's bin tellin' me fer this last week or more!' His expression turned serious; he gestured with his half-full glass: 'Yeh want moy say-so – 'n that's roight 'n proper, Moikey. It's the way we do things on the boats – boot yeh'll know that boy now.' He paused, took another long draw at his beer: 'Oi'll tell yeh straight, when she furst started mekin' oiyes at yeh, a few years back, Oi wouldn' 'a given yeh a thought. Yeh were joost a kid, same as 'er, 'n yeh'd not bin on the boats above a year or two. 'E'll never stick it, not fer long, that's what Oi thought – 'n ther were plenty of oothers thought so too. Boot yeh 'ave stoock it, 'n yeh've grown inter a good boater, 'n a foine young feller.' He broke off; Michael stood looking at him, his anxiety becoming unbearable as he waited for the man's final verdict. Henry watched him, his eyes twinkling in the moonlight, his amusement growing in proportion to the young man's nervousness, until he relented with another burst of laughter:

'Oi shouldn' keep yeh on the 'ook, boy! Oi wish yeh a long loife tergether, 'n may yeh 'ave lots o' foine kiddies!'

'Yeh mean it, Mr Caplin?'

''Course Oi do, Moikey! Yeh're a credit teh yer Dad, 'n teh yer real folks, 'ooever they were. Yeh'll mek 'er a foine man, 'n yeh tek 'er wi' moy blessin'.'

'Thank yeh, Mr Caplin! Thank yeh…' Michael found himself almost speechless with delight. Henry transferred his glass to his left hand, stuck out his right; Michael switched his own glass, took it, felt his wrist start to go numb as Henry shook his hand enthusiastically.

An arm slid around his waist; Harriet stepped close beside him, as if she had been waiting for the moment, smiled up into his eyes as he bent to kiss her cheek.

* * *

'Oi'm bein' good, see? Oone point of ale, 'n Oi'll turn in early!' Albert led the two girls back to the boats outside the Globe. They'd spent almost an hour talking about Michael and Harriet, wondering how the boy's talk with her father was going, but Alby had been conscious all along of Ginny's wary eyes on him. He was feeling perfectly well – but then, they'd had a couple of long days, and an early night wouldn't do him any harm. Carrie, never one to say much of an evening, had seemed even quieter than usual – but they had both, separately, put it down to Michael's absence.

He saw them back into the butty cabin, getting a quick smile from Carrie as he ruffled her hair, and giving Ginny's shoulders a quick squeeze, and then let himself into the motor where he stirred up the range and set about making himself a last mug of tea.

In the cabin of the *Antrim,* Carrie quickly changed into her nightdress and snuggled down under her blanket which Ginny folded onto the sidebed for her. Ginny sat on the edge of the folded-down crossbed, idly munching on a digestive biscuit, looking down at the younger girl, the tousled mop of dark hair visible on her pillow: *She's quoite a pretty kid now she ain't so grubby!* She was thinking back, remembering how she had herself been catapulted into the life of the boaters when she was a year younger even than Carrie, when she became aware of the younger girl's quiet sobs. She reached out, put her hand on the child's hair: *Poor kid, she moost be missin' 'er Mam!* A hand crept out from under the blanket, gripped hers; she allowed it to be drawn into an embrace, clutched to Carrie's chest, as the little girl cried on in near-silence.

Chapter Twenty-Eight

'Cor, Booger! S'too bloody 'ot fer this game!' One of the wharf hands paused to wipe the sweat from his brow with an already-damp sleeve. Ginny looked at Alby with a smile on her face; he nodded, and she disappeared down into the motor's cabin.

Two months had passed – the shocks, the tragedy and the joy of the early spring had slipped quietly behind them. Alby had settled into a less strenuous routine, taking turn and turn about with Ginny at the butty's helm in the pounds, steering the pair breasted through locks, while Michael and the girls shared the lock-wheeling. The smile rarely left Michael's face now, unless it was to be replaced by a huge grin – the occasional reminder of Billy's impending marriage when they met making him think ahead to his own, now planned for the following September.

Ginny's concern for her Dad's health had eased with the absence of any further scares; and nothing had been heard of her erstwhile if unwanted saviour, either. Carrie was the only one whose mood and manner had, if anything, declined – Ginny frequently found herself silently consoling a weeping child at night, and she no longer seemed to find such solace in Michael's company, despite often being allowed to steer the motor boat. Now, she would take herself quietly off to bed when she was ready, rather than clinging to him until he put her down for the night. All three of them were aware of her introspection, but each separately assumed it was simply ongoing grief for her parents.

Little Josh, by comparison, had begun to bounce back from the tragedy with the robustness of youth. Each time they met the Hanneys he seemed more like his old cheeky, active self, under Vi's loving protection and guidance: 'Oi said as 'e'd coom good if soomeoone cared about 'im, din't Oi?' she said when Ginny commented on it.

Early June, a blazing hot day, and they were loading again at New Warwick Wharf. With the new regime of orders, trips to and from City Road had become intermingled with all manner of other work; but now it was the old routine of mixed cargo for the central London basin, for a trip or two at least. Ginny emerged from the cabin clutching a handful of bottles, grinned at Alby who was leaning against the cabinside smoking his pipe, not unthankfully respecting her instructions that he wasn't to help with the loading.

''Ey, lads, 'ave a rest, get oone o' these down yer!' The wharf men looked up as he spoke, then glanced at each other:

'We ain't s'posed ter drink on the dock, Alby.'

'Aah! Oi won' tell 'em if you don't! We've 'ad these toocked in the counter wher' it's noice 'n cold – boot if yeh don' wan' 'em…' The men climbed out of his hold and each took a bottle of the pale ale, mumbling their thanks as they knocked the caps off and gasping their relief as the cold beer went down their parched throats. Ginny handed a bottle of lemonade down to Carrie, who was helping to stack boxes in the hold; Michael, sorting cases on the wharfside, helped himself as Alby too took a long swig.

''Tis 'ot under 'ere, ain't it?' He remarked; the wharf foreman laughed:

'Yeah! Canopy keeps the sun orf, but there ain't no air, is there?' He took another pull at his bottle, then gave him a searching look: ''Ave yeh 'eard anythin' from Braunston since yeh passed there on yer way 'ere?' Michael shook his head.

'Aah...' The man paused: 'Yeh go in there for yer mail, each trip, is that right?'

'Yeah – Ginny and Oi get letters from ar Grandad, soometoimes.'

'Ah – well, word is yeh're going ter find somethin' yeh don't expect next time. Yeh'll be there, what, Thursday?'

'Yeah, should be.' Michael sounded wary; Alby and Ginny were listening closely.

'Ah, well. From what we've 'eard, there's goin' ter be some woman there as wants ter interfere in yer lives. Yeh know Mr Vickers?'

'Yeah, 'course.'

'Well, 'e's bin told not ter contact yeh, 'case yon girl' he nodded at Ginny 'don't show up. But 'e's got the word out, on the quiet like. Wonderful thing, the ol' towpath telegraph, ain't it?'

'Yeah, roight!' Michael's agreement was heartfelt; Ginny was looking at Alby, fear in her eyes:

'What we goin' ter do, Dad?' He hushed her as the man went on:

'*Word is* – this ain't official, like, y'understand – but the *word* is that yeh're to turn up there like yeh know nothin'. And yeh're *not* to worry.'

'But...' Ginny still sounded terrified. The man gave her a big grin:

'That's what we've 'eard. I used ter work for Ben Vickers years ago, and I'd trust 'im with me life, girl. So if 'e says don't worry...' Ginny regarded him with wide, fearful eyes, but she swallowed hard and nodded. Alby stood up, slipped his arm around her shoulders and gave her a squeeze:

'Everythin'll be all roight, yeh'll see, loove.' She just nodded again, reassured if unconvinced, and turned into his embrace. Michael walked over to them, squeezed her shoulder, gave her a smile as she looked around at him:

'Nothin' ter woorry 'bout, Gin.'

'Boot, Moikey…' He smiled again, tapped the side of his nose in that 'wait and see' gesture; and turned in time to catch a stricken look on Carrie's face as she watched them.

It was mid-evening before they were loaded, clothed up and ready to go. Normally Alby would wait until morning to depart, but Michael was eager to get up the Camp Hill flight that night; a message had come informing him that Henry Caplin's boats would be lying at the Grand Union Company's Sampson Road depot that night, just by the top lock. So they double-worked the pair, bow-hauling the butty, up the six single locks, tying at last, hot, tired and sweaty, just before nine o'clock.

Henry and Suey Caplin took Alby to the local pub for a beer while Harriet and Sam brushed up their reading and writing under Michael's watchful eye. He tried to cajole Carrie into joining in – she had started to learn at first, but over the intervening weeks seemed to have lost interest; now she just turned away and went to sit with Ginny in the gathering dusk. They sat, side by side, on the gunwale in front of the cabin, not speaking, each seemingly lost in her own thoughts.

A little later, the lesson over, Michael and Harriet emerged from the cabin:

'Yeh want ter go fer a drink?' He asked her; she looked up at him with the still-shy smile that he loved so much:

'It's a loovely noight – let's go fer a walk, can we?' He just smiled back, bent to kiss her cheek, then took her hand. As they strolled away, lost in each other's company, Ginny paid them scant attention, her thoughts still on their next visit to Braunston and the possible fate that awaited her there. Only Carrie's green eyes watched them go, holding a look of utter desolation; and only Sam saw that look as he climbed from the cabin to join them in the fresh evening air.

He sat down beside her, put a hand over hers where it lay in her lap:

'Yew h'okay, Carrie?' She looked around, and he saw the tears welling up in her eyes as she leapt to her feet and ran to the stern of the boat, climbed aboard and vanished into the cabin. He turned puzzled eyes on Ginny:

'What's oop wi' 'er?' Ginny sighed:

'She ain't got over losin' 'er folks.'

'Boot… She were better'n that, last toime we saw yeh!'

''Ow d'yeh mean, Sam?'

'Well… She were 'appier, 'n bein' wi' Moikey – yeh know! Joost then… she looked loike the end o' the world 'ad coom!'

Ginny didn't reply – she sat reflecting on the last few weeks, back over the time since they'd taken the little girl in. Maybe Sam was right – she did seem to be getting more and more unhappy as time went by… But it was too much for Ginny to cope with, her own troubles were too much in the forefront of her mind to be able to take on Carrie's as well… *Mebbe Sam's roight – boot Oi'll think about it later, when Thursday's over 'n doon with…* For now, all she could do was shake her head and descend once more into her own worries.

Chapter Twenty-Nine

'Moikey, yew stay 'ere 'n keep Carrie coomp'ny, Ginny 'n Oi'll go ter the h'office. 'N yew, girl' Alby spoke to the child 'keep out o' soight, h'okay? If that bloody woman foinds out we've got anoother orphan kiddie wi' oos Gawd knows what she'll troy 'n do!'

'Yes, Mr Baker.' Her voice was listless, subdued. He looked at her for a moment as if to say something more, but then just shook his head and climbed from the cabin into the June sunshine. Michael went to sit beside her on the sidebed:

'Coom on, Carrie, cheer oop! She ain't goin' ter take Ginny away, yew wait 'n see.' The little girl didn't look up, but wriggled her shoulders, and seemed to shrink even further into herself.

'It ain't that, is it?' He slipped his arm around her: 'Yeh're still missin' yer Mam 'n Dad – boot yeh've got oos now, eh? T'aint the same, Oi know, boot we do loove yeh, really we do!' The thin shoulders under his embrace began to shake silently; then she looked up at him. Her words came in gulps, between her tears:

'Oh, Moikey! – Oi thought everythin' – would be h'okay – if Oi was with yew! Boot – they want ter take – Ginny away! 'N yer Dad's – not well! Oi 'eard – what Sister Mary said – 'e could die! 'N… 'N… Oi'm goin' ter be all alone…'

Michael stared at her, incredulous:

'Carrie! Whatever do yeh mean? We're never…'

A knock on the cabinside interrupted him; Paul Merson's head appeared in the hatches:

'Mikey? Mr Vickers said to get along to his office.' Michael looked up:

'Oh – h'okay, Paul. Oi'll be roight there.'

'Right away, he said?'

'H'okay! Oi'm on me way!' He returned his attention to the girl: 'Oi'll be roight back, Carrie. Stop frettin' – we ain't goin' ter leave yeh all alone, whatever 'appens! Oi'll talk to yeh later, roight?'

She gave him a tearful nod as he climbed from the cabin.

'Oh, Mikey – come on in. Thanks for joining us.' Ben Vickers welcomed him into the office. Vickers was standing over his desk, his fingers splayed on its surface as he leant forward. The protagonists were ranged to either side of the small office: To the left, Loretta Hope-Tanswell, smartly dressed as ever, her yellow hair in waves over the shoulders of her jacket, stood next to a burly police sergeant whose expression was impassive. To the right, Alby, with a face like thunder, stood with his arm protectively around Ginny's shoulders; she was trying to look untroubled but without a lot of success.

'What is it, Mr Vickuss?' Michael pretended the ignorance that had been suggested.

'Miss Hope-Tanswell, the lady here, has a court injunction which requires her to take one Virginia Thompson back with her to be delivered to a Buckingham Council children's home.' Michael looked mystified:

'Oi don' oonderstand, Mr Vickuss – what's that ter do with oos?'

'In a moment, Mikey. This girl, Virginia, is an orphan, you see. She has no living family who can look after her.'

'Yes – well, Oi s'pose she'd be best off in a 'ome, then, eh?'

'I think we'd all agree with that, Mikey. I don't think any of us would stand between a child and a decent upbringing, would we?'

'No...' Michael still sounded puzzled; Alby gave him a quizzical smile as he shook his head in agreement. 'So 'ow's this ter do with oos, Mr Vickuss?'

'She believes that your sister, Ginny, is the girl in question.'

'What? Boot that's stoopid! Ginny's moy sister!'

'I don't dispute that, Michael. But your own name is really Thompson, isn't it? You ran away from home in 1940 – and took Virginia with you two years later!' Loretta interjected.

'That's roobish! Tell 'er, Dad!'

'Oi 'ave already, boy. She won' listen.'

'If Virginia is your daughter, Mr Baker, you'll have her birth certificate?' Loretta asked, a confident smirk on her face.

'Er – well, no. Yeh see, we don' alwes 'ave toime ter stop fer things loike that. She was born in Birnigum, 'n we 'ad ter get goin' roight away.' Alby caught the glint in Vickers' eye as he fabricated his story.

'How about Michael's?'

'Er – no, Oi ain't got one fer 'im, neither.' Loretta turned to the policeman:

'You see, Sergeant, it's all a pack of lies! These are the Thompson children from Wolverton – they are the right ages, they *look* like old pictures and descriptions of them, and they *don't* look in the least like their supposed father, do they? And with no proof that they are his children… Now, can we take Virginia and get away, please? I have to get her to the orphanage in Bradwell as soon as possible.'

'Hold on just a moment, please.' Vickers held up his hand: 'Sergeant – would I be right in saying that you are here, at least in part, as an impartial observer?'

'In part, sir, yes. It's my job to see that the law is obeyed, but fairness is a part of that duty, I would say.'

'You would have to agree that Miss Hope-Tanswell has little real evidence that this' – he indicated Ginny – 'is the girl she's looking for?'

'From what I've heard today, no, she hasn't, sir. But the injunction is clear:' He took the paper from Loretta and read out: 'The girl Virginia Thompson, possibly known as Baker, believed to be living on a canal barge. That would mean this young lady, sir.'

'Would you take a look through these, Sergeant?' Vickers picked up a sheaf of papers from his desk and handed them over. The sergeant read through them one by one as he went on: 'You'll see that some are signed with a cross – many of our boatmen cannot read or write, so I have taken down their statements and had them make a mark. A few are in the men's own handwriting, including the one from Rueben James, my chief storeman.' Silence reigned while the policeman read; at last, he dropped the papers back on the desk and looked around:

'All of these statements are from men who claim to have known these two children from birth, and can witness that they are indeed Mr Baker's offspring.' He addressed Loretta.

'But – that's nonsense! They're fakes!'

'All of them?' He asked.

'Of course! They have to be!' The sergeant looked around their faces again:

'Well, well. There seems to be no argument that Virginia Thompson belongs in the council's home – but which Virginia?' He turned to Ginny: 'You say you are not Virginia Thompson?' She shook her head vehemently:

'No, Oi'm not! Oi'm Ginny Baker!'

'And so say all of you?' He looked around again, to a chorus of assent, and sighed:

'Well! Now what do I do?' As if to relieve his dilemma, a knock sounded at the door which then swung open.

'Mr Vickuss, can yeh… Oh, sorry! Oi din't know yeh was busy!'

'That's all right, Joe. What can I do for you?' The young man looked around:

''Allo, Mr Baker, Moikey, Ginny – 'ow are yeh?' Alby and Ginny were looking astonished, but a smile crept over Michael's face; he spoke before the others could get a word out:

‘’Ello, Mr Caplin, we’re foine. What brings yew ’ere?’ Joey looked from him to Vickers, carefully keeping a straight face:

‘Oi was ’opin’ Mr Vickuss could ’elp me out – me snubber’s joost boost in Nelson Lock, ’n Oi was ’opin’ ’e could let me ’ave a new ’un. Coomp’ny’ll pay, o’ course.’ Vickers turned to Loretta and the policeman:

‘Joe Caplin here is another boater, but he works for a different company. We all try to help each other out when it’s necessary, you see.’ He spoke to Joe: ‘Sure, Joe. Go and see Rueben in the stores, tell him I’ve said it’s okay.’

‘Roight – thank yeh, Mr Vickuss.’ Joe turned to go, but Loretta put out a hand to stop him:

‘Wait a minute! Mr Caplin?’

‘Yes, Missus?’ A frown of annoyance crossed her face, but she let it go:

‘You don’t work for Mr Vickers’ company?’

‘No.’

‘But you know Mr Baker, and these children?’

‘’Course! Yeh get ter know pretty mooch everyone ’oo works the cut, even if they’re on diff’rent jobs.’

‘So you’d know – how long have Michael and Ginny been working with Mr Baker?’ He gave her a puzzled look:

‘Well, since they’m been ’bout six or seven, Oi s’pose.’

‘Since they were six or seven?’ Her tone held a wealth of scorn, but Joey ignored it:

‘Well, kids don’ ’elp with the boats ’til they’re old enooff, see? ’Fore that, they’re usually kept insoide or chained on the cabintop, so’s they can’ fall in.’

‘So you’re saying that these are Mr Baker’s own children?’ The sergeant asked.

‘Yeah – ’course they are! ’Oo’s else’s would they be?’

‘You’ve known them since they were small?’

‘Yeah – Moikey’s only ’bout five year younger’n me, we used ter play tergether soometoimes – yeh remember, Moikey?’

Michael chuckled:

‘’Course Oi do, Joe!’ Joey looked around:

‘Can Oi go now? Only Oi’ve got an urgent load fer Sam’son Road, see.’

‘Yes, go on, Joe. And get that new rope from Rueben, okay?’ Vickers told him; he left, with a last glance around the gathering in the office. Loretta was looking furious; she turned on the policeman:

‘You don’t believe that nonsense, surely? He’s been put up to it, for certain!’ The sergeant’s gaze that held hers was stony:

‘I would have said that was as close as we’re likely to get to an independent witness, Miss.’

‘But… It’s arrant lies! They’re…’

‘I’d be careful what you say, Miss. That young man doesn’t even work for this company, so I can’t see that he’d be a part of any conspiracy, can you?’ He turned to Ben: ‘You had no idea he would be here today, I take it, sir?’

‘No, that’s right, Sergeant. As you say, he isn’t one of my crews, so I would have no way of even knowing his whereabouts, let alone that he might come in here. His own people would normally provide his needs, but they don’t have a depot here.’

‘I see, sir.’ He lowered his eyes to Loretta once more: ‘I think we should leave and let these good people get back to their business, don’t you, Miss?’

‘But…’ He cut her off:

‘It would seem that you have the wrong girl for all of your certainty. Now, I suggest you let the whole thing drop before any tempers get any more frayed. All right?’ The look on his face suggested that it was his own temper he was referring to. He ushered her out of the door and followed her with a last apologetic glance over his shoulder.

Ben Vickers looked around his office, at the relieved joy on Albert’s face, the triumph on Ginny’s, and last, at the conspiratorial smirk on Michael's. He raised a hand to stop them before any of them could express their pleasure:

'I think we got her on the run, don't you?' he asked quietly. Michael chuckled:

'Worked a treat, didn' it? 'Ow'd yeh get 'old o' Joey?' Vickers laughed:

'My master-stroke! I rang the Grand Union depot at Bulls Bridge the other day, found out who was likely to be passing here today. When they told me Joe, I got them to call him to the phone and we organised things. As the sergeant said, an independent witness! The statements were easy – no-one wanted to see you taken away, Ginny!' She had been staring at him in disbelief:

'Yew fixed it all?' He nodded, smiling; she ran to him and threw her arms around him:

'Thank yew! Oh, thank yew so mooch!'

'Michael suggested I collect signed statements to the effect that you're really Albert's daughter, because he knew that woman couldn't have any proof otherwise – so he should take the credit!' Michael laughed:

'Boot yew gettin' Joey ter coom boy at the roight moment was real genius, Mr Vickuss!'

A knock sounded at the door once again; Vickers chuckled:

'Come on in, Joe!' Joey Caplin entered again, a huge grin on his face this time:

'Was that h'okay, Mr Vickuss?'

'Brilliant, Joe! You deserve an Oscar!' Joe looked blank:

'What the 'Ell's a h'Oscar?'

Chapter Thirty

Fred Morris got up from his knees, straightened his aching back with a groan: *I never did like weeding!* He glanced at his watch: past twelve, time enough to go in and get some lunch. He picked up the pile of dead weeds, took them to the compost bin and dropped them in, then headed for the kitchen door. As he stepped inside, he heard the front door open, and footsteps hurrying down the hall; then the door facing him flew back:

'Ginny! What on earth are you doing here?' The girl rushed into his arms:

'Oh, Grandad! We decoided to coom 'n see yeh on the way boy!' Over her shoulder he saw Michael's excited grin, and the smile on Albert's face.

'Everything's all right, I take it?'

'Woonderful!' Ginny stretched up to kiss his cheek and he kissed her back; he shook Albert's outstretched hand, and then embraced his grandson as Ginny let him go. Finally, he held out his hand to the little girl who stood shyly in the doorway:

'And you must be Carrie?' She nodded and took his hand, her eyes averted; he bent his knees to get down to her level:

'I'm so pleased to meet you – Michael and Ginny have told me so much about you in their letters!' She raised her eyes and tentatively returned his smile as he stood up again:

'So! To what do I owe the pleasure of this unexpected visit?' He beamed around at them: 'You came over on the bus, I take it?'

Michael nodded, as Ginny began to explain:

'Yew remember that woman from the council? Well…' Ginny went on to explain everything that had happened: '…Boot Oi was too oopset, when we 'eard that she was coomin' back, ter wroite to yeh. Oi'm sorry, Grandad…'

'Oh, don't worry! I can imagine how you were feeling, my darling. But – you really think you've put her off for good and all?' Albert chuckled:

'Oi reckon so, Fred! That was the good bit 'bout 'aving the copper ther'. If she doos troy agen, we've got the papers Ben Vickuss arranged, 'n we can call 'im as witness ter back it oop. Ben's got 'is name, 'n 'is noomber, writ down in 'is office.' Fred laughed:

'And getting Joe to come in and support your story! That was brilliant, wasn't it? He's the fellow who married Gracie, isn't he?'

'That's roight, Grandad' Michael confirmed: 'We stopped 'n 'ad a coop o' tea with them yesterday, 'fore we each set off agen. Gracie's 'avin' anoother baby in September – 'n little Jack's two year old now!'

'Where are my manners? You've got time for a cuppa and a sandwich, have you?' Four heads nodded eagerly: 'Right then! Tell me the rest of the news while I get the kettle on!'

* * *

With the dramas that had filled the first half of 1947 at last concluded, the routine of the boats returned to its normal sequence of load, cloth-up, clean-down; then the more enjoyable period of travel to their destination before the hard work of unloading and the boredom, albeit often very brief, of waiting for the next orders. Biggest subject generally of conversation and speculation was the impending nationalisation of the waterways; but to those select crews directly involved, the upcoming marriage of Billy Hanney and Sylvie Benchfield was uppermost in their minds.

With the threat to Ginny removed and Alby's continuing good health, Carrie became more relaxed, more settled; she drifted some way back to her old reliance on Michael, even if she showed little of her previous devotion to him. As the weeks passed, he had begun showing her how the engine controls worked, and she had taken delight in being able to make the big Bolinder change speed and even direction at her command, although the heavy clutch rod was still too much for her. But despite it all, she held to a quiet reserve, speaking little unless she was spoken to first. The hints of her distress, even her enigmatic conversation with Michael the day of Loretta's downfall, had been forgotten in the triumph of that occasion; and, it had to be admitted, his thoughts were very much divided between Billy's nuptials and his own betrothal.

At the end of July, Braunston's available mooring space was once again chock-a-block – but now the sounds emanating from boat cabins and pub bars were those of pure joy. The wedding went off without a hitch, except for a slightly embarrassing pause after the priest pronounced Billy and Sylvie to be man and wife, broken when he suggested in a deliberately loud stage-whisper: 'You *may* kiss the bride!' Which Billy did, to a ripple of amused applause.

From the church to the Old Plough, where the party began; down to the waterside, where many water-cans full of Best Bitter were passed around; and back to the Plough at re-opening time. It was getting late when the massed ranks of boaters, their wives and children, and sundry others who had somehow got swept up in the proceedings, followed the happy, and by now exceedingly merry, couple, back to the canal and the pair of bright, clean, newly-docked boats which Ben Vickers had arranged for them. Most of their personal possessions had been put into the butty cabin during the course of the day; now they vanished inside to the sound of ribald cheers from the towpath. Kim Warden was staying on his parents' boats that night, to give them the maximum privacy; he would join them the following day as they set off to work empty to Brentford for orders.

Michael had refrained from over-indulging, knowing that Alby was certain to make the most of the occasion, and recognising that he would be the one to have to get them under way the next morning. But he was, none-the-less, quite tipsy – their path had crossed that of Henry Caplin two days before, and the memory of that evening spent in Harriet's company after a not-too-lengthy bike ride combined with the occasion to leave him with a feeling of joy beyond his ability to describe. Meandering back to their boats, he guided Alby down into the motor cabin and left him to drop the cross-bed and settle himself. He stepped back into the butty's well and sat on the gunwale, gazing happily up at the stars in the midnight sky.

Carrie, who had spent the day playing cheerfully with the other boat-children, and Ginny, had returned to their beds a while before; but now Ginny emerged from the cabin in her night-dress and came to sit next to him. He put his arm around her:

'Ain't it a loovely noight, Gin?' He sensed her silent nod in the darkness: 'Yew were h'enjoyin' yerself with Stevie, weren't yeh?'

''E's moy *friend!'*

'Ah. Yeh goin' ter marry 'im, oone day?' She wriggled shyly:

'Dunno – mebbe!'

'*Aah!'*

'Not fer a long toime. If Oi do, at all!'

'Oi should 'ope not – yeh're only thirteen!' She giggled, but then turned to him with a serious light in her eyes:

'Moikey?' He frowned at her tone:

'What is it, Gin?'

'It's Carrie. She was foine all day – boot tonoight, Oi showed 'er Billy's new boats as we walked down…'

'Yeah?'

'Well – she went all quoiet. 'N joost now Oi woke oop, 'n she was croyin'.'

'Croyin'?'

'Yeah – joost softly loike, boot Oi could 'ear 'er. Oi got oop, 'n asked 'er what was wrong, boot she joost turned 'erself away.'

'Is she still…?'

'Yeah, Oi think so.' He hesitated, but then got up and let himself down into the cabin. The little girl was curled up under her blanket on the side-bed facing the wall, and he could hear the soft, muffled sound of her distress. He drew out the stool and sat down beside her, put his hand on her shoulder:

'Carrie?' She shook him off, but he put his hand back:

'Carrie, loove – what's the matter?' She said nothing – but this time, she let his hand remain in place. He shook her very gently:

'Carrie – please tell me what's wrong?' After a moment, she wriggled around to look at him, her eyes red-rimmed, but still she didn't speak:

'Coom on, Carrie – 'ow can yeh be sad on a day loike this? Billy 'n Sylvie… oh! Remoinds yeh of yer Mum 'n Dad, doos it?' The shake of her head was almost angry at his failure to understand:

'Then what *is* it? Please tell me, Carrie!' She pushed herself up on her elbows, spoke through the hitching of her breath:

'It's *them!* They're married…'

'Yes?' He was puzzled by this odd statement.

''N they've got their own boats…'

''Course – that's 'ow it is! When folks get married, they wan' ter get off on their own.' She just stared at him, as if willing him to understand; then, out of the blue:

'Oi loove yew, Moikey!' He reached out to her:

''N Oi loove yew, Carrie – yeh know Oi do!' She hesitated, but then leant forward into his embrace, spoke despairingly into his jacket:

'*Boot yeh're goin' ter go 'n leave me!'* Now, he was totally confused:

'What? Whatever d'yeh mean?'

'Oi thought, when Mam 'n Dad doied, if Oi could be wi' yew, it'd all be h'okay…'

'Yeh *are* wi' me, silly!'

'Boot – yeh're goin' ter marry 'Arriet…'

'That's roight, but… oh, bloody 'Ell!' The penny at last dropped: 'Yeh think, when Oi marry moy 'Arriet, Oi'm goin' ter go 'n leave yew?' He felt her head nod against his shoulder:

''N that's whoy yeh've been so quoiet, whoy yeh 'aven't given me a cuddle in so long? 'Cause yeh thought Oi was goin' ter leave yeh?' Another nod:

'Oh, Carrie!' He held her away to look into her tearful eyes: 'Oi'm never goin' ter leave yeh! When we get married we're goin' ter coom on *these* boats, wi' yew 'n Dad 'n Ginny – the three o' yeh'd never manage without me, would yeh?' She shook her head, essayed a tentative smile:

'Oi do loove yew, Carrie – Oi care about yew, joost as Oi do 'bout Dad 'n Ginny. Yeh're moy new little sister, roight? Oi'll never leave yeh alone, yeh oonderstand?' The smile was stronger now:

'Yeh mean it, Moikey?'

'Of course Oi do, silly! 'N there was Oi, thinkin' yeh didn' loike me any more!' He smiled as she shook her head: 'Oi've missed our cuddles, Carrie. Yeh know, grown-oops need cuddles too, soometoimes…' The smile shone in her eyes as he drew her close again, felt her arms go around him and hold him tightly.

Chapter Thirty-One

The blaze of the stars was spectacular, trying to outshine the streetlights of Birmingham; their breath misted in the bitter air as Albert Baker and his crew made their way up to the road above Farmer's Bridge Junction. A few yards more, and they pushed through the doors into the welcoming warmth of the Prince of Wales.

Christmas 1947; a combination of luck and devious planning had conspired to bring old friends and relations together for the holiday – as ever, a riotous evening was to be expected on Christmas Eve, and a quieter day of rest on Christmas Day, while everyone recovered:

'Alby! Moikey! Wha'yer 'aving?' Billy called to them from the bar. They eased through the crowd to his side:

'Two points o' moild, 'n a lemonade each fer the girls' Alby told him as he embraced Ginny and Carrie in turn, kissing each on the cheek, to the embarrassment of Ginny and the delight of Carrie.

'Ma 'n Dad're over in the corner' he told them before turning and waving to attract the attention of the laughingly flustered barmaid. Stevie had risen and hurried over:

'Allo, Moikey, Ooncle Alby. All roight, Carrie?' But his arm had slipped surreptitiously around Ginny's waist; she looked up into his eyes:

'Ello, Stevie.' The others were slapping him on the back and wishing him a merry Christmas as he smiled back at her:

'Ello, Ginny.'

Equipped with full glasses, they all retired to a corner booth where Bill and Vi Hanney were ensconced, with Sylvie, Kim Warden and young Josh. He looked up with sheer joy on his face as he saw his sister:

'Carrie!' He leapt to his feet and flung his arms around her.

'Josh! S'woonderful teh see yeh! 'Appy Christmas!'

'Yew too – 'Appy Christmas!'

The two squeezed into a bench side by side, and began to talk nineteen to the dozen, catching up on their lives since they'd last met. For months their only sight of each other had been brief encounters on the move, a shouted hello, an exchange of 'ow are yeh?s as the boats passed. Now they set to to make up for lost time.

Among the adults several conversations were running at once, their threads inter-twining:

'Only days, now, 'n the cut'll be nash'naloised.' Bill, observing.

'Ah. Oi wonder 'ow it'll be?' It was old ground of course – but still, with the turn of the year almost upon them, the hot topic.

''Arriet not about, Moikey?' Vi asking:

'Nah. 'Enry 'n Suey're down Brentf'd, waitin' fer orders, Oi should reckon. We passed 'em two days back.'

'Saw her then, did yeh?' Sylvie enquiring:

'Oh, ah! In the New Inn, top o' Bugby.'

'Give 'er a Christmas kiss, did yeh?' Kim, being cheeky; Michael gave him a playful clip around the ear.

'Yeh've 'ad no more trooble from that 'Orrible-Tinsel woman, Gin?' Stevie, looking concerned despite his humour. Ginny laughed, dug him in the ribs with her elbow:

''Ope-soomthin', yeh silly beggar! Dad reckons we won't, not now. 'E thinks we put 'er off properly, wi' Joey's 'elp!'

'Aye! 'E did a brilliant job, eh?' Alby, overhearing.

''E did, Dad!' Michael, agreeing.

'Any idea where they are?' Sylvie, wondering.

'Aven't seen 'em fer a few weeks – pity, Oi'd boy 'em a drink fer Christmas!' Alby, not knowing.

'Let's drink to 'em any'ow! Joey 'n Gracie!' Bill, raising his glass.

'Not fergettin' little Jack 'n baby Rosie!' Billy, joining him. Nine glasses raised; a tenth joined in as Carrie picked up her lemonade:

'Joey 'n Gracie!' Her child's voice carried over the hubbub as they all drank.

'Soomeoone tekin' moy name in vain?' A voice called from the street door; they all looked around:

'Joey!'

'Get oover 'ere, boy! What'yer drinkin'?'

Joe Caplin fought his way through to them, shook hands all round:

'Oi'll 'ave a point o' best, if that's h'okay, Alby!'

'Gracie not with yeh?' Michael asked him.

'She's stayin' on the boats wi' Rosie 'n Jack. Oi'll tek 'er a bottle o' stout back wi' me later, boot she sends yer all 'er loove.'

'Wher' yeh toied, Joe?' Bill asked.

'Sampson Road. Came oover on the boos – Oi'll not stay too late, boot Oi 'ad ter 'ave a beer wi' yeh fer Christmas, eh?'

'Bloody good ter see yer, Joe!' Billy told him.

'Yew too, mate! 'Ow's married loife, then?'

'Bloody brilliant! Yeh know Sylvie, don't yer?

'Course Oi do!' He bent to kiss her cheek: 'Not mekin' Vi 'ere a grannie, yet, then?'

'It won't be too long, we hope, Joe!' she replied, blushing slightly.

''N Yew, Moikey – lookin' forrard teh yer marryin'?' Joe asked.

Michael gave him a wide grin:

'Oh, aye, Joe! Oi can' wait!'

'September, did Oi 'ear?'

'Yeah – Oi'll be noineteen in March, 'n we thought then'd be roight, after 'Arriet's birthday.'

'Good fer yew, mate!'

Time passed, and ale was drunk. Josh fell asleep, cradled in Vi's ample lap; Carrie soon followed suit, her head on Michael's shoulder, his arm around her waist. The conversation turned once more to the impending changes for the canal system:

'Won' affect yew all as mooch as it will oos, o' course.'

''Ow's that, Joe?' Bill asked.

'Well, see – Gran' Union *Carryin'* Coomp'ny's part o' the Gran' Union *Canal* Coomp'ny, roight? 'N we – Oos, 'n Dad, 'n all the oother Gran' Union crews, we're goin' teh get nash'naloised, too, en't we?'

'Yeh'll be workin' fer the Gov'mint?' Alby asked.

'Ah, that's about it. Boot Fellers's 'n all the oother proivate coomp'nies, loike Clayton's, 'n 'Arvey-Taylors, 'n all the rest, 'cause they *are* proivate, will go on joost loike before.'

'Oh… Boot we'll be payin' our tolls teh the Gov'mint?'

'They'll be roonnin' the cut, so yeah, Oi s'pose yeh will.'

'Aah. Well, at least, if the Gov'mint's roonnin' things they'll want it all shipshape, won' they?'

''Ow d'yeh mean, Bill?'

'Well – they've got plenty o' mooney, roight? 'N if they puts soome inter drudgin', 'n fixin' things oop, we'll be able teh get about better. 'N if things are goin' better, mebbe we'll get more trade back on the cut, eh?'

''N they'll be getting' all the toll mooney as well, loike Joe joost said. That should 'elp, too, shouldn' it?' Alby agreed.

'Should do, Alby. They're puttin' our rates oop 'n all, so we've bin told.'

'What? Puttin' yer pay oop?'

'Yeah, s'what they've said. Better rates fer the job, all round.'

'Booger! Oi wonder if Fellers's'll put our'n oop, too, Alby?'

‘’Oo knows, Bill? If they don’, folks’ll be goin’ oover teh Grand Union, though, won’ they?’

‘Bloody roight! Me ’n all, if the pay’s mooch better!’ Joe laughed:

‘If they’ve got jobs enooff fer yeh all! We don’ know what we’ll be called, even, yet – moight still be Gran’ Union, boot they moight ’ave a new name fer oos.’

‘Goin’ ter be a ’ole lot diff’rent, ain’t it?’

‘Aye. A ’ole new start fer the cut, eh?’

‘Let’s ’ope so, Bill!’

Chapter Thirty-Two

'Ah, go on, 'Enry – yeh've got ter give 'em a fair crack o' the whip!'

'Oh, mebbe, Alby. Boot in three moonths all the've doon is ter foind a new name fer oos 'n decoide ter repaint ar bloody boats! 'N bloody awful they'll look, 'n all!'

Good Friday, 1948, and a good many boaters were gathered in the Five Bells, in Brentford High Street, their regular evening haunt whilst waiting there for orders. On January 1st, the old independent canal companies had ceased to exist, their assets taken over by the Labour government's nationalised industry. The Grand Union Canal Company was no more - its canals part of the national network, and its carrying fleet a part of the new British Waterways operation. Henry Caplin, a long-time employee of the former, was less than impressed with what he had seen so far of the latter; Alby Baker was perhaps, more forgiving, and more prepared to await developments:

'Yeh've got ter give 'em toime, mate! They've only been in charge a few weeks, yeh can' expect 'em ter wave a magic wand 'n 'ave everythin' roight in no toime, can yeh?'

'Well, mebbe – boot ther's no soign of any drudgin' bein' doon, no-one out fixin' any o' the bloody locks, nothin' 'appenin' at all. With all the bloody mooney the gov'mint's got, whoy en't they getting' on with it?'

'They will Oi'm sure, 'Enry. They'll need toime ter get their act tergether, see what's needed, 'n decoide what ter do furst.

It'll 'appen in toime – after all, as Oi've said before, ther's no sense in them roonnin' things if'n they don' mek the best of it! They'll want everythin' workin' the best it can, stands ter reason – so they'll 'ave ter fix it all oop, sooner or later.'

'Oh, mebbe yeh're roight, Alby! Boot after all the years o' seein' things getting' wuss 'n wuss… Coom on mate, 'ave anoother?'

'Moild 'n bitter, please, 'Enry.'

'Stout fer yew, Suey?' Henry asked his wife; then he turned to a secluded corner booth, and raised his voice:

''Ey, yew two loove-birds want a drink?' Michael looked up from his girl's face, paused his quiet conversation:

'Same as Dad please, Mr Caplin. 'N a shandy fer 'Arriet?' She nodded her agreement as he glanced at her. Henry passed on the orders to the barman, then turned the other way to where a noisy game of bar-billiards was going on in the background:

'Sam! Ginny! What d'yeh want?'

'Lemonade please, Mr Caplin?'

''Ave they got that Coca-Cola, Dad?'

'Coomin' oop!' He turned back to Alby: 'Bloody Yankee drink 'e's got 'ooked on! What 'bout young Carrie?'

'She's outsoide playin' wi'the oother boatee kids – she'll be foine.'

Fresh drinks supplied all round, they returned to their discussions:

'So what's this new paint job loike then, 'Enry?' Caplin grimaced:

'We seen a boat re-doon, at Bulls Bridge as we coom boy. Broight yeller panels, broight blue borders – no loinin'. Looks bloody drab 'n 'orrible.'

'What's the lett'rin'?'

'Same blue fer the letters, with a little bit o' green fer shadin'. No *stoyle* ter it at all, no… joost plain 'n 'orrible. Everythin's blue or yeller, ther's no *colour* about it!'

'Doosn' sound too bad, 'Enry?'

'Hah! Yew wait 'til yeh see it!'

''N they're doin' away wi' all the flowers 'n the lan'scapes!' Suey sounded scandalised; even Alby was taken aback at this:

'What? No roses? No castles?'

'Not a oone! They say as it'll save tóime 'n mooney on the dock, so they ain't goin' ter put no decoration in 'em at all!' Henry replied.

'Bloody 'Ell! Tha's a bit steep, mate!'

'Yer tellin' me! They're goin' ter send oos off in bloody borin' lookin' boats, wi' not even any colour insoide of 'em!'

'Yeh can stil 'ave yer 'angin'-oop plates, though, can yeh? 'N yer brasses?'

'Oi s'pose so – 'aven't 'eard nothin' 'bout them.'

'Booger! Oi'm glad we're fer Fellers's, ther's no talk of 'em changin' ar boats, not as Oi've 'eard, any'ow.'

'No reason, is ther'? Yew loocky boogers ain't bin nash'naloised, 'ave yeh?'

'Aye, mebbe we're loocky…' Alby broke off at the sound of a loud gasp from the corner, followed by a frightened yell:

'Moikey!' Both men turned to see what was wrong, to find Michael bent over holding his stomach, and Harriet with her arm around him, her face creased with worry.

'What is it, Moichael? What's oop, boy?' Alby hurried to his side, Henry and Suey on his heels; Michael looked up, his face grey:

'Me toommy, Dad! Christ, that 'urts!' He gave another gasp as a fresh wave of pain hit him.

''Elp 'im, Mam, Dad!' Suey bent to him, eased him up straight:

'Wher's it 'urt, Moikey?'

'Down – ah! – 'ere.' He pointed to the right side of his groin: 'Oi've 'ad a few twinges – boot Oi thought as it was only indigestion! Boot – a-ah!' Suey raised her head, called to the barman who was looking on, concerned:

‘’Ave yeh got a telephone?’ He nodded. ‘Can yeh call a h’amb’lance fer ’im? Oi think it’s ’pendercoitus – moy brother ’ad it, when we was kids. They ’ad ter h’operate on ’im, ’n pretty quick, too!’

By now Ginny and Sam had dashed over:

‘Moikey – what’s wrong?’

‘It’s ’is toommy’ Suey told them: ‘Oi reckon it’s ’pendercoitus, loike yer Ooncle Frank ’ad when ’e was young, Sam.’

‘Will ’e be all roight?’ Suey smiled:

‘’E should be foine – barman’s callin’ a h’amb’lance. They’ll ’ave ter get ’im ter the ’ospital – boot ’e’ll be roight as rain in a few days! Ar Frank was any’ow, when ’e ’ad it.’

Minutes later, a gleaming Daimler ambulance pulled up outside the pub, to be promptly surrounded by a crowd of curious children. The ambulance men hurried inside, a stretcher between them; and, moments later, hurried out again with Michael lying on it, still groaning. A quick look had left them with the same instant diagnosis as Suey, so a quick dash to the nearest hospital was seen to be the order of the day. Alby went with them; Carrie, among the youthful crowd of onlookers, let out a yell when she saw the stretcher’s occupant:

‘Moikey!’ Alby grabbed her, gave her a gentle shake:

‘’E’s goin’ ter be foine, Carrie – it’s joost a bad toommy. Yew go in teh Ginny, now, she’ll look after yeh. Oi’ll be back soon – h’okay?’

‘Yew sure ’e’s all roight?’

‘’Course Oi’m sure! ’E’ll be ’ome with oos ’imself in no toime, yeh’ll see! Go on, now.’ He shoved her gently towards the pub door; she went reluctantly, her eyes on the stretcher as the ambulance men closed the doors behind it.

In the Five Bells, everyone was standing around in a hushed silence, shocked by the sudden, dramatic events. Carrie entered and made her way over to Ginny, who took her in her arms:

'Nothin' ter be oopset about, Carrie – Moikey's 'ad a bad turn in 'is toommy, boot the 'ospital will soon 'ave 'im roight. Dad's gone ter make sure 'e's h'okay – 'e'll be back later.' The girl nodded, not entirely convinced but unable to do anything.

'Coom on, Carrie – would yeh loike a glass o' lemonade? Or they got that new Coca-Cola – would yeh loike that?' Henry spoke softly to her; she nodded shyly:

'Oh – can Oi troy the Coca-Cola, please, Mr Caplin?' She looked around; Suey was comforting Harriet who still looked deeply shocked.

'Thank yeh, Mr Caplin.' She took the proffered glass, sipped at the dark contents, and smiled up at the tall boatman: 'That's noice!'

'We'll go 'ome ter bed when yeh've drunk that, shall we, Carrie?' Ginny suggested.

''Ow long'll Moikey be in the 'ospital?' She asked; Suey looked around:

'They 'ad ar Frank in 'bout four days when 'e 'ad it.'

'Will we stay 'ere 'til 'e's back?'

'That's oop ter Dad' Ginny told her: 'If we get h'orders termorrer, 'e'll 'ave ter decoide what ter do. Boot if we 'as ter go, 'e'll be out ready fer when we get back, eh?' Carrie just nodded, sipping at her drink.

Chapter Thirty-Three

It was almost seven o'clock when Bob Renwick strolled along the line of empty, moored boats, looking for one pair in particular. A smile lit up his lined face as he spotted them, bent to knock politely on the butty's cabinside; moments later the hatch slid open and a pretty face with blue eyes and a head of golden hair appeared:

'Oh, 'ello, Mr Renwick! Kettle's on – would yeh loike a cuppa?'

'I'd love one, Ginny. Is your Dad there?'

''E's insoide 'avin' 'is breakfuss. Coom in, 'ave a seat on the step.'

Renwick did as he was bid, stepping over into the well and down into the cabin. Albert acknowledged him with a wave of half-eaten toast from his seat on the stool, and Carrie gave him a shy smile from the corner of the sidebed. Ginny dug out a spare mug, and poured the tea:

''Elp yerself teh sugar, Mr Renwick.' He smiled his thanks. Alby finished chewing:

'Yeh've 'eard about Moikey, Mr Renwick?' He smiled again:

'Better than that, Albert – I've just spoken to the hospital on the phone. They tell me the operation went very well and he's doing fine.' Ginny treated him to a beaming smile of her own, and Carrie's eyes lit up as Alby replied:

'Oh, that's grand! Thank yeh fer callin' them – we've been really worried, even though they said las' noight it was a simple job. They were joost tekin' 'im down the h'operatin' room when Oi coome back 'ere.'

'Oh yes – appendicitis is nothing to worry about these days! He'll be as right as ninepence in a day or two. They'll keep him in for another couple of days just to be sure.'

'Can we go 'n see 'im?' Carrie asked eagerly, but Renwick shook his head:

'He's still out from the anaesthetic at the moment.'

'Can we go later?' she persisted; he gave her a sympathetic look:

'That's the other reason I'm here:' He raised his eyes to Alby: 'We've got a load of aluminium that has to be taken to James's foundry in Birmingham as soon as possible – and I haven't got any spare boats. Or, to be truthful, I can find boats but I haven't any crews for them! How would you feel about taking a trip with just the three of you? I know Carrie's very young…' Alby waved him to silence:

'She's not as yoong as Ginny 'ere was when we went three-'anded back in th' war! 'n she's a good little boater – Moikey's taught 'er teh 'andle the motor, so we can do it for yeh, no trooble! 'S long as yeh'll keep an oiye out fer Moikey for oos, 'til we get back?'

'Of course I will! He can stay with me and Ivy when he comes out of hospital; or perhaps we can put him on the train to join you in Birmingham if they let him out in time?'

'Aye, that'd be good – if yeh don' moind?'

'Of course not – the company will pay for his train fare, I'm sure. Get the manager at James's to call me when you arrive, and I'll send him on his way!'

* * *

They had all had a rather sleepless night, concerned for Michael despite the doctors' assurances. It had been quite late when Albert returned, having made his way back across Brentford on the bus, but, none-the-less he'd found both girls still awake, eager for his news. Now with their minds set at ease by Renwick's information, they quickly manoeuvred the boats alongside the lighter and stood back to allow the dockers to tranship the ingots of silver-grey aluminium into their holds. The total load was only thirty-eight tons, less than they would usually carry – but that would help them to make up time, travelling more quickly in stretches where the water was shallow after so many years of inadequate or non-existent dredging. With such a clean and easy-to-handle load, they were away at lunchtime, the boats mopped down, brasses polished.

That night they reached Widewater lock, helped by a good road most of the way. At Ginny's insistence Alby remained on the boats in charge of the motor, while the girls worked the locks; he took this with poor grace, uncomfortable that the hard work was being done by two children while he, as he put it, 'took 'is ease' at the tiller. No beer, and an early night – they were all tired after the day and their poor rest the night before, and aware of the need for an early start the next morning.

Another long, hard day saw them stop at last at Bulbourne, at the top of the Marsworth flight. They might have gone further, but they found themselves missing Michael's youthful strength and the unremitting commitment to 'get 'em ahead' that Albert had so successfully instilled in him over the last eight years. To get even so far had meant each of them putting in much more effort than would usually have been needed; both girls were weary and foot-sore from running around the locks, and both had blisters from the continual winding of paddles. That night Albert had insisted:

'Oi'll be lock-wheelin' termorrer – the two o' yeh can' go on loike this! Yeh can manage the pair in the locks, can' yeh, Carrie?'

'Oi dunno, Mr Baker...' She replied doubtfully, as Ginny protested:

'Dad! Yeh can't do that, what if yer 'eart goes dicky again?'

'Oh, Ginny! Oi've bin foine now fer a year 'n more – tha's all better now. Oi can' let yew two knock yerselves oop the way yeh've bin goin'.' She gave him a stern look:

'Well – we'll do Maffers, roight? Get 'em down the seven, then mebbe we'll see. Carrie can tek 'em through from there?' She looked at the younger girl, who gave her a nervous nod:

'Yeah – Oi think Oi can, Ginny. Moikey's only let me roon 'em inter locks a few toimes – boot Oi'll manage! We can't 'ave yew getting' bad as well, Mr Baker!'

He held up his hands in surrender:

'H'okay! Now, Oi'm goin' ter get a beer 'fore Oi go ter bed – yew two want anythin'?'

'No Dad – we'll get an early noight ready fer termorrer.' Carrie nodded in agreement:

'Oi'm toired out, 'n all!'

'All roight – see yeh in the mornin'.'

A bright and early start the next day, as well. Awake at six, a quick mug of tea all round and Alby started the engine – one task neither Carrie nor Ginny was yet up to – and they were away before seven. Alby grumbled his way down the seven locks, still unhappy at the girls doing all the hard work; but, at the bottom, as they singled the boats out for the short run to the next locks, Carrie joined him on the motor:

'Yeh still want me ter tek 'em from 'ere, Mr Baker?'

''S long as yeh're 'appy ter do it, girl.' She gave him a grin:

'Oi can manage 'em, don' woorry!' He grinned back:

'Good fer yew, girl!' He gave her the tiller and moved to stand on the gunwale at her side, where he packed and lit his old pipe. Puffing contentedly, he looked back, gave Ginny a wave where she stood in the hatches of the butty eighty feet behind; she waved cheerfully back.

Even three-handed they made pretty good time over the long descent from the Chiltern Hills: Peter's Two, Nag's Head Three,

Corkett's Two, all fairly close-set groups of locks in which they kept the boats breasted for easier working; then the four single locks at Horton, Slapton, Church and Grove, and at last the long level run through Leighton Buzzard. At first Alby had felt a twinge of conscience at leaving the boats in the care of two young girls, the oldest of whom was still a couple of months short of her fourteenth birthday. But all the way Carrie had managed the motor boat with little cause for concern, making Albert look on her with a profound but quiet pride: He'd taught Michael all the boy knew about boating in the eight years they'd been together, and now his adopted son was making a good job of passing that knowledge on. And today he'd found a real pleasure in lock-wheeling, something he rarely did as Michael or Ginny would usually be the ones to cycle ahead, setting the locks. The only thing dampening his enjoyment was the fact that they faced a bad road – another pair must be travelling ahead of them, far enough in front to be out of sight and unaware of their presence, but close enough that most of the locks were set against them, the bottom gates and paddles open. The extra time and effort lost in closing up and filling the locks before their boats could enter was just what they didn't need on this trip, short-handed and in a hurry! Even so, early afternoon saw them through Leighton Lock and driving along the Jackdaw pound towards the three locks at Stoke Hammond.

Bouncing along the uneven towpaths, his windlass tucked into his belt, he'd felt the smile widening on his face: *Oi said as 'ow Oi'd be foine! Oi 'aven't 'ad a turn in more'n a year, that trooble's all cleared oop long ago! 'N it ain't 'ard work, after all...* Along the three miles of the Jackdaw he had jumped onto the motor again, heaving the bike onto the cloths in front of the cabin until it was needed again. Hammond Three were literally on top of each other, so he'd work them on foot, but he'd take the bike to get ahead to Talbot's…

At the three locks, he set out with the smile still on his face in company with Ginny, to work the pair through. Carrie was gaining in confidence all the time; by now, she was slipping the breasted boats into the locks with no more than inches to spare each side with hardly a thought, and bringing them to a halt by reversing the fickle Bolinder just touching the bottom gates, exactly where they needed to be. The intermediate basins are so short that careful working is needed if the pounds are not to be flooded as the boats descend, but in less than half an hour they were dropping in the third and last lock, with not a drop of water wasted. Albert finished winding up the paddle and turned to sit on the balance beam – it had been a strenuous effort, and he could feel the weariness creeping into his bones. And then, suddenly, a sharp pain struck him, making him gasp; he bent over, a hand on his chest, as the ache surfaced in his left arm as it had before.

Ginny had heard his gasp – now, she dropped her windlass and dashed across the gates to his side:

'Dad! Are yew all roight?' He felt her hand on his shoulder, raised his own with an effort and put it over hers:

'Joost a bit toired, Ginny.' He spoke without raising his head, and she knew he was lying:

'Oh, Dad! Yeh're 'avin' a turn again, ain't yeh?' She looked around, close to panic, but the pub was closed now, in mid-afternoon, and no-one was about. She left him sitting there and dashed to the pub door, hammered on it – but there was no response. She hurried back to him:

'Dad? 'Elp me push this gate open, h'okay?' He nodded, his head still bowed; the lock was empty now, and they eased the heavy gate back:

'Now stay 'ere whoile Oi get th' oother one, roight?' He nodded again, and she hurried around the lock, heaved the opposite gate open, and then rushed back around to him. From the lockside she called down to Carrie:

'Pull 'em in below the lock, Dad's not well!' Carrie looked up and nodded, her worry clear on her face, but she drew the boats in to the bank and jumped off with a rope to hold them steady. Ginny ran down to her, scrambled over into the motor cabin and searched through the bits and pieces in the ticket-drawer. She found what she was looking for and gave a sigh of relief:

'The pills Sister Mary gave oos, ter give 'im if 'e 'ad another turn!' She called to Carrie before hurrying back up to where Albert still sat on the lock-beam.

'Coom on, Dad, swaller oone o' these, h'okay?' He took one of the pills from her and put it in his mouth; she watched as he swallowed it, concern and relief mixed in her expression.

Carrie had dropped the rope through a mooring-ring to hold the boats; now she came up to them, fear and pain in her face, and handed him a glass of water:

''Ow are yeh, Mr Baker?' Her voice was hushed, scared; he looked up at her, essayed a smile:

'Oi'll be h'okay, Carrie, don' yew fret.' But he still looked far from well, and his words did little to reassure her; she raised her eyes to Ginny:

'What'll we do, Ginny?' The older girl seemed unsure; she took her arm, led her out of Albert's earshot:

'Ther's no-one about, Oi've troied the pub. We can't get any 'elp 'ere – we'll 'ave ter go on.'

''Ow far?'

'Oi dunno. If we could get 'im ter Sister Mary it'd be best, wouldn' it?'

'We can, if we get a move on!' Ginny thought:

'Yeah, Oi s'pose we could. Mebbe we can get soome 'elp soomewher' along the way, boot if we get goin' we can be in Stoke Bruin tonoight, can't we?'

'Yeah! Ther's only Talbot's, Fenny, 'n Cosgrove locks – we can tie at the bottom o' Stoke 'n roon oop fer the Sister, can' we?' Ginny paused to think:

'Yeah – it'll be late 'fore we get ther', moind – Can yeh manage the boats in the dark?'

''Course!' The little girl glanced over at Albert: ''Specially fer 'im. 'E gave me a new 'ome when Oi needed it, din't 'e?' Ginny smiled at her:

'Coom on, then! Let's get goin'!'

'Shall we leave 'em breasted?'

'Yeah – 'ere teh Talbot's, 'n Fenny. Boot we'd better single 'em out from ther' ter Cosgrove, wi' those toight bends boy Tinker's Bridge 'n around Target Turn. We don' want ter risk getting' stook.'

'H'okay, Ginny!'

They went back to where Albert sat and Ginny helped him to his feet:

'Coom on, Dad, back on the boats. We'll get yer teh the Sister, h'okay, 'n she'll 'ave a look at yeh.' He tried to wave her aside:

'Oi'll be foine in a whoile – joost let me 'ave a bit of a rest!'

'No, Dad, we're goin' ter get movin'. Yew can rest in the cabin, roight? Carrie 'n me'll manage the boats fer now.'

'The two o' yeh can't roon the pair on yer own! Don' be daft, girl!' She looked at him – he was still quite grey in colour, and his face was suddenly haggard:

'Don' *yew* be daft, Dad! Yeh're in no state ter do anythin', so we're goin ter get yeh ther', roight? We can manage, joost yew watch!'

Still grumbling, he nevertheless allowed her to lead him to the boats, help him over into his own cabin where she settled him on the sidebed, resting in the corner. She quickly made a brew of tea from the kettle, hot on the range, and gave him a big mug, well sugared. Taking one each for herself and Carrie, she cast off the line from the bank as Carrie put the engine into gear, jumped back into the butty's well as they gathered way and turned into the curve which leads away from the bottom of the locks.

Chapter Thirty-Four

The boats forged ahead, bow-waves making a double vee in the still water along the short pound to Talbot's lock. The spring day around them brightened each time the sun shone through the scudding clouds, but soon another would hide it again, returning them to a darker, vaguely threatening world. Ginny watched the weather, expecting any one of the grey thunderheads to greet them with a sudden drenching, but the threat of rain remained just that.

At Talbot's bridge around halfway along, Ginny jumped off with the bicycle and pedalled furiously on to set it ready; Carrie slipped the boats in with barely a nudge of the side, and they quickly had them down to the lower level. Clearing the lock, Ginny threw the bike back onto the motor's cloths and stepped aboard; she eased past Carrie to go down into the cabin:

''Ow're yeh feelin, Dad?' Alby looked up:

'Not seh bad, Ginny. The pain's getting' easier – prob'ly that pill o' Sister's.'

'Roight. Are yeh comfy ther'? Can Oi get yeh anythin'?'

'No, loove, Oi'm foine. Oi'll be oop ter lend a 'and soon as Oi feel oop ter it.' She put her hands on her hips, her sternest expression on her face:

'Yeh'll do no sooch thing, Albert Baker! Yeh'll stay roight wher' yeh are 'til Sister's 'ad a look at yer! Carrie 'n me'll get yeh ther', don't yew woorry!'

Moving slowly, which only added to her concern for him, Alby pulled his watch from his waistcoat pocket:

'Three o'clock now, girl – yeh'll be loocky teh mek Stoke bottom 'fore ten ternoight, even if yeh go 'Ell fer leather.'

'That's ar problem, Dad – yew joost sit back 'n leave it ter oos.' She gave him a sudden grin: 'We can' stop, any'ow – neither of oos knows 'ow ter start that injun! So it's Stoke or boost!' He looked up again with an answering smile:

'What would Oi do without yeh? Either of yeh?' She just smiled at him as she climbed back up into the cool spring afternoon.

In less than an hour, thanks to Carrie pushing along as fast as she dared, they arrived at the derisorily shallow Fenny Stratford lock. Another pair of Fellows, Morton and Clayton boats had just entered from the opposite direction and were rising in the lock; Carrie held the pair back under the railway bridge to allow them room to pull out. The boatwoman saw them and hurried over:

''Ello, Ginny, Carrie – we 'eard about Moikey. Is 'e h'okay?'

'Yeah, 'e'll be foine, thanks, Mrs 'Ampson.'

'Tha's good! 'Ow 'bout yew two? 'N yer Dad – wher' is 'e?'

''E's insoide, 'avin' a breather.' Ginny answered, unwilling to share their problems and well aware that he could get into trouble for leaving the pair in the charge of two children.

'What – with a lock ter be worked?' Enid Hampson sounded doubtful; she looked up as a holler sounded from the boats in the lock:

'Coom on, Missus, we're away!'

''Old on, George, ther's soomat wrong!' she shouted back; the boatman stopped his boats, still in the lock, and stepped off as she asked again:

'What's oop, Ginny? Soomat's amiss, ain't it?'

The girl relented:

'Yeah – it's Dad – 'e's 'ad anoother bad turn. 'E's got a bad 'eart, see, 'n Sister Mary told 'im ter tek things easy – boot wi'

Moikey in 'orspital, 'n a roosh load fer Birnigum, 'e's been workin' too 'ard!'

'Oh, moy! What're yeh goin' ter do?'

'We're mekin' fer Stoke bottom – Oi'll get the Sister to coom 'n see 'im when we get ther'.'

'Yeh could mebbe get a doctor round 'ere soomewher'?' George Hampson had come over to join them.

'Yeah, mebbe – boot Oi'd rather the Sister saw 'im.'

'That's roight! Yeh know yeh can troost 'er, don't yer?' Enid agreed.

'Ther's joost the two o' yeh ter work the boats?' George asked. Ginny nodded; a frown creased the boatman's forehead as he said:

'If ar John was 'ere, we'd send 'im with yeh…'

'Well 'e ain't, George, is 'e?' Enid's annoyance sounded in her voice; her son's abrupt departure for a job 'on the bank' obviously still rankled.

'We can manage – ther's only this'n 'n Cosgrove to do!' Ginny sought to assure them: 'Moikey's taught Carrie 'ere ter roon the motor, so we'll be h'okay.'

'Yew sure?' He sounded doubtful: ''Ow old are yeh, Carrie?'

'Oi'm ten!' She told him forcefully ''N Oi've bin steerin' the motor fer almost a year now!' Ginny chuckled:

'She doos foine, 'n all! Oi've never roon the motor, boot Moikey's been tekin 'er with 'im since she joined oos las' year.'

'H'okay – boot yew go careful now, roight? Yeh'll stop at Stoke, will yeh?'

'Yeah – Oi s'pose we'll 'ave ter.'

'H'okay – we'll get word ter the coomp'ny ter get a pair teh yeh teh tek over the load, shall we?'

'If yeh would, Mr 'Ampson.'

'Roight then – yew two go easy now. Be careful – yeh'll be goin' in the dark 'fore yeh get ther'.'

'We'll be foine, Mr 'Ampson!' Carrie insisted; he gave them a worried smile:

'Roight – best o' loock ter yeh! We'll work yeh through 'ere, h'okay?'

'Oh, thank yeh!' He nodded and turned away, went to run his own boats out of the lock. Carrie ran the pair in and Ginny and Enid quickly opened the paddles, pushed back the gates when the level was made.

'Go steady – 'n good loock!' Ginny looked back and waved as she jumped onto the butty; Carrie was already away in front, the boats singled out now for the long pound to Cosgrove. Enid gave her a wave back, a worried look still on her face, then hurried to her own boats as George pushed in the clutch.

The smartly-turned-out pair of boats forged along, sweeping around the many long turns of the eleven-mile pound as the afternoon wore on. Several pairs passed them in the opposite direction and each steerer gave them a slightly puzzled look as he waved his greeting, surprised to see two young girls apparently alone on the boats. One or two called across to ask if all was well and where their captain was; each time, Ginny called back that he was resting in the cabin.

At the tiller of the *Sycamore,* Carrie found herself caught up in a whirlpool of emotions: She felt elated to have sole charge of the motor boat and was thoroughly enjoying the challenge of handling it, all the time allowing for the loaded butty trailing in her wake, making sure that Ginny had as easy a time as possible in steering the unpowered craft around the bends and under the bridges. At the same time she was worried about Albert, only too well aware of the hurry to get him to the Sister for the help he needed, and scared of the responsibility she had assumed, both for the boats and for him. If he had another attack, she would have to deal with it, with Ginny eighty feet away at the end of the towline. But each time she glanced down into the cabin he looked all right, and usually caught her eye and smiled reassuringly. She kept the throttle wound as far open as she dared, the fuel rod pulled right out, the old Bolinder vibrating with its heavy, even beat, only easing down slightly for the very worst of the turns.

Away behind her, Ginny leant on the curved wooden tiller of the *Antrim.* Her eyes were on the waterway before her, watching the twists and turns of the motor boat, concentrating on keeping her silent charge placed in the deep-water channel, avoiding the risk of grounding in the bends by going too close to the inside. It was second nature to her after six years of practice, but on this occasion she took extra care, knowing that any delay now only increased the danger to her dad. Part of her mind sat with him in the motor's cabin, wondering how he was feeling, mentally urging him to sit quietly and rest until they could get him to the help they knew was waiting at Stoke Bruerne. Time and again she berated herself for not taking him into her cabin – it would be easier for her to look after him if anything was to happen, rather than Carrie, who had enough to do to keep control of the motor boat. But, she reflected, the motor was his home, he and Michael had always shared the close confines of its cabin, so he had his own surroundings, his own things all around him, if he needed anything.

Dusk was falling at about seven-thirty as they flew over the aqueduct between Wolverton and Cosgrove, above the gathering gloom in the Ouse valley below. At Cosgrove lock Ginny stepped down quickly to check on Alby:

''Ow yeh doin', Dad?' He looked up with a smile:

'Oi'm mooch better, Gin. The pain's all gone – Oi joost feel so bloody toired!'

'Won' be long, now. Coopl'a hours, 'n we'll be ther'.'

'Aye – don' woorry 'bout me, girl. 'Ow's Carrie doin'?' Ginny laughed:

'She's doin' joost great, Dad! Oi think she's h'enjoyin' 'erself ter tell yeh the truth!'

'Good fer 'er! 'S good practice fer 'er, ain't it?'

'Yes, Dad – now, yew tek it easy, we'll soon 'ave the Sister to yeh.'

She clambered out with a last smile at him and walked to the fore-end to light the *Antrim*'s old oil-lamp headlight; the *Sycamore* had an electric light, saved from an old motor-car many years before, wired through a switch which Carrie could reach from the tiller. But she left it off, preferring to steer by the fading evening light reflected in the stillness of the canal, as they set off on the last lap of their epic journey.

Darkness had fallen long before they passed Castlethorpe Wharf; still, Carrie did not ease down the throttle. Following the gleaming trail of moonlit water, she kept the boats driving ahead, leaning, scared and excited, on the long brass tiller and gazing into the gloom before her. Running into Acre Wood she became aware that the night around her was growing darker, darker than the surrounding woodland merited; looking up at the sky she realised that cloud was building up rapidly, thick, heavy and black over them, carried on the gusting north-west wind. She shivered, drawing her woollen pullover more tightly around her shoulders; and then the rain hit her, driving as cold and fierce as an angry wildcat, into her face. She reached down, groping, found and flicked on the switch for the electric headlamp – but the light just shone back into her eyes, reflected from the curtain of water. Angrily she flicked it off again, and hunkered down in the hatches, peering through the storm, trying to keep track of the banks, the twisting channel in front of the boats.

A touch on her leg; she looked down:

'Yew h'okay, Carrie? Oi 'eard the rain on the cabintop.' Alby was peering up at her, concern on his face. She nodded, raising her eyes to peer ahead through the deluge, called down to him:

'Oi'm foine, Dad! Yew sit down, tek it easy!'

'Yew can' manage in this, girl! Oi'm coomin' oop.' He made to push past her out of the cabin.

'No! Oi'll be… Dad!' Carrie had seen him stagger, clutching at his chest, and sit back down heavily on the sidebed: 'Dad! What's oop?' He shook his head, looked up at her:

'Joost a twinge – Oi'll be h'okay.' He sounded breathless. Trying to watch him whilst still keeping the boats in the channel, Carrie called down:

'Tek anoother o' Sister's pills!' Glancing between him and the streaming darkness outside, she saw him take a tablet from the bottle on the table, throw it back down his throat and wash it down with water from the glass which stood beside it. He looked up, caught her eye and smiled:

'Oi'll be foine, Carrie! Yeh're doin' a grand job, child.' Relieved but still uneasy, she just nodded and went back to the job in front of her. Rain lashed into her eyes, blinding her to the road beyond the boat's fore-end; it needed all of her concentration to stay in the deep-water channel in the middle of the canal, to avoid running headlong into the bank at one of the many bends, to pass cleanly through whenever a bridge loomed suddenly out of the murk. Still she kept the throttle wide, the Bolinder driving at full power, the boats flying along as if they were running through clear, bright daylight.

In the cabin Alby sat still, his head resting back against the cabinside. The pain in his chest was slowly subsiding now, the breathlessness easing; but a smile creased his weathered face: *Dad! She called me Dad...* The smile grew a little wider: *Sounds loike Oi've got* two *daughters now...*

Eighty feet away, the fore-end of the butty clove the rain-lashed water in their wake. Ginny leant on the slide, crouching down to keep as far out of the weather as possible, the curved wooden tiller tucked under her arm, peering in her turn into the obscuring darkness of the storm. She could barely see the motor boat ahead of her through the gloom, the white band around its stern flitting in and out of sight in the driving rain. Racked with anxiety, her heart was racing – but she forced herself to stay calm, knowing she could do nothing to help either her dad in his illness, or Carrie, in her headlong flight to reach the help he needed.

Past another derelict wharf, with a sway-backed farmhouse; the rain at last began to ease a little as Carrie was able to relax momentarily on the long straight where, many years before, Michael had first put his hand on a boat's tiller when he was the same age as she was now. Around the hill upon which stood the village of Grafton Regis; almost in sight of her destination now, the storm slowly losing its power, the winds softening – around the tight bend under Bozenham Mill bridge, a few gentle turns and they were cruising along past the weirs below Stoke Bruerne locks. At last, with a heartfelt sigh of relief, she eased down and let Ginny run the butty alongside her, snatching the sterns together and then leaping over with the back-end line to hold them against the bank while Ginny tied them securely.

'We made it!' She sounded as delighted, as weary, as she felt. Ginny grinned at her:

''Course we did! Oi knew yeh could do it.'

They faced each other almost shyly, the last of the rain falling gently now, running through their sodden hair, trickling down their wetly smiling faces. Carrie gave a deep sob, and threw herself into Ginny's arms; the older girl held her as she burst into tears, and found herself also crying from the sudden release of their shared, prolonged tension.

Chapter Thirty-Five

Sister Mary Ward sat relaxing in the sitting-room of her cottage beside the top lock, the gentle rattle of her knitting-needles the only sound. She glanced up at the clock on the mantelpiece: Gone half-past-nine! A last cup of tea and she would take herself off to bed.

Then she turned, startled – a thunderous knocking at her door, a voice calling 'Sister! Sister Mary!' Wondering who it could be, but realising that someone needed her help – and urgently from the sound of it – she hurried to the door and snatched it open:

'Ginny! Whatever is it?'

'It's Dad, Sister – 'e's 'ad anoother turn! Can yeh coom, quick!'

'Of course, my dear – just let me get my bag. How is he?' She turned and picked up the ready-to-hand medical bag she kept by the door.

''E's restin' in the boat. We've brought 'im 'ere so yeh could see 'im.'

'Oh! When did he have this turn?'

''Bout two. We were at 'Ammond Three, 'n 'e was took bad at the bottom.'

'You've kept him resting since then, have you?' She ushered the girl out, following her and closing the door.

'We 'ave, Sister. Oi gave 'im oone o' the pills yeh left fer 'im, 'n Oi wouldn' let 'im do anythin', all the way 'ere.' Ginny picked up the bicycle and turned to head back down the flight.

Sister Mary asked: 'You're at the bottom, are you?'

'Yeah – Oi boiked oop teh get yew.' They hurried along, Ginny wheeling the bike; the Sister gave her a puzzled look:

'Didn't I hear that Mikey's in hospital in Brentford?' Ginny nodded:

'That's roight. He got 'pendercitus, 'n they took 'im in three days back, 'E should be coomin' out soomtoime soon.'

'So, who's on the boats with you?'

'Joost me 'n Dad 'n Carrie.'

Sister Mary's feeling of amazement was growing:

'And you're loaded?'

'Yeah. Thirty-eight ton o' aluminum fer Birnigum.'

'So you two girls brought the boats all the way from there on your own?'

'Yeah.'

'Good Heavens! How old are you, Ginny?'

'Thirteen, nearly fourteen. Carrie's ten now.'

'Good Lord! Loaded boats, and in the dark too, for the last little while – did you come through that storm, too?'

'Ah, we did! That was quoite nasty, couldn' see wher' we were goin'!'

'Goodness! You should be proud of yourselves!' Ginny shrugged:

'It was Carrie mostly – Moikey taught 'er to steer the motor, so she 'ad to bring oos along. Oi've always 'ad the butty.'

'That child deserves a medal! You both do for that matter!'

* * *

Once Ginny had set off on the bike, pedalling furiously into the darkness, water spraying from the tyres on the wet towpath, Carrie had climbed wearily down into the warmth of the motor boat's cabin. Alby watched her with a smile as she checked the state of the kettle, murmuring to itself on the range:

''Ow're yeh feelin', Mr Baker?'

'Oh, Oi'm h'okay, Carrie loove. Sit yerself down 'n Oi'll mek soome fresh tea.'

'No yeh don't! *Oi'll* get the tea, yew sit ther' 'n tek things easy.' Alby laughed:

'Yeh've spent too mooch toime listenin' ter Ginny, yeh sound joost loike 'er!'

'Well, she's roight! Wait 'til Sister's seen yeh 'fore yeh get doin' things. Oi don' want…' She gave a strangled sob: 'Oi don' want yeh ter die…'

Alby stared at her, then patted the bench at his side:

'Coom 'ere, girl, put that kettle down.'

She replaced it on the range, tears welling in her eyes, and went to sit beside him; he slipped an arm around her slim waist, held her close:

'Oi ain't goin' ter die, not yet, any road oop! Loike Sister said before, Oi'll be foine if Oi tek things a bit easy. Oi've been roight as rain, fer ages now, 'aven't Oi? It was only 'cause Moikey's away – Oi s'pose Oi was troyin' ter do too mooch.' Carrie nodded, her head resting against his chest:

'Yeh moostn't do that, ever again!'

'Don' woorry choild, Oi don' intend teh!' He looked down at the tousled wet head leaning against his jacket: 'Carrie?' The head nodded again:

'Mmm?'

'Back ther' in the rain?'

'Mmm?'

'Yeh remember what yeh said?'

'Mm… Oh!' The head was raised, and wide green eyes gazed into his: 'Oi called yeh… Did… Did yeh moind, Mr Baker?' He shook his head, chuckled:

''Course not! Oi'm so proud of yeh, 'specially after terday – 'n if yeh want ter think of me as yer new dad, Oi'd be even more proud.'

The head settled against his chest again:

'Thank yeh, Mr... Dad. Oi'll never ferget me real dad, o' course, but – 'e's gorn, 'n yew've looked after me.' The eyes lifted to meet his again: 'Oi loove yeh, Dad!'

He bent to kiss her forehead: ''N Oi loove yew, Carrie.'

She wriggled in his arms, making herself comfortable; in moments, mentally and physically exhausted, she was asleep.

Not long after he felt the boats rock, and looked up with a smile as the hatch slid back. The doors swung open and Sister Mary let herself down into the cabin; Alby gently laid Carrie on the sidebed as he got up and moved behind the curtain which shielded the cross-bed, beckoning the Sister to join him.

She emerged a few minutes later, closing her medical bag:

'Ginny? I'm going back to my house to call an ambulance. Oh, don't worry...' she held up a hand at the scared look in Ginny's eyes: 'he's going to be all right, I'm sure. But I want the doctors there to take a look at him just to be on the safe side. I expect they'll want to keep him there for a few days, to keep an eye on him. You stay here, make sure he rests until they get here.'

'Oi will, Sister. Will they be long?'

'Half an hour, maybe – they'll have to come from Northampton I expect, at this time of night.' She smiled at the girl, seeing the strain and tiredness in her face: 'You know what day it is, Ginny?' The youngster shook her head: 'It's Easter Monday! Have you two eaten today?'

Ginny shook her head again: 'Once the ambulance has been, you and Carrie are coming to my house for a meal, you understand? And you can stay the night rather than sleeping in the boats on your own, if you like.'

'Thank yeh, Sister! Boot it looks loike Carrie's already asleep.' She looked down at the younger girl, still curled up on the sidebed. The nurse nodded:

'She'll be much better for good hot meal inside her even if we have to wake her up. The poor child must be absolutely dog-tired – and so must you! Now I'm going to call the hospital – you wait here with your Dad. I won't be long.'

* * *

''Noight, all!' Tom Kingsley raised a hand in parting salutation to the remaining crowd as he stepped out of the Boat Inn into the damp, chill night air. Born in the cabin of an L.B.Faulkner horse-boat during the First World War, he was now running his own pair of boats for the same company, even if he had the benefit of a two-cylinder National engine in place of the old horse. Emily had stayed with the boats to keep her eye on the children; they were tied up near the tunnel with their load of gravel destined for Olton, on the outskirts of Birmingham.

He made his way around the end of the derelict second lock, stepped up to cross over the balance beams of the remaining lock, stepped carefully down again onto the lockside outside Sister Mary's cottage. He wasn't drunk – but he'd had a few beers, and more than one boater had lost his life slipping into a full lock in the dark after a night in the pub.

Something caught his eye, and he looked around again – yes, it looked like the Sister's white headdress, bobbing towards him through the darkness: *Soomat's oop, she's nearly roonnin'!*

'What's amiss, Sister?' he called as she approached.

'Who... Oh, Tom! It's Alby Baker, he's had another heart attack.'

'Is 'e h'okay?' Concern for another boatman rang in Kingsley's tone.

'I think he'll be all right but I'm calling an ambulance, getting him to the hospital for a check-up, anyway.'

'Wher's 'is boats?'

'At the bottom, on the old wharf.'

'Ah…' She felt the boatman's gaze for a moment: 'Be better if they were oop 'ere fer the h'ambulance?'

'Well – it would be easier, perhaps?'

'Ah. Well yew tell 'em ter coom 'ere, then.'

'Tom?'

'Leave it ter me – yew go call 'em, roight?'

Chapter Thirty-Six

Ginny watched her adopted father over the rim of her tea-cup: *'E don' look too bad...* Apart from dark shadows under his eyes and a slight paleness, Alby seemed close to normal; he glanced up and smiled at her, taking a swig of his own tea.

She had brewed up after the Sister had left, leaving Carrie still curled up asleep on the sidebed. Alby sat within the bed-hole partly hidden behind the curtains; she perched on the step below the cabin doors next to the range. Neither had spoken for a little while, content to relax in each other's company, lost in their own thoughts. Ginny was feeling much happier now, knowing that the Sister had seen her Dad, although she would be happier still once the doctors at the hospital had looked him over: *Wher's that h'ambulance?*

'Won' be long now, Ginny.' She smiled back at him, knowing he had sensed her concerns. Then she jumped at the sound of a loud knocking on the butty cabin next to them – it was too soon, surely, for the ambulance to have got to them all the way from Northampton? She stood up and poked her head out of the open hatch, to be greeted by the sight of a number of shadowy figures on the towpath; one stepped forward and the light from the cabin limned his face:

'Mr Kingsley?'

'Aye, it's me, Ginny. 'Ow's yer Dad?'

'Better – 'e's restin'. Sister's sendin' fer the h'ambulance.'

'Oi know – Oi met 'er oop top o' the floight. We're goin' ter get yeh oop ther', 'n all – easier fer the h'ambulance men, see?'

'Boot...?'

'Don' woorry!' He chuckled: 'Ther's a boonch of oos – yew joost sit toight, we'll 'ave yeh ther' in no toime!' He turned to the men behind him in the shadows: 'Ned? Yew knows yer Bolinders – get 'er started! Fred, Caggy – mek sure they're breasted good 'n toight 'n we'll be away.'

A rush of water from the lock drew Ginny's attention; Kingsley chuckled again:

'That's Norman 'Ambridge 'n 'is boy – they're settin' 'em fer oos.'

''Ey – yew tek care wi' moy boats, yoong Kingsley!' Alby's voice sounded from within the cabin.

'Don' yew woorry, Alby, we won' scratch yer paint!'

The hissing of the blowlamp was already issuing from the engine-hole; the rattling of control linkages announced that Ned, George Hampson's brother, was preparing to kick the engine over. A clang, a wheezy 'ker-fuff thump!', and a billow of black smoke from the chimney was followed by a muffled curse from below. Moments later, and Ned's second attempt resulted in a loud 'whumpf!' and another cloud of smoke – but this time the aged engine, still hot from their frantic dash along the pound, picked up and settled down to its usual off-beat idle.

Not a word was said or needed as the boatmen cast off the moorings. Tom Kingsley steered for the now-open lock as the other two men pushed the deeply-laden boats out from the bank, and then hurried to close the gates behind them and whip up the top paddles.

An uphill pair had left the flight set against them, but with two men to set the locks ahead, and three more to work the boats through, it was barely twenty minutes later when they emerged from the top lock and tied them outside Sister Mary's cottage. An elderly Crossley ambulance was waiting on the road by the bridge, having only just beaten the boats to it; The ambulance men hurried over as Alby climbed from the cabin and took him in charge as he stepped over onto the bank, followed by Ginny and a reawakened Carrie. He turned to hug them both:

'Yew two stay 'ere, look after the boats, roight? Oi'll be foine – Sister'll let yeh know 'bout things, h'okay?'

'Of course I will, Alby' she confirmed from beside him, then led him away to the ambulance. He stepped inside with a quick wave for the girls; the doors were closed, and he was gone; Sister Mary gave them a reassuring smile:

'He's going to be just fine, don't you worry about him! I'll telephone in the morning to see how he is and what the doctors say, all right? Now you're coming in with me for a hot meal!'

'Don' yew fret about yer boats, Ginny – we'll move 'em oop boy the mill fer tonoight, ther's room fer 'em ther" Tom Kingsley told them; Ginny turned to him:

'Thank yeh, Mr Kingsley!' She looked around the gathered faces: 'Thank yeh, all of yeh! Yeh've been – joost brilliant! Thank yeh…' She could feel the tears rising in her eyes; Tom put his hands on her shoulders:

''S no trooble, Ginny. We're all boaters, 'n we look after ar own, roight? Yeh'd do the same fer any of oos.'

'Of course…'

'Now – yew go 'n get that 'ot meal insoide o' yeh. Oi'll coom boy in the mornin', see as yeh're h'okay.' She went to speak again, but he put his hand up: 'Go on, girl!'

She gave him a beaming smile and nodded, despite the tears of gratitude running down her face; then she took the half-asleep Carrie by the elbow and guided her to the cottage door in the wake of the Sister.

* * *

Ginny rolled onto her back, her eyes still firmly closed, fighting the need to wake up despite the fact that someone was shaking her. She felt so warm, so cosy – it couldn't be time to go to school yet?

'I'll be up in a minute, Mum' she mumbled, and went to roll over again, but the shaking wouldn't stop. Lost somewhere in the shadows between waking and sleeping, she forced her eyes open; a face swam slowly into focus above her, but it wasn't her mother's face. A kindly face, nevertheless – round, smiling, with gentle eyes and a white headdress of some kind… She felt a frown crease her own face, puzzled by the presence of a stranger in her room; the face spoke to her:

'Wake up, Ginny! Mr Vickers is on the telephone.' It was the sound of the voice more than anything which at last brought her awake, brought back the memories of the day before – she sat bolt upright, suddenly scared:

'Sister! What's oop – 'ow's Dad?'

'Shhh, it's all right, Ginny – your Dad's fine, I've just spoken to the hospital and they say he's much better. I've told Mr Vickers and he wants to speak to you now, if you're up to it?'

'Oh – yes!' She swung her legs out of bed, discovering to her surprise that she wearing only her knickers: 'Oh! Where am I?' She looked around, puzzled; the Sister laughed:

'In my spare room! Look, Carrie's in the other bed!'

''Ow'd we get 'ere?'

'You both fell asleep after dinner last night so I put you both to bed here. Oh, you needn't worry – Tom Kingsley kept an eye on your boats, he's been by this morning to see how you were.'

'Oh, roight – is 'e still 'ere?'

'No – he's had to get started, they've a load for Olton on board. He said to give you his best wishes.'

'Oh! 'E was so koind las' noight – they all were!' Sister Mary chuckled:

'That's boaters for you! Now dear – Mr Vickers?'

'Oh – yes! 'E's 'ere, is 'e?'

'No, dear, he's on the telephone. You slip your frock on and come downstairs, and I'll make you some breakfast while you talk to him.'

Moments later in the neat surgery which occupied the front room of the cottage, the Sister handed her the telephone's big black handset. Ginny looked at it uncertainly; Sister Mary smiled, and guided it to her ear:

'You talk into this end, Ginny!' With another doubtful glance at her Ginny spoke into the mouthpiece:

'H – hello?' She jumped as Ben Vickers' voice sounded in her ear:

'Hello, Ginny – how are you?' *'E could be standin' next ter me!* As if reading her thoughts, he went on: 'Marvellous, isn't it? I'm here in Braunston, and you're in Stoke, but we can talk as if we're in the same room!'

'Y – yes, isn't it? Oi'm h'okay, Mr Vickuss. 'N Sister says Dad's better terday – yeh know what's 'appened?'

'Yes, Ginny – I'm so pleased he's all right, but Sister says he'll have to stay in hospital for a few days, so that they can make sure he's recovered. Now listen – Mikey's on his way to join you...'

'Moikey's coomin'?' she interrupted him; he just laughed:

'Yes, he's on his way! They let him out of hospital last night and he stayed with Bob and Ivy Renwick – Bob's been keeping in touch with him and keeping me informed as well – and they've put him on the train to Northampton. He can get the branch line from there to Stoke Bruerne and he should be with you about lunchtime, I expect.'

'Oh, that's woonderful! Thank yeh, Mr Vickuss!'

'Right. Now – I don't want you three trying to move the boats today, you understand? You're to have a day off, have a rest after your efforts of yesterday – and you can all go and see your

Dad in the hospital. I've spoken to the ward sister and she's agreed to let you all go in at any time. It's very much against their usual rules, and she was a bit sniffy to start with, but when I explained the situation she came 'round. And – talking about yesterday: I'm so proud of you two girls, we all are, of the way you brought the boats all the way from Stoke Hammond on your own, and through that appalling weather. George Hampson's been in touch to make sure you're all right; so's his brother Ned, who I gather helped work the boats up the locks last night. I've told Mr Anderson, the Fleet manager, and he wants me to pass on his congratulations too, and his best wishes to your dad.'

'Thank yeh, Mr Vickuss!' Ginny found herself close to tears again: 'Ev'ryoone's been so noice, so koind…' She heard him laugh gently; he unconsciously echoed Sister Mary's words:

'That's the boaters for you, Ginny! Always there for each other when you need them. Now go and have some breakfast. Michael will be there soon and then you can go and see your dad. Tell him hello for me, and say I need him back on the job as soon as possible!' She could hear the smile in his voice, felt her own spread across her face:

'Oi will, Mr Vickuss! 'N thank yew again!'

Chapter Thirty-Seven

Nellie Collingwood walked back into Paterson Ward, casting her smile at each of the beds' occupants in turn. Not long qualified, she was still unsure of herself, nervous of her responsibilities. Her immediate duties completed, her task now was just to keep an eye on the ward and its incumbents until Matron's rounds later in the afternoon; then it would be serving dinners, clearing away, distributing their medications before her shift finished.

Most of the men in her care were reading books, newspapers, magazines, during the quiet period of late afternoon. Visiting had just finished, the hubbub of conversation faded, the wives, girlfriends, mothers all departed; she glanced at the new arrival lying back in his bed, eyes closed: *Poor old chap!* No-one had come to see him despite Matron's words when she'd told the staff of his presence.

Nellie had been ready to disapprove of him:

'Mr Baker is a canal boatman. He has suffered two mild heart attacks in the last twenty-four hours, and was brought in to us late last night. Dr Hollins has seen him and prescribed as you will see on his chart; he is to stay with us for three days minimum, for observation.'

A bargee! They're no better than gypsies! She'd expected to find a grubby, uncouth man in her ward, and had been almost startled to be greeted cheerily by the stocky, clean-shaven fellow in the bed, had responded with a more-than-habitual smile to the grin on his lined, weather-beaten face, the twinkle in his dark grey eyes.

Now she wandered over to speak to him. He opened his eyes, looked around with that same cheerful grin:

‘’Ello, nurse!’ She smiled back at him:

‘No visitors, Mr Baker?’

‘Ah, ther’s toime yet!’ His voice was so distinctive – rather high-pitched, the accent very Midlands, maybe Birmingham, but with a rolling quality that echoed the West Country. She felt her smile growing wider:

‘That’s true, Mr Baker!’ Matron’s instructions had been explicit, her tone indicating her own strong disapproval of the situation. And they had drawn a gasp of astonishment from the nurses – he was to be allowed visitors at any time, unless being attended by the doctor. And more than the regulation two persons, if more than two turned up! She made a show of tidying the covers around him:

‘Who are you expecting to come?’ She asked. He chuckled, a delightfully carefree sound:

‘Moy kids, Oi ’ope! Moy boy, ’n the two girls.’

‘Where will they be coming from?’

‘Oh, the girls’ll ’ave been on the boats las’ noight at Stoke Bruin. Moikey should be along, too – ’e’s’ joost coom out of ’orspital ’n all!’

‘Oh?’

‘Yeah – they took ’im in at Brentford, Froiday. ’Pendercoitus – boot Oi ’ad a message terday that they’ve let ’im out, put ’im on the train ter meet oos.’

‘Appendicitus? Did they operate on him?’

‘Aye. Boot they say ’e’s roight as rain now.’

‘That’s good! How old is he?’

‘Noineteen, now. Ginny’s near fourteen, ’n Carrie’s ten.’

‘They all live on the barge with you?’

He gave her a sidelong look:

'In the boats, yes.' He smiled at her conspiratorially: 'They ain't barges, nurse. Barges are dirty big things as work in the docks 'n the rivers – our'n are boats, narrerboats, to give 'em their roight name. 'N we're boaters, not bargees!' He chuckled again: 'Quickest way ter oopset a boatman, call 'im a bargee!' Nellie felt a flush rising to her face:

'Oh, I'm sorry! I didn't understand there was a difference!' He laughed aloud now:

'No reason whoy yeh should, girl! Not offen yeh get an ol' boatee in 'ere, Oi s'pose!'

'No, indeed! I think you're the first, at least since I came here.' He put out a hand, took hers and gave it a squeeze:

'Fergive me fer teasin' yeh, eh? 'N moy name's Alby, h'okay?' She smiled at him, relieved at his understanding:

'Of course – Alby!' she glanced around: 'I'm Nellie – but don't let Matron hear you call me that! We're not allowed to be on first-name terms with the men here.'

'Don' woorry, Nellie, Oi won' tell 'er!'

'I should go and check on the others – will you excuse me?'

'O' course, girl! Yeh've got yer job ter do.'

'Can I get you a paper, or a book to read?' He shook his head, chuckling again, beckoned her to bend close:

'Wouldn' serve no purpose, Nellie – Oi never learned teh read 'n wroite!' She stared at him, astonished: 'We don' get the chance o' no schoolin' – never in oone place long enooff, see? Moikey, 'e can read 'n wroite, went ter school when 'e was small, 'n now 'e's teachin' soom o' the other boatee kids.'

'Good for him!' She'd recovered from her surprise, now: 'You'll be all right?'

'Oi'll be foine, girl. Yew get about yer job.'

'I'll come and talk to you again, in a while, if that's all right?'

'Aye – that'd be noice.' She gave him a smile and turned away.

Minutes later, as she bent over old Mr Paget in the end bed, the door at the far end of the ward opened. Nellie looked up, to see a group of people standing there looking bewildered; she hurried towards them wondering who they could be, then caught Alby Baker's wave as she passed his bed: *They can't be his children, surely?* She'd assumed that the boatman's son would be pretty much a younger version of the man himself, but this young man was tall and well-built, his thick, unruly hair a sandy-blond colour. As she drew closer his soft grey-green eyes turned on her, and a smile crinkled their corners:

O-oh! What a handsome fellow... She put on her best nursing smile, held out a hand:

'Mr Baker?' He nodded, took her hand, sending a tingle up to her elbow:

'Yes – Oi'm Moichael. 'Ow's Dad?'

'Oh, he's doing very well, Michael. Come on over – Matron said you'd be coming when you were able to.' *And he's just my age...*

'Thank yeh, nurse. This is Ginny, 'n Carrie.' He indicated the two girls with him; Nellie smiled:

'Yes – your father's told me about you all. I'm so glad you were able to get here!'

'Ah – Mr Cook ran oos over in 'is car, 'e's waitin' outside.'

'That was kind!' She reluctantly let go of his hand and led them over to Alby's bed: 'I'll leave you together now. Call me if you need anything – my name's Nellie, Nellie Collingwood.'

'Thank yeh, Nellie.' She felt her knees tremble at his unaffected smile, and turned away before he saw the flush on her face.

They stayed for nearly an hour, until Nellie was beginning to get nervous in case Matron came. Although, she reasoned, if Matron had, however reluctantly, given permission for them to visit out of hours she could hardly blame Nellie for their presence! She had finished her round, checking, talking to the other patients, and then returned to her seat at the desk near the ward's entrance. She had tried to concentrate on her studies, but found her eyes drawn time and again to the tall, handsome lad sitting beside his father on the chair – the two girls perched on each side of the bed; the elder one, she saw, looked very much like her brother, but the little girl was more like Alby himself, short and dark: *Their Mum must have been a tall blond...*

When she caught their movement in the corner of her eye she stood up and went to them, waiting to one side as the girls each bent to hug and kiss their dad in turn. Michael took the old man's hand, and then bent to put his arm around him:

'Yew tek things easy, Dad, we'll be h'okay without yeh fer a whoile!' He glanced up at Nellie: 'And yew do as the nurse tells yeh, roight? Don't yew tek any nonsense from 'im, nurse!' She felt a blush rising as he addressed her, laughed to hide her embarrassment.

She followed them to the doors, paused while they turned to give their father a last wave:

'Will you be back tomorrow?' she asked the young man; he shook his head:

'Oi doubt it. We've got a load of aluminium on fer a fact'ry in Birnigum, 'n we'll 'ave ter get goin' in the mornin'. 'Ow long will Dad be 'ere, d'yeh know?'

'Matron said three days at least, but it'll depend on how well he is, how he responds to the treatment.'

'Oh... We'll be four days ter Birnigum 'n back minimum, mebbe foive or six, dependin' on what load we get. If 'e's still 'ere we'll coom boy then – boot Oi 'ope yeh'll 'ave let 'im go 'fore that!' *And I hope we haven't...*

'We'll just have to see how he is, Michael, what the doctor says.'

'O' course – we oonderstand. Tek care of 'im for oos!'

'Of course I will. How are you, now? He told me you've had appendicitis.' The young man grinned, making her heart jump:

'Bit sore! Boot Oi'm foine, thanks. 'N thank yeh fer lookin' after Dad.'

'It's no trouble, Michael.'

'Aye – well, goodbye, nurse.'

'Goodbye, and thank yeh!' Ginny echoed; Carrie gave the nurse a beaming smile.

'Goodbye, Michael, girls – have a good trip!'

A last cheerful grin, and he was gone. Nellie stood for a moment, watching him walk away down the corridor, then turned back into her ward and went over to the boatman. He smiled up at her as she sat down in the chair Michael had just vacated:

'You have a lovely family, Alby – you must be so proud of them!'

'Oh, Oi am! They're the best kids a feller could 'ave.'

'Your son, Michael – I'll bet he has all the girls after him?' Alby laughed:

'Oh, ah, 'e doos that – boot 'e 'ardly notices! Stoock on 'is 'Arriet, 'e 'is!'

'He's got a girlfriend, then?' Nellie kept her voice cheerful although her heart was in her boots.

'Aye – gettin' married in September, they are.'

'Oh! Well… I hope they'll be happy together…' He caught the slight catch in her voice, gave her a searching look, then smiled gently:

''E's a 'andsome devil, ain't 'e? Fer an ol' boatee's boy! Listen, child – yeh don' want ter marry a boatman! It's a 'ard loife, if yeh ain't born teh it – bad enooff if yeh are! Long hours, out in all weathers, back-breakin' work when yeh're loadin' 'n oonloadin' – t'ain't the loife fer a girl off the bank, troost me!'

Nellie looked up into his eyes, saw the compassion there and gave him a sad smile:

'Am I that obvious? I guess you're right, Alby, I was just being silly. But – he is a handsome fellow. You won't…?' He laughed gently:

'Oi won' say nothin', don' yew fret!'

Chapter Thirty-Eight

Michael had never felt so nervous or so scared, in all his life. He glanced around at Stevie, standing equally nervously by his side; they shared a mutually-reassuring smile before Michael turned his head further to look over his shoulder towards the church door, as he had been doing constantly for the last few minutes.

Both were dressed in their finest – new black moleskin trousers, made by Vi Hanney, sparklingly-clean white shirts set off by the bright colours of spiderwork belts and braces, new black waistcoats, sewed for them by Suey Caplin. Michael ran a hand over his slicked-back hair, disturbing it so that it sprang free into its usual tousled mop; from the corner of his eye he caught the shake of Vi's head, Stevie's sudden grin. He leant closer to his best man:

''Ow mooch longer're they goona be?' Stevie took his watch from his waistcoat pocket, glanced at its face:

'T'ain't toime yet, Moikey – 'noother coopla minutes ter 'leven.'

Michael just sighed, as anxious as he was nervous.

* * *

Five months before, Nellie Collingwood had had her wish. The doctor had kept Albert Baker in the hospital for the four days it took his boats to travel to Birmingham, pick up a return load and get back to Stoke Bruerne, partly, she suspected, out of astonishment at the rapidity of his recovery. But then, she reflected, he was an active, fit man, and that must have helped him to bounce back so remarkably – Doctor Hollins had prescribed tablets for him to take to prevent further attacks, and both he and Nellie had done their best to impress upon the old boatman that he must continue to take them every day, and to make sure he always had a supply on hand.

She had been on duty when his children came to collect him. Despite Albert's gentle admonishment and her knowledge of his approaching wedding, she felt her heart give a lurch as the tall, handsome young man strolled onto her ward and greeted her with that open, carefree smile. She had occupied herself, fussing over the boatman, impressing upon his elder daughter the importance of keeping him supplied with the medication, all the time aware of the young man's closeness. As they had left he had taken her hand in both of his own and thanked her for looking after his father, his soft grey eyes gazing into her own – she had stammered out that it was only her job as he smiled and squeezed her hand…

* * *

'Moost be toime now, surely?' Stevie checked his watch again:

'Joost.'

Michael sighed again:

'They won' be mooch longer, then.' Stevie chuckled:

'Broide's alwes late, mate! Look at Sylvie, when she married ar Billy.'

Michael groaned:

'Don' say that! Oi can' tek anoother ten minutes o' this waitin'!'

''Angover getting' to yeh?'

''S'not a bloody 'angover! Oi feel foine – it's joost all this 'anging about.'

'Nervous are yeh?' He glanced around at Stevie's innocent grin, laughed quietly at his own agitation:

'Bloody roight, mate!'

* * *

Since that fateful trip back in the spring their working lives had settled into a steady routine. Perhaps in acknowledgement of Alby's uncertain health, the company had had them on a regular traffic – bagged sugar from City Road Basin, where it was warehoused after arriving from abroad, to Fazeley Street, from where it was distributed by lorry around Birmingham. Their return load was cases of HP Sauce which suffered a similar fate upon arrival in London. It was, compared with the coal-shovelling or metal-handling that many other boaters had to endure, not overly arduous work; and stress-free because of its very invariability. Which suited Michael admirably, occupied as he was with the thought of his impending marriage…

* * *

In what was, perhaps, a subconscious effort to quell his nerves, his thoughts drifted back to the celebrations of the night before. Practically all of their immediate families and friends had managed to arrive in Braunston for the wedding, tying where they could between the turn and the locks; the women and girls had headed for the Old Plough in the village High Street for a few drinks, while the men had accompanied Michael when he strolled up to the Admiral Nelson beside the third lock, to enjoy his last evening as a single man.

Everyone had been in jovial mood – everyone, that is, except Henry Caplin. He had no reservations about his Harriet marrying her Michael, but the impending sadness of giving over his only daughter to the care of another man put him in a sombre mood;

and he had begun the walk to the pub exchanging grouses with his son, a fellow British Waterways captain:

'Still no soign o' that drudgin' they ortta be doin', Joey.'

'No, Dad. Cut's as bad as ever, ent it? Bloody gates leakin', paddles out all oover the place 'n all.'

'Ah. Yeh'd think they'd be getting' on with the job boy now, wouldn' yeh?'

'Yeah. T'ain't too bad down 'ere on the Joonction, moind – boot bottom road's 'bout finished! So's Stratford cut – been no boats down ther' fer years.'

'Oi know, boy. Ar jobs'll be on the loine 'fore long, yew wait 'n see!' Henry had always been a pessimist; but Joe wasn't prepared to give up just yet:

'Oh, it ain't that bad, Dad! They'll get 'round ter it in the end, yeh'll see.'

'Yeah? 'N wher's the loads coomin' from, eh? We're spendin' more toime sittin' on ar arses at Bulls Bridge every trip, waitin' fer orders!'

Joe had no answer for this; he fell silent until they walked past his own newly-painted boats:

'Look at 'em, Dad – joost docked. Don' they look 'orrible?' The pair were now painted in the latest British Waterways livery, with yellow borders around their blue cabinsides, and very plain, unadorned yellow signwriting for their names and fleet numbers.

'Bloody awful, Joe' his father agreed as they walked on.

''N ther's no proper flowers nor landscapes in 'em, neither!' Muttered disapproval rumbled around the gathering as he went on: 'They've put soome transfers on the cabin doors – boot they ain't nothin' loike the real thing.'

'Meks yeh wish we were with Fellers's, loike these loocky booggers!' Henry indicated their companions with a tilt of his head, waved a hand at Billy Hanney's pair which they were just passing. But Jack Warden gave a sceptical grunt:

'Oi wouldn' say that, 'Enry. We could be joinin' yer soon!'

The other Fellows, Morton and Clayton men turned to look at him, surprise on their faces; Alby spoke up:

'What d'yeh mean, Jack?'

'Oi've 'eard as 'ow Fellers's could be packin' oop.' He raised his hands at the chorus of jeers which greeted this statement: ''S roight – the dock-'ands at Fazeley Street was talkin' about it when we was loadin' ther' a coupl'a weeks back. Seems their foreman 'ad over'eard the manager 'n 'is depitty, 'n they was sayin' as the coomp'ny's been losin' money all this year. Reckoned the bosses moight close oop, sell out ter the gov'mint.'

'They'd be crazy ter do that!' The disbelief was a little less certain now, despite Billy's protest; his father sounded thoughtful:

'Loads 'ave been getting' scarcer, that's fer sure – 'n soome folk 'ave been leavin' the cut. Look at George 'Ampson, 'n 'is missus, both got jobs in that fact'ry in Leighton, wher' their John went. 'N Oi've 'eard 'is broother's goin' ter join 'im, 'n all.'

'Yeah…'

''S true, Bill.' All had heard of similar tales over the course of the year – Jack's suggestion suddenly sounded less far-fetched, at least to most:

'Boot Fellers's is a big coomp'ny – they can' joost pack it all in, joost loike that, can they?' Billy sounded scandalised: 'What about all the folks 'oo works fer 'em?' Jack shrugged his shoulders:

'Dunno, Billy. 'S all joost talk, moind – mebbe things ain't that bad at all, mebbe the men 'ad got the wrong end o' the stick, eh?'

'Let's 'ope so, Jack!' Voices echoed Bill's comment; Alby cut across the conversation:

'Coom on, yew sour-faced booggers! We're 'ere teh h'enjoy ourselves! Moy boy's getting' married termorrer, so we'll 'ave no more o' that talk, h'okay? Let's 'ave oos soome ale, drink ter Moichael 'n 'Arriet, 'n woorry 'bout the future when it 'appens!'

The evening had, from then on, been convivial – the beer flowed freely, and their merriment echoed across the lock until the early hours. Michael had deliberately kept his drinking in check, wanting to be at his best the following day, as had his best man; some of the younger boaters, knowing of Henry Caplin's strictures about his younger children drinking, had decided it would be funny to keep slipping half-pints to Sam when his father wasn't looking. The boy had eagerly supped all he could get, with the result that everyone (his father included) had laughed uproariously at his unsteady antics later as they walked back to the boats.

* * *

Michael glanced around the church, found his bride's younger brother seated a few rows back. Sam looked up, caught his eye, gave him a sheepish grin: *Boogger, 'e looks poorly!* Michael chuckled; his gaze travelled on: *'N Billy don' look mooch better!* Sylvie, next to her husband, gave him an encouraging smile; in the row behind them, Grace, little Rosie in her arms, beamed at him, and Joe, hand in hand with three-year-old Jack, gave him a thumbs-up gesture; Vi Hanney had a proud smile on her face as he caught her eye, and Bill, at her side, winked at him. In the nearest second-row pew, his dad gave him a beaming grin, one arm around the shoulders of a happily-smiling Carrie whose other hand clutched her little brother's…

Movement at the back of the church caught his attention, and his heart leapt…

Epilogue

'Dearly beloved brethren, we are gathered here today in the sight of God and in the face of this congregation…'

'Do you, Michael Henry, take Harriet, to be your lawful wedded wife, to have and to hold…'

'Oi do!' Bold, confident, and self-assured – Alby Baker's heart swelled with pride at the sound of his son's voice.

'Do you, Harriet, take Michael…'

'Oi do.' Quieter but just as confident – Suey Caplin smiled through the tears that rose in her eyes at her daughter's words.

In his second-row pew, Fred Morris stood with his arm around his grand-daughter's waist, watching and listening as his grandson and his bride made their vows: *I wish Ethel could have been here to see him – what a wonderful young man he's turned out to be!*

As if sensing his feelings Ginny glanced up at him; he gave her a gentle squeeze and smiled down at her; he caught the pride on Albert's face as, standing beside her, his arm around Carrie's shoulders, he gazed at his adopted son.

Fred raised his eyes again to the ceremony playing out before them: *His mother would be so proud! If only… Even Reg* – the thought came wryly to him – *what would he make of the man his son has grown into?*

'I now pronounce you to be man and wife together!' The priest's smile sounded in his voice. The young man and his new wife turned to face each other; their hands clasped, they leant forwards until their lips met…

A burst of applause echoed around the old church as Fred, surrounded by the ghosts of the past, watched the young couple take their first steps together into the future.

Ten-year-old Michael Thompson has had enough. Mentally and physically abused by his drunken father, treated like a skivvy by his mother, he's taken all that his miserable life can throw at him; but then the final blow comes when his dog is taken away as well: On a bitter cold night in January, 1940, he sets out to commit suicide – but all does not go according to plan…

A Boy Off The Bank tells a story of England's canals in wartime, of the pressure and the pain, the humour and resilience of the boating people. Tragic and heart-warming, it charts the progress of a job becoming ever more difficult, against the broader panorama of worldwide events, seen from the perspective of a narrowboat's back cabin. Published in 2006, this is the first part of a trilogy.

Departing from the detective novels for which he is known, in *Starlight* Geoffrey Lewis tells a tale of schoolboy friendship set against the backdrop of the Oxford Canal in the days when the commercial trade was in decline; the canal itself threatened with closure. In a story where the mood ranges from heartwarming humour to unbearable poignancy, he conjures up the world of the 1950s; factual events and real characters flit past in the background as he leads the reader through the long heat-wave of the summer of 1955, as it was seen by an eleven-year-old boy living in a little North Oxfordshire village.

Starlight was published in 2005 - for more information, please check our website at www.sgmpublishing.co.uk or telephone 07792 497116. ISBN 978-0-9545624-5-8. Cover price £6.99.

'Northamptonshire's own answer to Inspector Morse'

Image Magazine

'Impossible to put down'

ChoiceMagazine

'Plots brimming with unexpected twists'

What's On Magazine

These four D.I. David Russell novels may be ordered from any good bookshop. Just ask for:

Flashback by Geoffrey Lewis	ISBN 978-0-9545624-0-3
Strangers by Geoffrey Lewis	ISBN 978-0-9545624-1-0
Winter's Tale by Geoffrey Lewis	ISBN 978-0-9545624-2-7
Cycle by Geoffrey Lewis	ISBN 978-0-9545624-3-4

published by SGM Publishing.

SGM Publishing

35 Stacey Avenue, Wolverton, Milton Keynes, Bucks MK12 5DN

info@sgmpublishing.co.uk

www.sgmpublishing.co.uk